HEADSTRONG

BOOK ONE: IMPROVISE

MELANIE RACHEL

CONTENTS

It's that wonderful old-fashioned idea that others come first and you come second. This was the whole ethic by which I was brought up. Others matter more than you do, so don't fuss, dear; get on with it.

— **Audrey Hepburn**

CHAPTER ONE

H e was late.

She'd arrived early at De Roos and grabbed a booth tucked behind the wooden front door. She tapped the heel of her boot on the floor, turned to count the large fieldstones used to build the long bar on the back wall, and tried to guess where each of the customers had come from. Local? Tourist? Embassy?

At last, fifteen minutes past their meeting time and just before she stood to leave, Elizabeth Bennet saw him. Standing a few feet away, hands on his hips, canvassing the room before spotting her behind him, was Major Richard Fitzwilliam.

"Staff Sergeant," he said amiably.

"Sir," she replied with a grin.

He raised his hand to attract the attention of a waitress. When a buxom redhead wearing black pants and a tight t-shirt turned and saw him, he held up two fingers and she disappeared behind the bar.

"You made me wait," she chided, showing the display on her phone. "Hardly the way to say, 'Thank you for saving my life.'"

Major Fitzwilliam shook his head. "Last meeting ran long." He tossed his sunglasses down on the table. Elizabeth noted the tailored fit of his brown khakis and dark green polo shirt—casual wear that appeared expensive. *Everyone looks so different out of uniform,* she thought. He slid into the booth opposite her.

"A regular, I see," Elizabeth teased. She stretched her toes out in her boots, feeling comfortable at last. She'd spent her shift working on the embassy's computer network, including carting away some truly ancient desktops and swapping them out for newer models. Then she'd needed to update the software. The assignment was way below her pay grade and boring as dirt. But it was easy enough, and it meant she was stationed in Brussels, so she wasn't complaining.

Elizabeth had found the major surprisingly good-natured for an officer in the months since she'd arrived in Europe. She'd worried a bit at first that he was flirting with her, but it turned out he teased just about everyone. She knew now that Major Fitzwilliam was too dedicated a Marine ever to break the regulation on fraternization. That being the case, Elizabeth felt safe enjoying his friendly banter. It was a bit like having a charming and sarcastic older brother.

The major ran a hand through his sandy hair in a gesture that indicated a long day. "I am, but I'm not a lush, if that's what you're implying," he said flippantly.

"Well, sir, it would explain how you managed to purge thirty significant documents from your computer . . . don't you officers know how to back up files?"

"I'm still not sure how that happened." He exhaled dramatically and tossed his hands up in frustration. "The entire program for the conference next month, including the papers, and the translations, all in the correct formatting. I could have gathered them all again, but it would have taken forever to redo the translations. You didn't save my life, Staff Sergeant, but you sure saved my weekend."

"You're welcome," she replied, a little smug. "And because you are being so polite, *and* you're buying me a beer, I'll let you in on a secret." She arched one eyebrow.

"How do you do that?" he asked, leaning forward. "Move just one eyebrow?"

She shrugged. "Dunno. I can't roll my tongue or wiggle my ears, so it all evens out, I guess."

The corners of his mouth turned up. "You're damn cheerful for all the menial labor I saw you put in today." He leaned forward. "So tell me, what's the big secret?"

She raised both eyebrows before saying,

"First, you really *should* back up your files."

He rolled his eyes. "Yes, so I've been told." He motioned for her to continue.

"*You* didn't lose anything. The general logged onto your computer and tried to send the files to her own. She's the one who did the damage." Satisfied, she leaned back in her seat. "Sir."

"Son of a bitch!" Richard growled, banging a fist on the table. "I *knew* it! The old gorgon turned it on me before she even took a breath." He spoke through his nose in imitation of the general, "'It's *your* computer, Fitzwilliam.'"

"It's unfathomable, really," she said with a chuckle, "how the woman can command an embassy as well as she does and yet be so entirely computer illiterate. How difficult is it to transfer files?"

Elizabeth's playful mocking was interrupted by the arrival of what looked like a wine bottle and two substantial steins. The major allowed his eyes to linger just a bit too long on the prominently displayed breasts of their server, and Elizabeth grimaced. Was it really necessary to ogle the waitress? She made a face at him and he responded by lifting one shoulder and letting it drop before he poured them each a beer from the bottle. She lifted her stein and sipped from it.

"What is this?" she asked. "It's really good."

"It's Fou'Foune," he replied, taking a long draught of his own.

She took another sip. "Mmm."

Richard heard a happy "tap, tap" on the wooden floor and shook his head. Sometimes he forgot how young she was. *Twenty-two, twenty-three, maybe? Not so young for a Marine. I'm just getting old.*

"So," he said, leaning back, relaxing. "Few months in Brussels so far, right? Like it?"

Bennet nodded. "I'm hoping to get to see a bit more of Europe. They've had me everywhere *but* Europe. I was in Japan for a while, and that was nice, but my broken Spanish wasn't much help."

"I was in Asia a few years ago," he said amiably, reaching for his drink. "My Japanese isn't great, though. My Dutch is good, French is better, and my Arabic isn't terrible. I also speak a little Pilipino."

"Is that the same as Tagalog?" she asked.

He nodded.

"The Philippines," she mused. She gave him an assessing look. "I suppose you know Kali?"

Kali was one name for the knife fighting style he'd learned there. "I know enough."

She seemed to be waiting for more, but there wasn't much he was authorized to say about his work in the Philippines. "I now carve a hell of a Thanksgiving turkey," he said simply. "How'd you hear of it?"

"I like to read," she replied with a shrug. She took a drink. "I had a few tours in Afghanistan and Iraq and other places in the Middle East," she said, "but I mainly stayed on base setting up networks, working out kinks in the existing computer systems and searching for intrusions and vulnerabilities. I was in Africa, too, but I couldn't tell you where—we were usually in concrete bunkers doing our thing. It's been really nice to have normal off-hours, even a weekend here and there, do some sightseeing." She set her beer down. "Everything's so close here—it took me less than two hours to get to Paris. And the work—well, it's not exactly challenging, but that's okay."

He thought she didn't seem particularly concerned about it and asked her why.

"I'm planning to separate at the end of my six. So coasting for a few more months doesn't bother me at all."

He nodded. It made sense. "I'm getting pretty close to my ten."

"Are you thinking about separating?" she asked curiously.

He shrugged. "Haven't decided," he replied.

As Bennet set her mug on the table and reached for a menu,

Richard saw her frown and tilt her head slightly to peer around the end of the booth. She became very still, very serious.

"Sir," she said, in a low, urgent whisper and gestured behind him with a slight movement of her eyes.

Richard turned, careful not to move too quickly, and spied four men swaggering to the bar, dressed too warmly for the weather. They were looking around but not sitting. "Another . . . ?" he asked in a murmur, tipping his head behind him, towards the entrance.

She responded with a minute nod of her head, indicating the approximate position of a fifth man.

"Damn," he muttered.

He reached for his sidearm, but there was nothing there. They couldn't carry weapons outside the Embassy grounds, and he was suddenly glad they weren't in uniform. At least they'd have the advantage of surprise. They'd need it.

Bennet caught his eye. He pointed to her, the stein, and then down to the floor beneath her seat. He'd never fit in the small space between the bottom of the booth and the floor, but Bennet could. She'd be able to get in behind the sentry from that angle.

She nodded, grabbed her beer, dropped to the ground, and carefully eased into position. Richard knelt down near the edge of the table, remaining out of sight while he tried to assess the situation. He reached up to grab his own beer, took a drink, poured out the remaining liquid on the floor behind him, and hefted the weight of the stein in his hand.

The three men had moved into the restaurant, facing the other side of the room where everyone else was seated. One pulled a Luger, and then everything happened at once. There was an earsplitting shriek of gunfire into the ceiling that made his ears ring and his guts squeeze tight. The gunman's torrent of words was nearly drowned out by the screams of the customers and staff as they scuttled for shelter, but he caught enough. *Arabic,* he thought clinically, *but a terrible accent. Second, maybe third language.* There was a sudden flurry of movement as several young men who had been seated on a booth at the far end of the room burst through an emergency exit into the street, yelling for help. The repeated klaxon of the alarm was deafening, but it abruptly ceased when one of the shots that followed destroyed the old box housing it.

The attackers began arguing, the escape clearly rattling them. *They sure didn't map this out.*

Each man had what appeared to be a Luger. They shot randomly, angrily, at the overturned tables, the windows, the open kitchen. The sharp, ear-piercing ricochet of metal against the hanging pots was painful. There were screams and sobs as people hit the ground. Some tried to crawl away. Out of the corner of his eye, he saw a blur as Bennet made her move.

Elizabeth was hyper-aware of the grit under her palms as she sized up her target and counted. *One.* Several college-aged boys fled into the street. *Excellent.* The men in the center of the floor began to argue. *Two.* The young man standing guard stepped a little farther into the room. She grabbed her stein. *Three.* Heart pounding in her ears, she launched herself out from under the booth, moved into position, and swung. The heavy stein impacted the attacker's head with such force that it sent a painful jolt up her arm. In the second it took for the man to drop to his knees, Major Fitzwilliam appeared in front of him. He grabbed the man by the collar and delivered a powerful blow to the man's face, breaking his nose. The sentry slumped backwards and collapsed to the floor, where he lay motionless. Elizabeth grabbed the prone figure under one arm, the major the other, and they dragged him a few feet back, out of his partners' direct line of sight.

She took a quick look at the middle of the room as they both searched the unconscious man for weapons—his team was still shooting in the other direction, backs to the front door, screaming at each other, making too much noise to hear what she and the major were doing. They had not yet noticed that their man was missing. She grabbed the Luger from the attacker's slack hand, and the major shoved him up on one side, still hunting.

The tallest attacker flipped his long coat back to reveal a rifle.

"AKM," they hissed at the same time, and their speed increased. Elizabeth's hand closed around a second magazine and then the handle of a knife while the major grabbed a second handgun. The major held out his hand and she passed the knife over. Then they split up. He moved back to their table while Elizabeth slipped to the right and behind the bar itself. Once concealed, Elizabeth checked the condition of her weapon and ammunition—eight rounds in and eight in the magazine. She met the major's eyes. He gestured to a group of upended tables down the left side of the room—he would keep between them and the wall, and she would provide cover. She nodded once.

The firing stopped, and the jabbering began again. Elizabeth popped her head up over the top of the bar and took two shots. She ducked just as she heard four shots hit the front of the bar and two more hit the mirrored wall above her, splintering the glass. She dodged the shards as well as she could, then crept down the bar past the bartender and the waitress who were on the floor, curled into fetal positions with their hands over their ears. Once well beyond them, she rose just high enough above the counter to return fire with a pair of shots before dropping back to one knee.

There were a lot of civilians scattered around the room in the line of fire. She didn't have a lot of ammunition either—she'd have to pick her shots and hope for the best. She crouched again and scrambled all the way to the far end of the bar, took a breath, and peered over the top. The attackers were still aiming their weapons in the direction of her previous position. She steadied her weapon and squeezed off two rounds. One man went down.

They all turned at once, but the man with the AKM was struggling to reload it. She took two more shots. Even as fast as she dropped to the floor, she saw another man fall to the ground and she grimaced as she reloaded. *Eight rounds left*. As she worked her way back to the center of the bar, she heard the major firing from his position across the room, and then an angry howl. *They'll take cover*, she thought. *We need to get them now*. She peered over the top of the bar to see that both two remaining attackers were now behind tables, and the AKM was pointing directly at her.

Her eyes locked on the rifle.

"Down!" the major ordered. It must have been shouted, because she heard it clear as a bell.

Elizabeth dove to the ground and pressed her hands to her ears as an entire wall of bottles above her exploded in a thunderous hail of bullets.

Richard sneered as at least thirty rounds were fired at Bennet's position. *Did he just empty his clip to shoot up the booze?* He uncovered his ears, but it hadn't done him much good to protect them—he could hear nothing more than a buzzing sound. He ducked as the second attacker whirled to fire randomly at him, but fortunately the man was unable to properly handle even his smaller weapon. He managed to clean out most of the front windows and not much else. A few jagged pieces of glass still clung to the frames, sending bright shafts of refracted light across the polished wooden floor. While the shooter reached for another magazine, Richard aimed and fired, striking the man in the arm when he turned at the last moment. *Shit.* That resulted in more wild shooting around the room, the bullets rising too high, Richard hoped, to hit anyone.

Bennet popped up from behind the bar like a freaking jack-in-the-box, taking three more shots and briefly drawing attention away from him so he could move. The remaining two attackers, both wounded, backed up across the room towards the emergency exit, speaking excitedly, weapons still aimed inside. *Damn, is that Russian now? No . . . I think that's Turkic.* Richard squeezed off several more rounds. One man went down, but the slide on Richard's pistol didn't retract. Out of bullets. He shoved the gun into his waistband and kept an eye on the fallen man as he moved from one source of cover to another. Bennet was watching their exit from a kneeling position behind the end of the bar on the other side of the room, weapon still in one hand but without a clear shot, holding the other hand up, palm out, as a sign to everyone to remain in place.

He drew the knife from his belt.

As the last attacker scrambled over the body that was now lying across the threshold, he lit a rag stuffed in a bottle and cocked his arm back to throw it inside. Just as the man was about to release the bottle, Richard whipped the knife at him. There was a flash of metal and a scream and the bottle's trajectory changed.

Time slowed down for Richard. He was caught in no-man's land: too far away to leap the overturned tables and chairs to grab the Molotov before it exploded and burned, not far enough away to escape the blast. All he could do was watch the arc of the bottle and the tiny flicker of the flame as he imagined his life ending in fire. There was even time to consider the irony that it was the Embassy assignment his father had insisted he take that would kill him in the end. *Killed by the world's stupidest terrorists*, he thought, and then, hopefully, *maybe the flame will go out*.

As he was helplessly watching the bottle sail beyond his reach, Bennet sprinted from behind the end of the bar. She caught the bottle in one hand and ripped the burning rag out of it with the other. The flame reached the fuel on the cloth and flared before she dropped it and stomped on it. She picked up her firearm from where she'd left it and began to retreat to cover.

His heart rate slowing just a bit, Richard got to his knees and crawled to the terrorist closest to him. The man's arms were curled around a backpack. Richard watched him closely and eased the pack away so he could check it for weapons. He glanced as a blur of long black hair flew past. A teenager with tears on her cheeks and her mouth open in a scream he couldn't hear was running across the floor. "Stop!" he yelled, but who knew if her hearing was any better than his? He spied Bennet leaving cover to intercept the girl.

A limp hand brushed his fingers, and Richard's attention jerked back to the body. Startled, he pulled the pack into his arms and sprang away as he saw the man's eyes focus on the backpack, his lips moving. He couldn't hear the words, but he saw the grim smile and could read the man's lips. "Allahu Akbar," he mouthed. His thumb twitched against a cell phone in his other hand, searching for something.

Time sped up again as Richard leapt to his feet. As though he were throwing a discus with both hands, he used the straps to toss the backpack through the air with all his strength.

"Bomb!" he yelled. Bennet's arms wrapped around the girl, sending them both to the ground a split second before the backpack sailed inches over their heads. It traveled through the largest of the shattered windows and out onto the street corner nearest the alley.

There was the roar of an explosion outside, the acrid odor of gunpowder and smoke, the whizzing of shrapnel, broken pieces of wood and glass shrieking back inside through suddenly heated air. He stayed down and hoped Bennet had found cover.

Once the worst of the debris settled, he remained prone for a second to mentally review his injuries before emerging to survey the damage. The remaining glass nearest the detonation had been blown from the windows, and the heavy front door had been knocked off its top hinge and was leaning precariously into the room. The booth where they'd originally been seated was in three large pieces. He shifted to look behind him. The other end of the room, where most of the civilians were hiding, seemed mostly intact other than the holes high up on the wall, same as the kitchen.

He reached forward to pull himself up. The back of his hands and forearms had taken the brunt of the flying glass, but he felt a damp trickle of warm blood on his neck as well. His ears were ringing. *Maybe a few stitches*, he thought, rather stunned that he had escaped with so little damage. He shook his head, and tiny bits of glass rained from his hair.

"Anyone critical?" he called, sitting up slowly. He couldn't hear his own voice, and he shook his head a bit, irritated. It didn't help his hearing, but it did make him feel a little nauseous. *Like being shot at by circus clowns.* He flinched at the pain in his arms. *Still hurts.*

He gazed more carefully around the room. He counted two wounded over by the front windows. Around the room, people continued to simply appear, heads rising above the debris like moles, most faces white with shock, some only now reaching out gingerly to one another. He saw injuries from the flying glass and some minor wounds—there was one corner where there seemed to be several more serious injuries. It was difficult to see over the toppled booths and splintered tables laying on their sides. His eyes flew back in the direction he'd tossed the backpack. *Where is Bennet?*

He pushed himself up to begin triage, closing his eyes against the dizziness for a moment and then moving towards the first prone figure. He instructed the woman's husband to hold pressure on her wound, then shifted to the next casualty.

Elizabeth's head was throbbing, her ears ringing. She could feel her t-shirt sticking to her back. There was a strong, sharp metallic smell filling her nose and mouth that made her gag. She spit out blood—she had bitten her tongue—and felt a body shifting beneath her. The teenaged girl she'd tackled and covered shrugged her off, and she let go as a man in his mid-forties ran over to sweep the girl into his arms. Elizabeth saw only a bobbing ponytail as he carried her away.

She pushed herself up to her hands and right knee and waited for a moment, expecting the room to stop spinning and her ears to cease ringing. When neither happened, she tumbled over into a sitting position and stared dumbly at a thin metal splinter protruding from the side of her left leg, close to her kneecap. *I should feel that.*

She glanced over at the bar to see the bartender poking his nose above the bar and then standing. She met his gaze, and he nodded. His face was pale, and he'd been cut up by flying glass from the bottles, but otherwise he appeared well. He reached down to help his coworker up.

With a grunt, Elizabeth hauled herself to her feet and balanced most of her weight on her good leg. There was an ache in her shoulder and a small, sharp pain just above her left eyebrow. She passed a hand across her face and stared at the smeared blood. *Oh,* she thought blearily. *That explains it.*

The major was crouched near some of the wounded giving

instruction and trying to take a casualty count. She leaned on whatever was still standing as she hobbled over to provide aid.

She touched his shoulder. "You all right, sir?" she asked, her voice loud and hoarse. He looked down at his bloody arms, but she gestured to his neck, just below his jaw. He put his hand up to touch where she indicated, and his fingers came away wet and red.

"Close," Elizabeth yelled. He nodded as the room filled with Belgian law enforcement, and they both reached for ID.

Richard looked Bennet over. Her t-shirt was shredded and stained, more seriously on her left side. Her face was clear but for one razor thin cut just above her left eyebrow that bled profusely but he thought looked worse than it was. *Glass.*

"You okay?" he asked in a near shout. He stood and turned away from an officer who then retrieved his empty gun from his waistband. *They got here fast*, he thought, then remembered the boys who had escaped. He reached out with his free hand to help her to the nearest booth. The vinyl on the seat was torn and large pieces of foam still floated in the air. She blinked at him as the tiny yellow pieces swirled around them but did not respond. *Shit,* he thought, looking her full in the face, *her pupils are dilated.*

He watched her lips as she said, "Pipe bomb." He agreed without comment. Impossible to know whether there had been a detonation from the phone or whether the motion of the throw had set it off. No matter. Had it gone off inside . . . he glanced at the windows.

Bennet grimaced at him, nodded outside. "Game over," she said, completing his thought. She placed her weapon on the tabletop and eased herself back on the seat, extending her left leg along its length. It was then he noticed the shrapnel jutting out of her leg just to the side of her knee. She put her right arm heavily on the battered table, her red, blistered hand landing on a handle that had once been part of a stein. She clutched it in her fist and raised it to show him, meeting his gaze for a moment until her focus faltered. Richard sat heavily across from her.

"You still owe me a beer," Bennet said. She lay her head down on her upper arm and the fist clutching the handle dropped to the table. He could see her adrenaline draining away, and he struggled to read her lips. "This one doesn't count."

CHAPTER TWO

Off-Duty US Marines Thwart Terrorist Attack

Five gunmen were subdued by two American Marines at the De Roos Bar and Restaurant last night near the US Embassy in Brussels. The men are not known to be affiliated with any terrorist organization, and no group has yet claimed responsibility.

The attack began just after 6:00pm, when the men entered, shouted orders in Arabic, and began to fire weapons, reportedly Lugers and an AKM, a more modern version of a Kalashnikov.

The gunmen were apparently unaware that two US Marines were among the customers. Though unarmed, Major Richard Fitzwilliam and Staff Sgt. Elizabeth Bennet managed to incapacitate a terrorist stationed at the front door, disarm him, and engage the other four.

Four of the attackers were killed at the scene. According to witnesses, when the final attacker attempted to toss a Molotov cocktail into the center of the bar as he fled, Bennet was well placed to intercept it and snuff out the flame before it could ignite and explode.

A second bomb was discovered and thrown outside by Fitzwilliam seconds before it detonated, greatly reducing its impact. Several police at the scene were struck by shrapnel in the blast, but none sustained serious injuries. The final terrorist was wounded and taken into custody as he attempted to flee.

Most of the fifty-seven customers and fifteen staff in the restaurant at the time of the attack were treated at the scene. Twenty-one were transported to the hospital and seven were admitted, including Bennet. While several of the wounded are in serious condition, all are expected to survive.

Both Marines were modest when asked about their role in ending the attack. "It could have been a good deal worse," said Fitzwilliam, who has been working as an international analyst and interpreter for the Embassy. "Bennet was able to snuff out the Molotov, and the pipe bomb detonated outside, where the area had already been cleared of civilians."

When Bennet was reached for comment by phone this morning, she said, "We're Marines. We're trained for situations like this. I'm just glad nobody was killed." When asked where she was assigned at the Embassy, she replied, "IT."

Will Darcy tossed his morning paper aside, appetite gone. He picked up his cell phone and hit the speed dial for his cousin. It went directly to voicemail. Again. Will rolled his eyes, but if he wanted a reply, he'd have to leave a message this time. Richard's rules.

"Richard, I just saw the news," he said tersely. "They didn't have names until now, but I was up all night. Call me as soon as you're free." *If he doesn't call me back this morning,* he thought, quickly calculating the time difference, *I can be on the next plane. I may be on the next plane regardless.* His next call was to his uncle.

Senator Terrence Fitzwilliam answered on the first ring. "William," he said warmly, "I was just about to call you. I assume you saw the news segment?"

"Not yet. Richard's in the *Times.*"

"Really?" his Uncle Terry sounded pleased. "I haven't seen that one yet."

"Have you heard from him?" Will asked, trying not to sound annoyed. On the front page, above the fold, was a color photo of his cousin in a tattered, blood-stained polo shirt exiting a Brussels restaurant half supporting a woman whose shirt was just as gory, her face obscured by blood, two startling green eyes staring vacantly out at the camera. They were surrounded by Brussels law enforcement, and he thought he could detect an Embassy official in the background of the shot, immaculate suit and tie a jarring contrast to his cousin's appearance. It wasn't something that should make his uncle happy.

The sight of Richard's injuries thoroughly unnerved Will, particularly what appeared to be a neck wound. *Damn close to the jugular, Richard. You could at least have texted to tell me you were okay.* He drummed his fingers over and over on the stone kitchen counter.

"Yes, that's why I was going to call," came his uncle's reassuring hum. *Politician's purr,* Will groaned silently, his fingers slowing, clenching into a fist that he tapped on the counter instead. "It's been busy here since the attack, but I had a voicemail from Richard this morning saying he's fine. He needed stitches but wasn't admitted to the hospital. He's back on duty being debriefed and will call when he can."

A lot of stitches, from the looks of it. At least he's shut up in meetings and not just ignoring me.

It didn't improve his mood. Richard's ten years were coming up, and he had promised to consider separating. Will worried that this incident would encourage his cousin to remain in the service. With Richard's business savvy and ability to pick up languages, he knew of a dozen ways his cousin could step into a leadership role at FORGE without putting his life at risk every time he left the house. After almost eight years in the field, Richard had agreed to a desk job, but he'd been alternately bored and irritated with his work at the Embassy. Will had allowed himself to hope.

"Barker is apoplectic," his uncle laughed, referring to a long-time rival in the Senate. "Support offers are rolling in. Maybe I'll make another run after all."

After a short conversation, Will ended the call. He checked his watch. Georgiana wouldn't be up yet in California. He sent her a text asking her to call him first thing.

He set his phone down and read the story again before pushing the front section away. He'd heard about the attacks before heading to bed the night before and had stayed up waiting for names. He'd had a terrible feeling about his cousin, especially when he wasn't answering his phone, but Will tried to convince himself that Richard might just be involved in the intelligence effort following the attack.

Ignoring the oatmeal and fruit still sitting on the counter, Will opened the liquor cabinet and poured himself a whiskey.

"Damn you, Richard," he growled, sipping his drink and closing his eyes. "Just come home."

CHAPTER THREE

By the time Richard left the briefing room, he was exhausted. He'd been ordered to report the minute he was released from the hospital. All the glass flying around had done its damage. The ham-handed intern on call had taken forever, and he'd lost count of the stitches. He would have preferred to go back to his quarters, change clothes, and self-medicate with the bottle of whiskey Will had brought him when he'd last swung through on his way to a meeting in London. Instead, he'd left the hospital after midnight and was spirited back to the US Embassy before he'd even had a chance to learn anything about Bennet. Despite her leg wound, she'd insisted on walking out. At least she'd let him help her. It was foolish, of course, but he also admired it. The woman was cussedly stubborn and every inch a Marine.

He headed to his quarters where he changed out of his borrowed sweats and washed up as best he could without getting the stitches wet. He shaved, rubbing a hot washcloth across his face when he was done. The team from the embassy left him to sleep in a cheap plastic chair, his head on the table, as they conferred over his version of events and made plans to debrief Bennet in the morning. He finished getting ready, tossing on clean pants, a USMC polo shirt, pulling on a pair of new socks and his favorite boots. He yawned. *I hope they weren't expecting me in the office today*, he thought, and then, *I should remind them where I am*. The investigators had taken his cell phone, as though there might be some clue to the attack on it. They'd returned it, but he had it on the charger now. He picked up the cordless phone in the living room and made the call.

He was tired, his arms were stiff, and his neck hurt when he moved it the wrong way, but he wanted to see Bennet and he knew he had to call Will. His father had likely called him already, and he knew his younger cousin would be worried. *Like a mother hen*, he thought, and then felt ashamed of himself. *He comes by it honestly*.

It had been five years since George and Anne Darcy had died suddenly in a car accident two weeks before Georgiana's graduation from middle school. Neither Will nor Georgiana had ever really recovered. Will had always been a bit overprotective of his little sister, but he'd been just short of unbearable since the loss of their parents. On the other hand, Richard was sure that Will would have already been in touch with Georgiana, and he was glad. The thought of his youngest cousin hearing about the attack or seeing the videos of it online without being warned first made Richard cringe.

Still, once Will had him on the phone, it was likely to be a long conversation, and he needed to see Bennet. He'd been told she was recovering, but he felt guilty. She'd never been to De Roos before. She'd only been there because it was convenient for him and he'd suggested it. Besides, he felt like they were partners now, in a way. The hospital wasn't far. He'd just see if she needed anything and make his calls after.

When he arrived, he was asked for identification before being allowed up to her room, the door of which was flanked by two officers. Richard offered them a barely perceptible nod and walked inside.

Bennet was asleep, and he stood just inside the room, wondering if he should come back. He took a long look at her. One leg was in in a CPM cradle being continuously moved in a gentle circular motion. The cut above her eye was butterflied, no stitches. Her hospital gown gaped so he could see her shoulder was bandaged, but there was no sling. He couldn't tell for sure, but it did look like she had a pretty good lump on one side of her head under all that hair. He'd only seen her hair pulled back and secured above the collar. *She looks even younger with it down.* Her forearms, like his, were covered in gauze, as was her burned hand. Her color was better than it had been when they stumbled out of the ruined restaurant, but that wasn't saying much. He shook off the protective feelings that were surfacing. *I'm not Will, and Bennet's not Georgiana*, he thought. *She's a Marine, and she had my back.*

Elizabeth opened her eyes to a bright hospital room awash in white. White walls, white curtains, and a white ceiling. Her vision was blurry, and her teeth felt fuzzy. There was a muted, throbbing ache behind her eyes.

"Morning, Sunshine," came a deep voice from the foot of her bed.

Elizabeth swallowed, grimaced at the taste in her mouth. "Sir?" she croaked. Her throat felt like sandpaper.

"Major Fitzwilliam, the one and only," he replied, and she tried to focus on his face. She blinked. Better, but still blurry around the edges.

"Well, you look like crap," he said with a teasing grin. Then he asked, more seriously, "How're you feeling?"

She saw him more clearly then, as he moved out of the direct sunlight. His arms and neck were bandaged, and he had a few light scrapes along one side of his face, but otherwise he looked fine. She reached for a pink blob to her right, guessing it was a cup of water. She missed it the first time, and the major reached over to pick it up. He held it steady for her while she took a sip through the straw.

"Like someone threw a pipe bomb at me, sir," she said when she was through.

He grinned again, this time appearing more relaxed, and moved closer to her bed. "You must be feeling better if you're already giving me shit about that."

"I wouldn't know," she sighed, returning to the question. "They've got me on some first-rate drugs. I am literally feeling no pain," she said slowly, trying not to slur her words and leaning back. She held up her unbandaged hand in front of her and wiggled her fingers. Nothing. "Not feeling much at all, actually."

That wasn't entirely true. She could feel her left leg in a machine that was making a groaning noise as it gradually but continuously bent her knee and straightened it. *Oh yeah. Surgery.*

"You seem to have gotten off okay," he said, serious for a moment. "Second-degree burn," he told her, nodding at her hand. "The shoulder wound was superficial. You had surgery to remove some shrapnel from your knee, and you've got a concussion, which I'm pretty sure you already know. That'll happen when you tackle teenagers and dive into tables headfirst."

Elizabeth grunted a little. With a sigh and a slightly elevated eyebrow, she asked, "How many stitches did you get?"

He shrugged. "Lots. Too many. Why?"

"I bet I had more than you."

He snorted at that. "Trying to explain why you're lying around in bed while I have to work?"

She cleared her throat. "Do I need to explain this again? B.O.M.B."

He laughed full-out this time. "You can still spell. A good sign for someone with head trauma." He let out a breath. "I actually stopped by to see if you needed anything."

"I am in desperate, *desperate* need of a toothbrush." She closed her eyes. "And my phone. I have to call my sister." He glanced over at the side table and saw her phone was there. He picked it up, but the battery was dead. He looked in the drawer, but there was no charger.

"If you give me her number, I'll make the call."

"She'll freak out if someone else calls." Elizabeth forced her eyelids open. "But I guess if you tell her I'm busy being high . . ." The major shook his head. She recited the numbers, and he entered them in his phone. "I hope I got that right." She half-sighed, half-groaned again. The meds were making her feel sick and stupid. Were they supposed to give painkillers to someone with a concussion? "Ask for *Dr.* Jane Bennet." Her sister had earned a DNP—a Doctorate of Nursing Practice. It embarrassed Jane to be addressed that way, but Elizabeth insisted that she'd earned it. Jane would know she was all right if the major asked for her by title.

"Doctor, huh?" he asked. "Clearly she got all the brains."

Elizabeth gave him a half-hearted scowl. "You are so lucky I was there yesterday, Major I-speak-a-dozen-languages. It wasn't a scholar you needed."

The major chuckled.

Elizabeth closed her eyes again as a wave of nausea washed over her.

She could almost feel Major Fitzwilliam scrutinizing her. "Hey, you're looking kind of green," he said, after a moment. "You okay?"

"No," she said, grateful when he quickly grabbed a basin and held it under her as she sat up and heaved over the side of the bed. Dry heaves, in the end, for which she was thankful. When she was finished, he set the basin down and went the bathroom. He returned with a toothbrush wrapped in plastic and a tiny tube of toothpaste. He handed them to her.

"Thanks," Elizabeth muttered.

"You're welcome," he said. "I'm going to let the nurse know you're sick to your stomach so they can give you something for it. Unfortunately, I have to make some calls of my own after that."

"What time is it?"

He checked his watch. "Local time is 15:00."

"Wow." She thought about that for a minute. "The shooting was yesterday, right?"

"Yes," he said with a small grimace.

She picked up the pink cup in one try this time and took a sip. "And they're just letting you out of debrief?"

He nodded once. "About ninety minutes ago."

Elizabeth let out a short *humph*. "Sorry you had to do it alone. They spoke to me earlier, but I actually can't remember what I said. Something about Rosebud."

He stared at her.

"Yeah, that's the look they gave me, too," she said with a grimace. "*Citizen Kane*? Doesn't anyone watch the classics anymore?"

"You said that in debrief?" he asked. His cheek twitched and his lips quirked upward.

"Well, we'd already sort of exhausted everything else. Multiple times. I figured they'd leave if they thought the meds were kicking in."

He chuckled. "Not a bad strategy."

"Sorry, sir," she said abruptly, her eyelids dropping shut. The pain meds were putting her to sleep again. "I'm not trying to pull a Rosebud, but I have to stop talking now."

Major Fitzwilliam grunted at the announcement. She felt him lift the cup from her hand where it was beginning to tip over and replaced it on her tray. "Okay," he said.

She was drifting off when she felt the toothpaste and toothbrush leaving her hand and heard him setting items down on the table.

"See ya, Staff Sergeant," he said quietly. She was asleep before the door closed.

Richard found a courtyard wedged between two buildings in the medical complex and took a seat at one of the small outdoor tables. At this time of the afternoon, the area was deserted. He pulled his phone out of his pocket and placed his portable charger on the table, ready for use.

First, he tried the number Bennet had given him.

On the second ring, he heard a soft "Hello?"

"Hello," he said. "I'm calling for Dr. Jane Bennet?"

There was a soft huff on the other end, then, "This is she."

This is she? He thought. *Pretty formal for a sister of Bennet's.*

"Dr. Bennet, this is Major Richard Fitzwilliam, US Marines. . ." Before he could continue, he was interrupted.

"Is Elizabeth all right?" the voice asked, thoroughly panicked.

"She's fine, Dr. Bennet. She asked me to call you."

"Why isn't she calling me herself?"

Richard shook his head. *Bennet was right,* he thought. *Her sister is freaking out.* What had she told him to say? "She told me to tell you she was busy being high."

There was silence for a moment, then a *humph* that sounded nearly identical to Bennet's. "I'm sure she thinks that's funny. Is she really all right? What are they giving her? Does she have a concussion?"

"Wow, that's a lot of questions in a row." Richard ran a hand through his hair, trying to gather his jumbled thoughts. *How'd she know about the concussion?* "Uh, she *is* going to be all right, I don't know, and she does. Did someone already call you?"

"No, I think they called my uncle. I saw her photo in the paper."

Huh, he thought, impressed. Despite his crack about her sister having the brains, he knew from the few conversations they'd had that the staff sergeant was no slouch. *The Bennets seem a pretty smart bunch.*

Silence again, then, "Thank you for calling me, Major Fitzwilliam. Do you know when Lizzy might be able to call me, or is there a good time to call her? Her phone is going straight to voicemail. I'm afraid until I hear her voice . . ."

He felt a surge of sympathy for her that extended to his own cousin. "Sorry, I don't know. Her phone was dead, and she was sleeping when I left her. The meds are really knocking her out." He gave her the name of the hospital and Bennet's room number.

The next question was clipped, clinical. "What can you tell me about her injuries?"

He went through what he knew, and then, after another round of thanks from her, he hung up. Then something struck him, and he lifted his eyebrows.

"Lizzy," he said with a small chuckle. Bennet didn't look like a Lizzy to him. He was sure it would bug her. Yeah, he could have some fun with that.

He checked his battery and plugged in the mobile charger before checking the message icon for the first time in a full day and realizing he had over thirty messages.

"God," he groaned, scrolling through them. Most were numbers he didn't know, but it was easy to pick out Will's. He listened to the messages and tapped the screen to return the call. His cousin picked up before the first ring was complete. *Predictable.*

His cousin's baritone was taut, sharp. "Richard?"

"It's me, Will," Richard said. "How hard are you hitting the scotch?"

There was a pause. "Whiskey, actually."

"My mistake." He sighed. "I'm okay, Will. Really."

Will cleared his throat. "Your dad called."

"Oh, I'm sure that went well," Richard replied, resting his head in his hand. "Crowing, was he?"

"Do I need to answer that?" Will asked with a sigh. Richard imagined his stoic cousin running his hand through his hair. He always did that when he was unhappy or stressed.

He sounds wrecked. "No. Sorry I didn't call right after. My phone was confiscated when they heard me leaving a message for my dad. Just got it back and had to charge it."

There was a release of air Richard identified as anger, and then Will said, "Okay."

"Will," Richard said wearily, "I didn't go looking for this, you know. It might have happened in New York as easily as here." *I am too tired for this conversation.*

"I doubt it. You're in Brussels, Richard, a European hotspot for terrorist activity."

Richard almost laughed out loud but swallowed it. Sometimes his cousin sounded like he was eighty. "Hotspot?"

"Argh," Will groaned, frustrated. "You know what I mean."

"Sorry. You make it too easy sometimes."

"Richard . . ."

"No, honestly, I *am* sorry," he said, and he was. "I know you worry, Will, but really, I'm okay."

His cousin went straight to the heart of the matter. "Are you staying in?"

"I don't know," Richard replied bluntly, "and I can't think about it right now." *I really can't. Sleep. I can think about sleep.* He gazed up at the sky. "I tell you what. Send me a list of the jobs you're always nagging me about, and I'll look at them."

He could hear Will breathing for a moment before asking, "Really?"

It was difficult to believe one word could convey such a strong, quiet hope. Richard frowned. "I will *look* at them. No promises."

"Okay," Will replied quickly.

Richard suspected he was being handled. Will always seemed to know when to push him and when to back off. *Still.*

Maybe it was just the blood loss or the lack of sleep, but for the first time, Richard was starting to relent. While he had admitted that he needed to get out of the field, his work at the embassy had been unfulfilling. At this point, his cousins—Will in particular—likely needed him more than the Marines.

His own family didn't need him in the same way. Richard knew his father loved him, but Senator Fitzwilliam was a politician through and through, never averse to taking advantage of a good crisis. *This was a really good one*, Richard thought sardonically. *He'll get all kinds of points for having a son in the mix.*

That was probably unfair. His father did support Richard's military career, and he did care. It was just that once he was assured of Richard's health, he would move to wringing whatever he could from the publicity. There was no reason to call his older brother. Oscar had a highly developed network in the capitol. What with the attack being so close to the embassy, he'd probably known what was going on immediately after the Brussels police got the call.

Will—and, to some extent, Georgiana—sat at the other extreme. They'd likely be brooding over all the things that might have happened. When Aunt Anne and Uncle George died so suddenly, they had both handled things as well as could be expected, drawing even closer to one another than they had been. But their fears of losing someone else were always lurking just beneath the surface. Then, only two years later, his own mother had died. It had hit the entire family hard, but he suspected Will and Georgiana were terrified that the losses would just keep coming. Now, three years after her death, everyone seemed to be moving on at last. Except Will.

Will's worries seemed to be intensifying. Richard supposed it made sense. Georgiana had recently left New York for the summer business program Stanford offered to incoming students. Will was already having a hard time adjusting to his sister living on the other side of the country. Richard had not been at all surprised that she had chosen to attend Stanford over Harvard, or even NYU. As much as she loved her brother, she needed to establish herself on her own. She emailed and texted Richard constantly, telling him about her friends and classes, though she now seemed to be studying more than socializing. Richard thought she was probably even more circumspect with her brother, who, unlike him, could and would fly out to California the instant he thought she needed him.

He can be aggravating, but it's also nice to know someone cares that much. "Will?" Richard asked.

His cousin answered, his voice gruff. "Yeah?"

"Thanks."

After a brief, embarrassed silence, they moved on to talk about Georgiana, her studies, and how Will should discuss the news with her. The call lasted over an hour, and Richard decided he would return home and crawl into bed before trying to make any others.

CHAPTER FOUR

It was still dark outside, and Elizabeth pressed her hands around a cup of coffee, trying to get warm. She'd always done her work late at night or early in the morning—that was when the online chatter she used to track her targets really heated up. Once at the embassy, she'd re-trained herself to sleep at night and work during the day, but her stay in the hospital and the pain she was still experiencing had her sleep patterns in tatters. So she was tired and more than a little irritated that she'd been ordered to report for this appearance at four in the morning. She hadn't slept much, worried about being on time, only to have to wait for the major to arrive.

When he finally dragged himself in and dropped in a heap onto the dumpy little waiting-room sofa, tilted his head back and closed his eyes, she lifted an eyebrow and said, bitingly, "How did you become an officer when you're *always* late?"

"Don't start on me, Bennet," he groaned. "I got a wake-up call from the general at oh-two-thirty complaining that my 'celebrity tour' is causing her grief in the office. She was closing down some bar somewhere, and I couldn't get her off the line."

"*Celebrity* tour?" she asked, incredulous.

"Precisely." He opened one eye to look at her. "How's the knee?"

She tapped the brace. "Better. They have me back at work."

The major shut his eye again. "Head better too?"

She shrugged. *Ongoing battle.* "Mostly."

"I still owe you that beer," he said, half-asleep.

"Damn right you do, but I can't drink with the concussion. Trust me, I'll let you know. And I don't want any watered-down lager or cheap white wine. I want Fou'Foune."

That caused a small grin. "All right. You're on."

She rolled her shoulders and yawned. "You're so lucky this is radio. I am not in the mood to be shoved in a makeup chair and expected to make small talk." She finished her coffee and poured herself another cup. "How many more of these do we have to do? I mean, really, what is there left to say? We've talked about it for three weeks already. The whole thing was over in three minutes."

Major Fitzwilliam was half-asleep, head resting on the back of the couch. "Three minutes and thirty-seven seconds."

Elizabeth considered that. "Three-three-seven. Kind of like that. Lucky numbers."

He grunted. "Strange kind of luck, Staff Sergeant."

Elizabeth shrugged, even though she knew he wouldn't see it. "We're both standing here, sir."

He shifted, trying to get comfortable. "Sitting, actually. At four-thirty in the morning, thank you very much. After getting drunk-called by a general who thinks I'm her secretary."

Elizabeth grinned. "Are you sure she doesn't like you, sir?"

"Shut up, Staff Sergeant."

"No, I mean *really* like you. You're a catch, you know."

Major Fitzwilliam didn't open his eyes and his was voice calm and even. "Seriously, shut up. I'm too tired to crush you now, but I *will* retaliate. I know plenty of Marines who'd love to ask *you* out. Some even shower. Occasionally."

Elizabeth laughed. "Okay. I'll lay off since I've seen you throw a knife and I can't exactly run away." She sipped her coffee and sighed, content. "Between you and the coffee, I'm starting to feel almost human."

"Yeah," he mumbled as he fell asleep. "You're welcome."

As they waited for the program's host to arrive, they sat in the sound booth and chatted a bit. A sound tech was working on the other side of a plexiglass barrier.

"Shall I tell everyone the truth this time? You know, how I single-handedly kept five terrorists and two bombs from destroying De Roos?" he asked, leaning back in his chair.

"Why not? It wouldn't be the first time an officer took credit for my work," she shot back. "*Sir.*"

He laughed. "That hurts. You don't think I've earned my superhero cape?"

"Nope. You can't pull off the tights." She pressed the heels of her hands into her eyes. "Ugh. Now I have that image in my head."

Richard was about to joke "better off than on," when he saw a green light out of the corner of his eye and glanced up to see the tech grinning at them.

The host rushed in with stack of papers clutched in his hand and introduced himself before dropping into his seat and beginning the show.

They were five minutes into the interview being asked again why they had attacked the terrorist standing guard at the door, and Richard was trying not to smile at Bennet's epic eye roll. Instead, he answered diplomatically, "Well, he was isolated from the others, and we were in position to take him by surprise."

"But you had no weapons," the host insisted. "What made you think you could succeed?"

Richard sighed a little. *We're Marines*, he thought, and imagined hitting his head repeatedly against the tabletop. Surely it couldn't hurt any worse than answering these questions every day, could it? But then Bennet took over.

"We did have weapons, Henrik," she said smoothly. "Those heavy steins they use for the tourists. They might not be firearms, but they have great stopping power, right, sir?"

Richard didn't answer. *Great stopping power. Where does she come up with this stuff?*

Bennet's voice grew thoughtful. "In the Marines, Henrik," she said, "we have an unofficial motto: Improvise, adapt, overcome." She paused. "That's all we did here."

"And on that note," Henrik said jubilantly into his oversized microphone, "we need to move on to traffic. Thank you to Major Richard Fitzwilliam and Sgt. Elizabeth Bennet, recipients of Belgium's Order of the Crown, and US Marines through and through."

Fitzwilliam opened his mouth to say *Staff Sergeant*, but they were already off the air and Bennet just made a face. She stood up. As they walked out of the recording booth, he turned to her.

"Nothing like dropping pearls of wisdom and getting cut off for traffic," she quipped.

He shook his head at her. "Breakfast?" he asked.

She nodded. "Sure."

As they waited for their food, the major propped his head up on his hand and gazed groggily at her.

"So, Staff Sergeant, tell me something about yourself."

"This isn't speed dating, sir," Elizabeth retorted. "You have to be more specific."

"Do me a favor, keep me awake. We've been through how many of these things now? They didn't even send a handler for us today."

"Thank God," she groaned. She hated this whole press tour even more than the major seemed to. *We found ourselves in a situation, and we did what we were trained to do. I don't know why everyone's making such a big deal out of it.*

"Agreed," the major was saying. "But other than you're good at what you do, you have a sister who's a doctor, and you are a pain in the . . ."

"Hold up, there, now," she warned him laughingly.

"Other than those things," he replied, deadpan, "I don't know much about you. Home's in New York like me, right?"

Okay, I'll play. "Grew up in Meryton, upstate New York. Big country house in the family for four generations, lots of acreage, horses. Parents belonged to the country club. We played tennis and swam in the summers. Nice place, good town to grow up in. My family's in Montclair, New Jersey now." She gestured across the table. "You?"

He scratched the back of his head, and Elizabeth knew what he was thinking: *Why would they leave a family house like that?* She didn't elaborate.

"Manhattan boy," the major said. "My father's a senator. He commuted to D.C. my whole childhood, but now that we're all up and out, he spends his weeks down there and comes home when the House isn't in session. My mom died a few years ago of cancer."

"Oh, I'm really sorry to hear that," she said with genuine regret.

The major nodded, his eyes clouding over for a moment.

"Senator Fitzwilliam," she mused. "I've heard of him, of course. Wondered if you were related. Was that a weird way to grow up?"

He reached for the sugar and tipped it into his coffee. "Probably, but it was normal for us. Didn't see a lot of him, but he tried to be there for the big things. My mother was with us all the time." He paused. "He says he's not running for reelection. She'd have loved to have him home." He shrugged. "What about your family?"

"Umm," she said as she looked to the other side of the café to check for their waitress.

He tilted his head at her. "Look, I've heard a lot of horror stories from a lot of Marines. You aren't going to shock me."

She shrugged. "It's not shocking, just not all that interesting."

He waited.

She frowned. "My mother was bipolar. Lots of highs and lows, lots of what she called 'nerves,' and she didn't always take her meds. It made things kind of tricky."

"Did your dad help?"

She gave in to the inquisition. "I haven't heard from him in a long time. He left for good when I was a junior in high school. Jane was away at school and I didn't want her to quit, so I was sort of in charge."

"Sorry," he said. "That sucks." He took a sip of his water and then asked, "Siblings?"

"It wasn't fun," she said honestly, "but we coped. Four sisters. Jane's older, and I have three who are younger. They all live with my aunt and uncle now. Jane's a DNP in Newark at the hospital there. Mary started Montclair State this year. Kit and Lydia are still in high school. What about you?"

His forehead furrowed. "What's a DNP?"

Elizabeth smiled. "Doctor of Nursing Practice. She has a specialty in emergency medicine."

The major raised his eyebrows. "She's a doctor of nurses?"

"She's got a doctorate in nursing practice." She watched him squint and laughed softly. "I watched her graduate online—they streamed the ceremony. So, she's Dr. Bennet, though she doesn't like me to call her that."

"Pictures?" he asked.

Of course he'd ask for pictures. She pulled them up on her phone and handed them over.

"Wow," he said. He swiped the phone a number of times. "Geez, Bennet, is there anyone in your family who's not good-looking?"

She shrugged. "My sisters are all pretty, but Jane's clearly the most beautiful." She took her phone back when he held it out to her. "More importantly, she's an all-around amazing human being. She wants to wind up on one of those helicopter trauma teams." She tapped on her photo collection and smiled a little. "You'd never know it, but behind that toothpaste commercial smile, she's kind of an extreme sports junkie." She took a sip of her orange juice. "Now you."

He gave her a grimace, but Elizabeth detected his approval. *Jane gets the interest of men who haven't even met her yet*, she thought affectionately.

He cleared his throat. "One older brother, Oscar. Cousins Will and Georgiana. Oscar works in my dad's office as a campaign manager and strategist. Will co-owns his dad's company and is the CEO of his own. G has just started at Stanford."

"Underachievers, then," she replied, acknowledging him with a nod.

He snorted and added a little cream to his coffee before he drank it down.

"Stanford," she continued, pursing her lips. "She's smart."

Major Fitzwilliam nodded. "You're pretty smart yourself, Bennet," he responded. "I mean, you know, not *doctor* smart, but . . ."

She tossed a balled-up napkin at him.

"Your aim sucks, Staff Sergeant," he said as he caught it mid-flight.

The waitress arrived with their food. After she set down the plates and bustled away, Bennet picked up her fork.

Her eyes met his.

"No," she replied, her voice turning serious again. "It doesn't."

"No," he agreed, stabbing his eggs with a fork. "Praise the Lord and pass the ammunition."

And we'll all stay free, she finished silently.

They'd eaten half their meal in silence when the major looked up and asked, "Why didn't you go to college first and join as an officer?"

Like a dog with a bone. He's lucky I like him. "Timing," she explained, trying to remain nonchalant. "My mom died right before I graduated high school. My dad was still her beneficiary, so he got everything, and of course the house was always his. He paid for the funeral but didn't attend. He wrote my uncle to say he'd set up child support accounts for my little sisters, probably because he knew he would be taken to court if he didn't." She hesitated. It felt a little strange talking about it after all this time, but it was undeniably *easier* to talk about then it had been. "Then he sent a certified letter to tell Jane and me that as we were both out of high school, we were on our own."

Major Fitzwilliam squinted at her. "Were you?"

"Was I what?" She caught a passing waitress and asked for more coffee.

"Out of high school."

She shook her head. "No, not quite. I had a few months left. I'd been accepted to Rutgers, and I couldn't wait to go." She held out her coffee mug, and the waitress poured her another cup. "Anyway, my father paid tuition once a year, and Jane lucked out—he'd already sent the money for her junior year." Her eyes drifted to the ceiling, remembering. "Jane and I had college accounts, you know, those 529 ones?"

He nodded.

"I worked and added to mine, but I didn't understand how they worked. As a minor, I couldn't access the funds, and my father never signed them over to me. Technically, he owns the account." She shrugged. "Without that money, I couldn't pay the deposit to hold my spot, and if I couldn't draw on that account, I knew I'd never be able to come up with the tuition anyway. I tried to contact my father, but I didn't have his phone number and he never emailed back."

"Nice," the major said, shaking his head.

Elizabeth nodded. "He didn't release the rest of Jane's funds either, but she only had to find money for one year. My grades had slipped because I was busy taking care of the girls, so I had no chance at an academic scholarship. I quit the soccer team for the same reason. No senior season, no recruiting. My coach was unhappy, and my teammates made kind of a thing about it." She poked at her eggs. "And because I was still on my parents' taxes, I couldn't qualify for need-based aid. It was going to cost around fifteen grand a year just for tuition, another ten for room, board, books—I didn't want to take on that kind of debt."

"So you joined the Marines?" he asked, with a twinkle in his eye. He was laughing at her. "Seems an extreme response."

Elizabeth thought she should feel insulted, but it *was* sort of funny. She shrugged. "My uncle was a Marine, and he and my aunt are probably the people I admire most." She pulled a face. "Aunt Maddy was pregnant, but she and my two little cousins still came to stay in Meryton with us for a few months to finish out the school year. Then we all moved to Montclair, and I joined the Marines because they'd pay for school." She reached for her water and drank the entire glass.

"Tough way to earn a degree," the major said, raising his eyebrows at her.

She let out a short bark of a laugh. "You're not kidding," she agreed. "I never seem to do things the easy way, unfortunately."

"Lucky you had your aunt and uncle," he said thoughtfully.

"They're amazing people," Elizabeth agreed, warming to her subject. "Aunt Maddy just gave up her life for almost two months to move in with us so we could finish school in Meryton. Uncle Ed drove up on the weekends. After I graduated, they took on my three sisters with no complaint, turned the guest room over to Kit and Lydia. Mary moved into the room Jane was renting." She shook her head with a small smile on her face. "They're more family to us than our parents were."

He stuck his hand up to wave the waitress down. "When you go home, will you live with them?" The waitress brought the bill and he grabbed it.

"No way," she replied, pretending to be horrified. "Six kids, four adults, two dogs, a cat, and a hamster under one roof. I mean, they have a big house, but they are maxed out. I will definitely be getting my own place."

"Ah, I see," he chuckled. "You joined up for the peace and quiet."

Elizabeth tossed some money across the table. He rolled his eyes at her, but he took it. "Absolutely," she replied.

CHAPTER FIVE

Elizabeth closed her laptop and stowed it beneath the airline seat in front of her. She leaned her forehead against the window as she watched the airfield at Newark coming into focus, feeling the pain of a migraine beginning at her right temple. *All this traveling.* She rubbed her ear against her shoulder unconsciously before pulling out a plastic prescription bottle. *Hardly any left.* She shook two pills into the palm of her hand, stared at them blankly for a minute, then tossed them in her mouth and washing them down with the water she always carried.

Home at last, she sighed. *Home for good.* She was expecting to feel different, more excited. Instead, she felt no different than she had when she had finally received her discharge papers—sort of a numb acceptance that it was time, finally, to move on. *It'll just take a while to get used to it again.*

She pulled the bottom of her uniform jacket to straighten out the wrinkles, as she was wearing her dress blues on final orders from her commanding officer. She was proud to wear her uniform, but it was August. It was hot, the uniform wasn't comfortable for travel, and playing the part of the perfect Marine had become tiresome. It was not the understated way she had planned to end her military career.

She had seen Major Fitzwilliam at several more joint appearances, his level of frustration growing even higher than hers, so she had buried her own irritation and physical discomfort, attempting instead to tease the usually affable officer into a better mood.

Her time in the Marines had been more difficult and more gratifying than she had thought it would. Even on those late nights in Uncle Ed's den just after graduation, where she had asked about his experiences in the Marines and he had related a dozen or more stories to demonstrate that serving, while not glamorous, could be rewarding, she could not have begun to fathom how much the experience would mean. It had been brutal in many ways—physically, emotionally, and intellectually—and yet the challenges had done her good. She had always been an athlete, but the Marines had broken her down and built her back up. She would not exchange the experience for the world, not even the attack at De Roos or the recuperation and ridiculous public relations duty that had been its result. She had a confidence now she'd never had before, a sure knowledge of her own abilities and two college degrees she had slaved over to keep herself out of trouble and smooth her transition back into civilian life.

It had required nearly the entire time remaining in her tour to recover, the concussion taking longer than the knee. She'd spent most of her time going to physical therapy and talking to the international media until they lost interest and only the American press remained. She still suffered migraines from time to time when she allowed herself to become too tense or tried to work for eighteen hours staring at a screen as she might have in the past, but it was a small price to pay for all being a Marine had given her.

The landing gear hit with a jolt, slapping the tarmac hard like a plane on a carrier, and Elizabeth grimaced. Clearly a Navy pilot.

As everyone stood to gather their belongings, she pulled her duffel from the overhead and set it on the seat, the strap of her laptop case already slung over her shoulder as she waited for the door to open. Suddenly, the flight attendant winked at her and began to speak into his handset.

"Ladies and gentlemen," he announced in a sing-song voice. "We have on board with us Marine Staff Sergeant Elizabeth 'Lizzy' Bennet, who is arriving home from a long overseas deployment, including some time at the US Embassy in Brussels." Elizabeth closed her eyes. *Richard Fitzwilliam, I will kill you. Seriously.* She opened her eyes to see everyone in first class turning to look at her, recognition lighting the eyes of a few. She made a game attempt to return their smiles, but she froze as she watched them begin to whisper to one another. She really hated this part. *So close to just getting away.*

"If you would all please just wait a moment and allow Staff Sergeant Bennet to deplane first, I am sure her family would appreciate it." He went on to deliver the rest of his customary speech thanking everyone for flying with them, but Elizabeth didn't hear it.

As the door to the plane opened, she tossed her duffel over her shoulder and walked down the aisle. She smiled and thanked the passengers who applauded, a few shaking her hand, another few taking pictures with their phones, and did the same for the crew. Then she stepped smartly up the ramp, taking her own phone off airplane mode and seeing that Jane had sent her eight texts, her building excitement demonstrated by the increased use of exclamation points and question marks as her sister's arrival grew closer. Elizabeth grinned.

She might not feel much enthusiasm for being home, but seeing Jane was another matter. Elizabeth had talked her sister out of coming to Brussels. She was fine, and the plane fare was exorbitant. Besides, Jane had just settled into her new position in the ER. They texted and made weekly video calls, but it wasn't as good as being in the same room.

Lizzy! I can't wait to see you!

*Are you **actually** on the plane?? Lizzy??*

You aren't writing back. You must be on the plane!!! YESSSSS!!!!!

You're in your seat, you're on your way, you're coming home TODAY!!!!!!!

Took the day off because there's a MARINE COMING HOME. Are you on the
plane????

Aunt Maddy and Uncle Ed are coming to the airport with me. Can't wait! Rosa's for lunch? Wait, what time zone are you on?

We are going out tonight, girl! Charlotte is coming.

We're here. Waiting in baggage. Where ARE you??????????????????

Elizabeth laughed quietly. Jane was constitutionally incapable of using any kind of text language. She used medical acronyms fluently, but she could not bring herself to "dummy down" the writing, as she always said, her lovely nose crinkling just a bit between her eyes.

Every girl in Meryton who met Jane wanted desperately to hate her. In addition to being incredibly bright and physically beautiful, she had never suffered the routine adolescent phase of acne and awkwardness. Everything seemed so easy for her. She had been a cheerleader all four years of high school, captain in her senior year, while maintaining a straight-A average even though she took all the toughest courses, particularly in math and science. She even volunteered at the hospital over the summers and on weekends after games, often in the NICU where she held the premature babies when their parents could not.

Nobody else saw all the hard work Jane had put in to earn her grades, the gymnastic practice for the routines cheer required, her graduation awards. Their father thought cheerleading absurd, and their mother didn't place any importance on academics.

Only Elizabeth saw, understanding that her sister felt an incredible amount of pressure to be the perfect student, the perfect daughter, and that she did not always succeed. Because Jane was always perceived as a threat to someone's grade or someone's boyfriend, she made lots of acquaintances but not a lot of close friends, which mattered less because she and Elizabeth were entirely devoted to each other. They spent a good deal of their childhoods taking care of their sisters and keeping their mother from falling apart—it had forged a deep and lasting bond between them. None of the girls who wanted to disparage Jane dared say anything aloud, because they were all a little afraid of how Elizabeth might respond. Jane, for her part, made it clear—where she went, Elizabeth was welcome.

Despite her driven, type-A personality and appearance of cool beauty, Jane Bennet was the warmest, kindest, most thoughtful person Elizabeth had ever met. She was also a thrill-seeker—her free time, when she had any, was filled with adventures like diving out of airplanes, bungee jumping from bridges, para-gliding from the edge of cliffs. Elizabeth thought it might be Jane's way of exorcising the demons of Longbourn and didn't say a word against it—she had joined the Marines, after all. At least Jane didn't have people shooting at her.

Elizabeth's pace quickened as she stepped onto the escalator. She shifted her duffel to the other shoulder and began the trip down into baggage claim. She glanced up, hoping to see Jane waiting, but what she saw made her jaw drop in surprise and, to be truthful, a little bit of horror. Her first thought was that the major had orchestrated this to punish her for some forgotten prank, but then realized even he could not have done this. It had to be her sister. She blinked twice, hoping that her vision would clear and this would all be some terrible nightmare.

There were at least a hundred balloons in five different colors tied to form a rainbow and a ten-foot banner that screamed "Welcome Home Staff Sgt. Elizabeth Bennet," being held up by what looked like the entire Montclair High School cheer squad. The high school band struck up the Marine Hymn from the back of the hall, making her flinch at the sudden sound, and a huge television camera was shining a bright light in her face, causing the dull ache in her head to develop into a throb. She felt the now familiar panic rising but blew it out in a nervous burst of air.

Thankfully nobody was asking her any stupid questions. Then she saw Jane, hopping up and down gleefully, blonde hair swept up, clapping her hands together at her sister's dumbstruck expression. She was wearing a neon blue t-shirt that read "Bennet Sister" and when she turned to say something to the cheerleaders, Elizabeth saw that the back read "#1." It was another moment before the extent of her mortification became clear. Her other sisters were here too, all smiling. Mary hung back a bit, but she was so grown up and sophisticated, her dark straight hair cut in a short, angular, edgy sort of style that suited her. Kit and Lydia, light-haired and blue-eyed like Jane, were still the giggling girls she remembered. They were all dressed in t-shirts that matched Jane's with, Elizabeth guessed, their corresponding numbers.

Beyond them, it looked like the rest of Montclair had shown up to wish her well. Her uncle and aunt were perched just beyond her sisters, anxious to greet her, but—like their returning niece—a little overwhelmed by the level of activity. It was wonderful, Elizabeth thought, scolding herself, that so many people would want to welcome her back like this. Jane began to lose some of her bounce as she watched her sister's expression, and Elizabeth noticed. She would never disappoint Jane after she'd clearly gone to great lengths to put this together. *Game face, Bennet.* She shook her head as though she was coming out of her shock, plastered on a huge smile, dropped her duffel, and opened her arms. Immediately, she was engulfed by Bennet girls.

"You realize, of course," were Elizabeth's first words to Jane, whispered in her ear in the middle of the crush, "that the t-shirt you want me to wear literally labels me #2."

Jane squealed with laughter. "God, how I've missed you," she said. "Welcome home, sis."

Elizabeth hugged her tightly. "I've missed you too, Janie," she whispered in her sister's ear.

CHAPTER SIX

"Local girl?" fumed Elizabeth. "*Local?*" She looked at Jane incredulously and waved the newspaper in the air. "*Girl?!*"

Elizabeth held Jane's copy of the paper in her hand and continued to shake it with indignation. "I lived here for, what, thirty seconds before I left for boot?" She stared at the headline for a moment like it was in a foreign language. "What's wrong with *woman*? Or, you know, just *Marine*?" She tossed the paper on the desk in disgust. "Non-local Marine . . . " She laid down on Mary's bed with her arms crossed behind her head and glared at the ceiling. "They didn't exactly rush to get in touch with Uncle Ed, did they?"

Jane shook her head dolefully. "No, I think he found out on the news, too."

Elizabeth sighed. "I'm sorry, Jane. I wasn't in any shape to call, and I guess since we were off-duty, the wheels turned a little slower."

"It doesn't matter now," Jane said comfortingly. "You're home, and everything's great." She sat at the end of Mary's bed to gaze at her sister. "If you want an upgrade from the basement," she said, "Mary and I have talked about adding a bed here."

Elizabeth laughed, looking around the room. "Where could you possibly fit one?"

"You and I could use a bunk bed. They go on sale all the time online." She smiled hopefully. "It will be just like the residents' quarters at the hospital."

Elizabeth coughed. *Bad idea.* "Jane, I love that you thought of me, but I won't be living here very long. I'm going to get my own place."

"Oh," came Jane's quiet voice. "I just thought..."

Elizabeth sat up and grabbed Jane's hand. "Jane, honey, I love you. I love all of you. But it's better for everyone if I don't try to cram in here."

Jane nodded, her lips tugging down at the corners. "Okay."

"You're welcome to join me," Elizabeth added. She knew Jane wouldn't agree, and it probably wasn't a good idea anyway. She wasn't planning on much traveling, but with Abby in the picture, one never knew. Her regular hours were odd and her work, which would be largely conducted from home—well, it wasn't family-friendly.

Very few institutions needed a full-time professional to monitor their servers and networks for vulnerabilities and ward off hackers, so she planned to consult on a project basis. This way, she'd have full control of her schedule. She took great pleasure in identifying clues and tracking down both vulnerabilities and infiltrations and finding the bad guys by tracking them online. It was like a big puzzle, and Elizabeth loved solving puzzles. She knew with her background, certifications, and degrees, she could make a lot of money, and she was already anticipating what she would do with it. *I will never depend on anyone for money again*, she thought. *I'm in charge of my own life from here on out.*

"I don't know, Lizzy," Jane said slowly. "I still have the one student loan to pay back for grad school, and you know I contribute here . . . "

Elizabeth offered Jane a little smile and nodded. Despite her wild hobbies, Jane thrived on habit and routine. With so many children in the house, having a nurse on-call was a definite benefit. She also assigned and evaluated chores for the Gardiner children. Mary and Kit both drove, so they took turns getting the younger kids to their after-school activities while Aunt Maddy cooked and cleaned and worked from the house part-time. Lydia babysat and was about to get her driver's permit.

The rest of the family had been working together as a team for so long, Elizabeth couldn't help but feel a little outside of everything, even if there was nothing she would change.

The wind rushed through the open windows of Jane's little car, drowning out everything but raised voices as they zipped in and out of traffic. Elizabeth closed her eyes as they changed lanes inches from a Jeep's front bumper. She heard a horn in the distance as they sprinted ahead.

"You know, Janie," Elizabeth said with volume, beginning to feel a little nauseous, "I've not been to Rosa's in years. A few more minutes won't matter."

"Not you, too," Jane groaned, rolling her eyes. "My driving is fine. Never had an accident." She jammed her foot down on the accelerator.

"But how many have you *caused?*" Elizabeth asked, grabbing the hand rest.

"Funny," Jane said with a twisted grin. "Are you ready to see Charlotte?"

I'm ready to be out of this car, Elizabeth thought, closing her eyes.

They arrived at the restaurant miraculously intact to find Charlotte Lucas already waiting for them. She hugged them both before bumping Elizabeth with her hip. "This is so much better than all those video calls!" she exclaimed. The last time Elizabeth had been in the same room as Charlotte was three years ago at the last Gardiner-Bennet-Lucas Christmas when she'd been given unexpected leave. In the interim, the older woman had discovered indoor soccer.

"It's in a rink, so we play all year long. Totally recreational," Charlotte said, sipping from a gigantic margarita glass, running her tongue along the salted rim. "We don't slide tackle or anything like that."

"Then what's the point?" Elizabeth asked, deadpan. Jane handed their menus back to the waitress.

"The point is it's fun!" Char gave Elizabeth a crafty glance. "Speaking of which . . . we're allowed two players between 18 and 29, and now that I'm 30, we don't have any. You like soccer, right?"

Jane laughed and waved her finger at her sister. "Lizzy used to play center midfielder for the high school varsity," she told Charlotte. "She's a *very* good player."

"I haven't played on a team in eight years, Char," Elizabeth warned. "And I've never played indoor."

"Notice she said she hasn't played on a team, not that she hasn't played," Jane said, eyes sparkling as she reached for her iced tea. Elizabeth frowned at her sister.

"I can guarantee you will still be the best player on the team," Char said, beaming. "No throw-ins, and you can use the wall to bank the ball, that's all. Oh, and the field is smaller, like half the size. It's a high-scoring kind of game."

Elizabeth pursed her lips. *Might be fun.* "Can I let you know?"

"The first game of the session is in a few days. C'mon, you know you want to. A good player can never resist a high scoring game." Charlotte clasped her hands together and wheedled, "Please, please, please?"

Elizabeth grinned. She picked up a chip and loaded it with salsa. "Maybe."

Charlotte narrowed her eyes. "You're a tough negotiator, Bennet. I'll pay the guest fee for the first game so you can try it out, and I have an extra team shirt you can use. You'd be doing me a huge favor. Please?"

Elizabeth gave in. "What the heck," she said with a shrug. "I'm a sucker for a recruiter."

Jane shook her head as Charlotte hooted, raising her arm to summon the waitress. "Another margarita!"

When they finally stumbled into the house, Elizabeth was nearly asleep on her feet. She'd rested some on the plane, but the time difference was finally getting to her. Jane was their designated driver, and between the two margaritas and her jet lag, Elizabeth barely noticed the race-car driving.

As she passed her uncle's den on the way to the basement and her pull-out sofa, she heard him clear his throat. She paused and poked her head into the room.

"Uncle Ed? You okay?"

"Waiting for you girls to get home," he said gruffly, leaning back in the plush leather chair behind his desk. He had a bottle of scotch out and had poured himself a small glass. He held it up. "Would you like a drink?"

"No sir, thanks. I've had enough," replied Elizabeth wryly.

Her Uncle Ed smiled. He was a handsome man even at forty-seven. His hair was still light brown with only a hint of gray, and he remained in good physical shape. He was just under six feet tall, lean and wiry, with bright blue eyes that he shared with his sister and several of her daughters. "How many times have I told you not to call me sir?"

She yawned. Old joke. "Right, I know. You work for a living."

He chuckled. "Can I speak with you before you head downstairs?"

Uh oh. "Of course," she said and stepped inside.

He waved her into a chair and cleared his throat again.

"What is it, Uncle Ed?" she asked, knowing he usually made the sound only when he wasn't certain what to say.

"I just wanted to have a moment with my badass niece without your crowd of admirers," he replied, tipping his glass in her direction. "You're rather popular these days."

Elizabeth shifted uncomfortably.

He sipped his scotch and was silent for a moment. Then he said quietly, "I just wanted to tell you how proud I am of you."

"Thanks," Elizabeth said, brushing away the compliment.

Uncle Ed set down his glass and moved to stand before Elizabeth, placing a hand under her chin and gently tipping it up. "No,

Elizabeth," he said, waiting until she met his eyes. "I'm proud of you as a niece, always have been. You and your sisters have been a godsend to us." He dropped his hand and offered it to her. "But I'm also proud of you as a Marine."

Elizabeth felt a rush of blood to her face and a surge of pride as she stood to meet him. She looked him in the eye and took his hand. "I'm honored, Gunny," she said, her throat constricting. "Thank you. This means . . ." She couldn't continue.

Uncle Ed drew her in for a hug. "I love you, Lizbet."

"It means a lot," she said, speaking into his shoulder.

Uncle Ed released her, placing a hand on her cheek momentarily before stepping back. He toyed with something on his desk for a moment before handing her a slip of paper.

"What's this?" Elizabeth asked, holding out her hand to take it.

"It's the money you've been sending us each month." He sank back into his chair and put his hands behind his head, gazing past her right shoulder to a photo on the wall. "I know you love us, but trust me, I'm aware that we're a lot to handle. You're welcome to stay as long as you like of course, but this is your money. If you want to use it to find an apartment, you should feel free. Maddy and I can help you look around." He cleared his throat. "Your aunt will kill me if she knows I mentioned this, but I know you rode a motorcycle in the service. If you wanted to buy one here to get around, well, now you can."

Elizabeth saw the numbers on the cashier's check and suddenly felt completely sober.

"Uncle Ed, this has to be everything I ever sent you." She glared at him. "Six years of monthly payments."

He nodded. "That's right."

"You never used *any* of it?" Elizabeth wasn't sure how she felt about that. It had given her a sense of purpose, thinking she was helping back home. "I mean, I know it wasn't much, especially at first, but I thought you could use it for the girls—you know, help defray some expenses for clothes or food or something." *They took Jane's money—why not mine?*

Uncle Ed chuckled. "Don't look at me like that. Jane hasn't paid rent since the girls came to stay, even though it makes her crazy."

"I didn't know that," Elizabeth said honestly.

"You may not have thought it was much money, but it was more than generous given what you earned, Lizbet." He met her conflicted gaze. "It's something my mother did for me when I was away, and I remember how much it meant to have a little nest egg when I got home. Your aunt and I intended to do this from the start."

Elizabeth stared at the check in her hand. "I don't know what to say."

Uncle Ed grinned. "I didn't either. Just say you'll take it."

"Are you really sure?" Elizabeth asked, "I mean, I'll be making money before long, and you still have the girls."

"They're my girls now," Uncle Ed said firmly. "Mine and Maddy's. Have been for six years. Just like you."

Elizabeth let out a charged huff of air.

Uncle Ed grunted and pushed himself up to a standing position. "All right, I'm off to bed. You're dead on your feet—you should head downstairs."

Elizabeth kissed her uncle on the cheek. "You have no idea how much this means," she said softly. It wasn't even the money, though she was happy to have it. They'd thought about her when she was gone, still considered her one of theirs.

Uncle Ed met her gaze, his expression softening. "Actually, Staff Sgt. Bennet," he said fondly, "I believe I do."

Will was walking home when Richard called. He answered on the first ring.

"Hey," he answered, his voice warm.

Richard sounded confused. "There's lots of background noise. Where are you, cuz?"

"I'm outside," Will replied. "Just walking home from SCORE, then headed to training. Keeping busy."

Richard was quiet for a moment. "Oh right, the mentoring thing?"

Will sighed. "Yes, the mentoring thing, small business owners, all that. I've only been doing it for four years. Stop trying to distract me. Have you looked over the position description list?"

"Yes," Richard replied, "but that's not why I'm calling."

Will was disappointed. "You were serious about this, right? You weren't just trying to get me off the phone?"

"No, I'm thinking it through, Will. It's a big decision."

"Yeah," Will muttered. His good mood had evaporated. Richard had no intention of leaving the Marines. His cousin had just been stringing him along and he'd fallen for it.

Richard didn't seem to notice the change in Will's voice. "Listen, Will, I need a favor."

"Of course you do," he said with a grimace. "What do you want?"

"I want you to hire a colleague of mine. She's a friend and really good at what she does . . ."

Which is what, exactly? Will thought sourly.

There was some static on the line and then someone bellowed Richard's name. His cousin cursed softly. "This woman is going to kill me," he grumbled. "Will, I have to go. Watch for her résumé. I'll have Wanda set it up."

"No," Will said. "I don't want to hire . . ." But he was talking to himself.

———

Like everything in the Gardiner household, the basement was well-used but clean. There was a large flat-screen television mounted on the wall. Toy bins and bookshelves lined the wall opposite. A pull-out sofa sat in the middle of the room, anchored by a rug and a battered coffee table. Elizabeth tossed a skeptical look at the forest of half-dressed mannequins taking up the corner of the room nearest the foot of the stairs. She dressed for bed, but didn't have enough energy left to pull out the bed before she flopped onto the sofa face down. She fell asleep almost immediately.

Elizabeth was awakened by a small face hovering inches from her own. "Sarah," she grumbled, only half-awake.

"Cartoons," the four-year-old demanded, her dirty-blonde hair knotted and wild. She was clad in her blue and yellow footed pajamas and clutched a stuffed pink elephant by its tail. It was a sweet picture that contrasted sharply with the girl's imperious command.

"Mmm," Elizabeth said sleepily, rooting around, eventually locating the remote under her hip and pulling it out. "Here you go."

Sarah took it wordlessly, clicked on the television, and plopped on the ground in front of the coffee table, watching her shows at a volume that precluded further slumber. Elizabeth sat up as her phone buzzed in her pocket. *Wow, I was so tired I didn't even remember to charge it*, she thought, eyeing the battery indicator.

She glanced at the screen. *Abby. That was fast.* She checked the message—Abby was suggesting a call on Monday. She had no doubt her former commander would try to talk her into working for her again, but she'd also pass along other, less exciting jobs. The Abbot liked to take care of her people, and Elizabeth had always felt lucky to be counted among them.

Yes, she typed, and sent the message.

There was an earlier text from Major Fitzwilliam. *Are you home?*

Elizabeth rubbed her eyes and checked the time. 6:30 am. *Good gravy, kid,* she thought, looking at Sarah. *I will not last long in this house.* She rummaged through her belongings to locate the charger, plugged in her phone, and began to type.

Home, but sleeping! Or I was until a small human demanded her couch back.

Her phone buzzed again after a minute. *Hungover?* he replied.

She snorted. Jet lagged, yes, but two margaritas wasn't enough to put her down. *Not remotely.*

Another buzz. *I want you to interview at FORGE on Monday.*

FORGE. Elizabeth recalled the name, but not much else. Fortunately, the next message was an explanation. *My cousin's company. Mine too.*

He owned part of a company in Manhattan? He'd been holding out

on her. *Have a family bbq that night. Besides, might have something already.*
She'd promised Charlotte she'd play soccer, too. Maybe she could use
that as an excuse.

The major's response was lightning fast. *Have you signed a contract?*
Elizabeth sighed. *No.*

Take the interview. I'll make it early.

She grimaced. So much for not taking orders. *Do I need to dress up?*

Yes.

Strike one. *Already I don't want to work there.*

Too bad. You said you'd do it. I'll get a time for you and text back.

Elizabeth almost laughed. *When did I say I'd do it?*

You implied it.

"Not even," she said aloud. *I think I hate you, sir.*

Richard now. You're a civilian.

She sighed. Civilian. *And loving it.*

Elizabeth plucked some clean clothes out of her duffel and headed
for the stairs, startling when she blinked the sleep from her eyes and
found herself staring into the blank face of a mannequin. *At least this
early I might get a shower before all the hot water is gone.*

*Things are looking up. Money. Interview. I need to find Jane and Mary so
we can go shopping.*

After an early morning meeting on Monday, Will Darcy paused at
Wanda's desk in the outer office and handed her a stack of hard-copy
backup files. She passed over a few pages held together by a
paperclip.

"What's this?" he asked, holding it up to look at it.

"Elizabeth Bennet's résumé," Wanda said.

Will cocked his head at her, mystified, and Wanda rolled her eyes.

"The candidate Mr. Fitzwilliam recommended for an interview."

Will was annoyed. He'd spent the rest of the weekend irritated
with Richard, who hadn't been available to talk, and had taken out his
frustration on a heavy bag in the gym. That was followed by trying and

failing to get in touch with Georgiana. His trainer had worked him hard this morning, but it wasn't enough.

He was in no mood to do his cousin a favor, particularly if that included hiring or even interviewing someone who had no corporate experience. He had tried to speak to Richard again, but his cousin wasn't answering his phone. Will left a voicemail and several texts before he finally gave up. Well, he wasn't about to just cave in to Richard's demands. He didn't tell Richard how to do *his* job.

———

Elizabeth was sitting in Mr. Darcy's office. It was all clean lines with light blue-gray walls and white trim. There was a large window overlooking midtown Manhattan that let in a good deal of natural light. There were a few paintings and a large Japanese scroll that hung directly across from the large desk. She wondered what it said. *Richard would know.*

Eventually, she heard voices in the outer office, where Ms. Soames, Mr. Darcy's assistant, had her desk. Elizabeth turned toward the sound. As she quickly ran her hands down her skirt to smooth out any wrinkles, she caught her first look of him through the doorway. *Whoa.*

The CEO was much younger than she had expected, thirty or even a bit younger. His hair was a few shades darker than her own, cut short and neat. When he straightened, she could see he was tall, at least 6'2" if not a bit more, and fit. His jawline was strong, which she found immensely appealing. *Stop it, Bennet,* she told herself sternly. *You're here to interview, not get a date.* She thought she might have to thank Richard, though. *I guess it wouldn't be such a punishment to work here.*

Then he opened his mouth and spoke.

———

"This isn't a charity," Will announced loudly, exasperated. He pulled out his phone and checked his calendar. Yes, there was the interview. *It must be new.* Wanda's eyes widened, and she shook her head, but he didn't want to argue. He was still angry with his cousin and let it all come pouring out. "I don't have time to interview Richard's ex-Marine girlfriends or cast-offs or whatever, when they have no qualifications and nowhere else to go."

"Mr. Darcy," Wanda hissed. She had an expression of annoyed disbelief on her face, and he finally suspected he was in trouble. With an almost exaggerated slowness, she lifted her eyebrows tilted her head slightly in the direction of his office. *Shit.* He closed his eyes briefly before opening them and turning to face the music.

There, in the entry to the inner office, was—he checked the résumé again—Elizabeth Bennet. She was tall, standing approximately six feet in her two-inch black heels. A thin black belt around her dark green business suit gathered the folds of the suit jacket, accentuating her trim waist. Her chestnut-colored hair was pinned back neatly, leaving the length of it to hang down her back. One strand fell defiantly across her shoulder where the end curled into a lazy 'C.' Her pencil skirt was hemmed just at her knees, revealing lean, toned, shapely legs. *Athletic and lithe*, he thought. All she needed was a suitable hat and she'd have been the very model of a 1940s movie star, minus the garish red lipstick and overly painted face. He blinked before reason reasserted itself. *Probably broke and dumb as a rock.* Her piercing green eyes were bright with . . . what? Anger? No, that wasn't it.

"Nothing personal, Ms. Bennet," Darcy said firmly. His voice was not apologetic, and he struggled to appear impassive in preparation for the outburst of emotion he expected. "It's just that we don't offer interviews based entirely upon recommendations from people who are not employed here."

To his surprise, she seemed entirely unfazed by his comments. In fact, she appeared to be appraising him, her eyes taking him in. If he was reading her expression correctly, her assessment had found him wanting.

Elizabeth was incredibly irritated. *This guy is Richard's cousin?*

"I appreciate your honesty, Mr. Darcy," she said as soon as she could compose herself. *I am going to kill Richard. Bought a suit, took the train. I didn't even want this job.* She arched an eyebrow and spoke, placing a delicate emphasis on certain words. "I would have preferred, however, to be treated as a professional and have you say so to *me* rather than Ms. Soames." She returned to the chair to retrieve her computer bag. *Too bad he's an ass,* she thought. *All those good looks wasted.*

As she left his office, she stopped and stared straight into his eyes. "I told Richard I wasn't comfortable with this. I'm not used to being offered things based on who I know, but he insisted the company needed someone with my programming and cyber-security background, and I suppose he thought my security clearances might prove useful." She tucked her phone into a holster located on her waist but hidden by the jacket. When she looked up, she noticed her name on the lone document he was holding. It was her résumé. "Don't worry. I'll just tell Richard it wasn't a good fit."

She walked up to him and deftly removed her résumé from his hands. "But understand this, Mr. Darcy," she said, acid in her tone, "I am *nobody's* cast-off."

Elizabeth thanked Ms. Soames, smiled at her, and took three steps toward the door. Mr. Darcy hadn't moved, so when she turned her head, she was speaking to his right ear. "Oh, just one more thing. There may be inactive or retired Marines, but there are no *ex-*Marines. Once a Marine, always a Marine." She offered an icy smile. "Good day, Mr. Darcy."

Will let out the breath he had been holding as the door to the outer office clicked shut. *I'm going to kill Richard,* he thought. *I don't even need anyone in IT. And I don't believe he wasn't dating her. He must have wanted to, at least. She's beautiful.* He turned back to Wanda to see her laughing silently, her shoulders shaking.

"Oh, don't give me that look, Mr. Darcy," she said lightly. "She got you good." With a broad smile and a shake of the head, her hot pink flamingo earrings swinging merrily, she added, "And I must say you deserved it."

"Hold my calls," Darcy grunted and stalked into his office, closing the door firmly behind him.

CHAPTER SEVEN

Richard's phone began to vibrate, shimmying away from his beer. He figured it would be Will wanting to discuss Bennet, so he excused himself from the other officers at the table and walked outside. It wasn't Will. Instead, it was Bennet herself.

Not a good fit, Richard.

Richard was shocked. *What?*

He's not interviewing.

Well, that was just stupid. *Of course he is.*

He says he isn't.

The general had kept him busy all weekend. He'd known Will wasn't happy with him, but it wasn't like him to turn down a candidate like Bennet. *What did he say? Exactly?*

No response. Richard waited. Still no response. He opened his contact list and selected Bennet's number.

She picked up on the first ring. "What do you want, Richard?" she asked, clearly peeved.

"I want to talk to you," he shot back. "What the hell happened?" There was a long silence. "Bennet?"

She sighed. "So humiliating," he heard her mumble. She raised her voice a little. "He thought I slept with you to get an interview."

Richard's mouth dropped open. "He *said* that?"

Another silence before she replied, "He *implied* it."

He felt his stomach begin to clench and his shoulders tense. "What, *exactly*, did he say?"

She hesitated, and then, as though she was spitting something poisonous out of her mouth, repeated his cousin's words. They struck Richard like a hammer, particularly the parts about "ex-Marine girlfriend or castoff" and "not employed by the company."

This time it was Richard who was silent. Finally, he said, "Bennet, I'm going to have to call you back."

She muttered something Richard didn't catch, but when he asked her to repeat it, she spoke up, furious. "Don't *ever* set me up like that again," she snarled and ended the call. Richard hit the speed dial for Will.

"Richard," he heard his cousin say warily. "Before you say anything..."

"What the *hell*, Will?" Richard yelled, then lowered his voice as a young couple passing nearby picked up their heels and scurried down the sidewalk. "I send you an incredible prospect, and you call her a whore?"

"I didn't . . ." Will had the audacity to sound indignant.

Richard felt his cheeks burning. He never got this angry—at least, he never let it show. "You called her my cast-off. She's a smart woman, Will, she knows how to read between the lines. And before you say it, she only told me it wasn't a good fit. I knew that wasn't true, so I forced her to explain."

Will was silent for a moment before saying, weakly, "I didn't mean it like that, and I didn't know she was in my office."

"In what universe does *that* matter?" Richard hollered.

"Richard..."

"You want me to be a part of the company, you beg me to leave the Corps. For *years,* you've been on me, you put on the full-court press after De Roos, and the first time I recommend someone, you call her a whore and refuse to interview her?" He took a breath and when he spoke again, his voice was low, cold. "It's bad enough you would do that to Bennet, who happens to be one of the finest people I know, but it also shows that you haven't got any respect for me at all."

"You *know* that's not true," his cousin protested.

"It's not? You accused her of sleeping her way into an interview—with *me*. As if I would use the promise of an interview with the company to get laid? Or even better, to engage in that kind of behavior and then palm her off on you once I was done with her?" Richard began pacing as he spoke. "You didn't even interview her, Will, just insulted her after I had to convince her to even take the meeting."

Will sounded confused. "Why would you have to convince her?"

Richard threw his arms up. He squelched the urge to scream. Once he was under control, he brought the phone back to his ear with one hand and rested the other against the back of his head. He could feel a stress headache coming on. "How are you even in business, Will?" he asked, incredulous. "She's incredibly over-qualified, that's why." He knew Will couldn't see him counting on his fingers, but he did it anyway. "MPS in Information Security, experience in cyber-threat analytics and prevention for the Corps, programs her own software, experience setting up and repairing networks, sometimes under fire—and that's just the beginning." Richard had to stop briefly so he could regroup. His anger was increasing his volume again. "She plans to consult and within a day of getting home already has a line on some work. I basically ordered her not to sign a contract until you could talk to her." He pinched the bridge of his nose. "I was trying to get her on board before we couldn't afford her anymore." He paused as something occurred to him. "Oh, for God's sake, Will. Did you even read her résumé?"

"Didn't have time," Will said, but he sounded more apologetic now than insistent.

"You forgot all about her when you ended our call, right?"

Will exploded. "*You* ended our call, Richard. And I remember very clearly saying I didn't want to interview your prospect. If you were going to make an appointment anyway, a little more notice might have helped."

Richard shook his head. This was so disappointing. "You had

plenty of time to insult her," Richard said with a sigh. "Have you read her résumé now?"

Will grunted. He sounded embarrassed. "She took it with her."

Richard grinned. *That sounds like Bennet.* "Good for her."

Will sighed. "Not that I appreciate you strong-arming me, but I *am* sorry, Richard."

Richard shook his head. "The interview was meant to be a *formality*, Will. When someone like Bennet comes along, you hire the person and create the position afterward. I may not have a Harvard MBA, but I know how to build a team." He took a deep breath, letting it out slowly. "I thought that was one of the reasons you wanted me to come work with you, and you need to understand that it would absolutely be *with* you, not *for* you. If the only reason you want me there is to get me out of the Marines, I have to pass."

"Listen," Will replied. "Just give me some time to make it right."

"You think you can *fix* this?" Richard was skeptical.

"I don't know . . . I could reschedule the interview," his cousin said hurriedly.

"Don't you *dare*." Richard was again close to yelling, but he checked himself. "You want to offer her an interview only after I call to ream you out? Because you want *me* to join the company and she's the one standing in the way? Exactly how humiliating do you intend to make this for her?" He grunted. "That ship has sailed, Will. You'll never get her to consider us now."

There was a contrite sigh on the other end of the line. "I was in a shit mood and I said some things, but they were aimed at you, not her."

Richard rubbed his neck. "This was incredibly stupid, Will. Monumentally stupid. I'm so pissed at you right now . . ."

There was a pause, and then Will said, "I suppose I deserve it."

"You suppose? You *absolutely* do. But she doesn't." Richard sighed. "I'll try to talk to her later, after she's cooled down. Don't contact her until I do. And when you get the go-ahead, grovel. But don't offer her another interview."

"Are you sure . . . ?" Halfway through Will's words, Richard once again disconnected the call.

Will let his cell slip from his fingers to the desk. He blew out a giant breath and leaned back in his chair. At least he'd been alone with the office door closed when Richard had called. He hadn't been hauled out on the carpet like that since he was an undergrad and his father found out he'd cut economics class to drive out to the beach with some of his frat brothers.

He tried to get back to work after that, but he couldn't concentrate. He kept thinking about how Elizabeth Bennet had made him feel two inches tall without even breaking a sweat. She was in the right—he hadn't checked in with Wanda this morning, and he'd been negligent not to check his calendar himself. Richard had been the first to invest in FORGE when he'd been working to get it off the ground and had never asked him to hire anyone or offered advice unless asked for it. God, he was a shitty cousin. Will rested his head on his arms and closed his eyes. He was so tired.

He'd had another nightmare last night, a twisted mess of car metal, bombs, Richard, Georgiana . . . it was similar to how he'd felt after the accident. He hated having things like this hanging over him. He needed to make this right or he wouldn't sleep tonight, either.

Richard had promised him a decision one way or the other by the end of the month. It had him on edge. Now he'd likely blown that relationship, at least temporarily, but that wasn't Elizabeth Bennet's fault. *She thought she was doing Richard a favor.*

Regardless of the situation, he thought an apology like the one he intended to offer ought to be done in person, and soon. If someone had treated Georgiana the way he'd treated Elizabeth Bennet, he'd have been livid. So he left work a little early, took a quick trip home to change out of his suit, got in his car, and headed for the Holland Tunnel.

A little less than forty minutes later, he was in Montclair, looking for Gracechurch Street. *It wasn't a bad drive at all*, he thought. *The one time I wouldn't have minded a bit more gridlock . . .*

Stop stalling, he told himself. *You know you have to do it. It's the right thing.*

He located the address and parked across the tree-lined street not far from Watchung Plaza. The house was nice, a modern home painted in a slate-gray and styled to look like a Craftsman to fit in with the neighborhood. Will noted the wide covered front porch, belt lines, paneled door with stained-glass inserts, and white elephant columns, noting that the construction was certainly more custom than most typical modern replicas. The house was deceptively small from the front, but Will could detect that the lot was deep and there were two wings in the back, though so artfully done you might not notice if you weren't looking carefully. *Taste without excess*, he thought admiringly. He took a breath, then let it out. *Okay, Will. Time to go pay what you owe.*

He took the three steps up to the front door and rang the bell. He shifted anxiously from one foot to the other until the heavy wooden door opened, and he was greeted by a middle-aged man perhaps twenty years his senior. The man was wiry but muscled under his red USMC t-shirt, and he gave Will the once-over much as Elizabeth Bennet had before she put him in his place. *Kind,* he thought with chagrin, remembering how she'd remained professional in the face of his insults. *Given the circumstances, she really was remarkably kind.*

"May I help you?"

"I certainly hope so. My name is Will Darcy, and I'm looking for Elizabeth Bennet. She had an interview scheduled at my company this morning."

The man stepped out onto the porch and closed the front door behind him.

Well, that's not a good sign. Will stood his ground.

"She wouldn't say what happened," the man replied, looking Will in the eye, "but the hours of angry mumbling leads me to believe it wasn't pleasant."

Will looked the man straight in the eye. "It wasn't, and it was my fault. I'd like a chance to apologize to her, if she's willing."

The man stared at him for a long moment. "Let me make this clear," he said in a voice that was dangerously low. "If you are here to offer a *genuine* apology, I will allow that to happen so long as Elizabeth wants it to happen. If she does not, you will leave immediately and not try to contact her again. I don't care who your cousin is. Got that?"

Will nodded. "Got it. Full disclosure, Richard's on her side."

The man grunted a little. "I'm Ed Gardiner. My wife is Madeline. We're barbecuing in the backyard. Come on through, we're just waiting for Elizabeth and Charlotte to get back from an early game. Should be any time."

"Game?" Will asked, but Ed had already opened the front door and walked through. Will followed. The interior of the house was open and airy, the ceilings higher than a true craftsman but with the wide wooden beams that spoke of solidity. The colors were true to the style of the home, as were the built-in bookcases with pane-glass doors and the wood floors, though these had been stained darker than was traditional. It was messy, with sports equipment, clothing, toys, books, and other things tossed about and pegs in the wall near the front door covered in layers of clothing, but it was clean and there was an underlying order to things. He wondered how many kids they had. His heart ached just a little at that. He hated going home to an empty house.

As he stepped through the back door onto the deck and then down into the backyard, he saw a small crowd of people milling about. There were kids playing, teens listening to music, and a few adults speaking to one another. Two large dogs were playing in the back corner of the yard, near a large oak tree. The grill was hot, loaded with burgers. As Ed stepped over to it, a beautiful woman with long blonde hair handed him a spatula and moved away.

"Nothing burned, Uncle Ed," she said with raised eyebrows.

"Good thing it was you and not Lizzy," he said with a grin. As he turned to contemplate Will, the grin faded. "Everyone, this is Will Darcy."

The blonde held out her hand and gave him an amused look. *She knows what happened.*

"I'm Jane," she said. "Lizzy's older sister. Do you like hamburgers?"

He shook her hand. *Firm grip.* "Thanks, but I'll wait for your sister."

"Okay," she said, sincerely, waving one hand gently to indicate her family, "but don't say I didn't offer when there's nothing left. These people descend on food like locusts."

Will smiled tightly and rubbed his damp palms on his trousers. "I'll remember," he said.

He heard someone calling out from the side yard and steeled himself. A short African-American woman about his age came through the gate first. Her highlighted hair was arranged in raised curls and she held a soccer ball. She danced into the yard, whooping.

"You should have come!" she said gleefully, leaning in to hug the woman he suspected was Mrs. Gardiner and two girls about four and six. "She played angry, and it was spectacular!"

Will could almost feel the glare of Elizabeth's uncle on the back of his neck.

The older girl held up her hands, two blonde pigtails bobbing merrily. "May I please have that ball, Charlotte?" she asked sweetly.

"Of course, Moira," Charlotte replied, and handed it over. She turned to Mrs. Gardiner. "Moira is so polite!"

Moira skipped over to a boy of about ten he presumed was her brother and executed a perfect throw-in—right into the back of his head.

"Hey!" he yelled, outraged. Moira skittered away, and he ran after her. Mrs. Gardiner sighed and followed. Will was left standing by himself as Charlotte laughed and moved towards Jane.

He raised his eyes just as Elizabeth Bennet herself came around the side of the house and entered the yard. Her dark brown hair was pulled back from her face with a wide blue hairband. She was wearing the same uniform as Charlotte—a red soccer jersey and black shorts. She also carried a sports bag on her shoulder and held a pair of turf shoes by their laces in one hand. On her feet were black rubber sandals. Without the heels, he judged her to be about 5'10 with much of that height in her legs. Will tried not to notice how sexy she looked in soccer shorts. *Don't gawk,* he thought. *Her uncle will have you murdered and your body dumped at sea.*

At that moment, Elizabeth spied who was in the backyard with her family and stopped in her tracks to glare at him.

"Mr. Darcy," she said coldly.

Will cleared his throat. "Ms. Bennet."

She lifted an eyebrow. "I assume Richard gave you the address. Any specific reason for your visit?"

Richard? Not a chance. Will nodded. "My assistant, actually. I'm here to offer you an apology."

Everyone within earshot stopped, waiting for Elizabeth's reaction before reacting themselves. She gave him a calm once-over.

"Did Richard send you?"

Will shook his head. "No, he wanted me to let him contact you first, but I owe you an apology. If you're willing to hear it, I'd hate to wait. He's not always . . . prompt."

She cocked her head to one side and studied him for a moment, then nodded.

"Okay," she said, "but you *will* actually have to wait, at least a bit. I'm going to grab a shower and change first." She gestured to the ice chest. "Help yourself." Without another word, she disappeared into the house.

Will felt a little of the tension leave his shoulders, and everyone went back to talking with one another.

"Jason and Todd," Mr. Gardiner hollered suddenly, making Will jump, "get off the slide *now!*"

"We're playing king of the hill, Dad!" the younger boy declared from the top of the slide.

"No," his father said decisively, "you are *not.*" The boys groaned and complained but slid down one at a time.

Charlotte stepped up to Will. "You're the guy who made her so mad today?"

He shrugged. "I believe so, yes."

Charlotte smiled widely. "You have to come make her angry *every* week before our game. I will pay you, buy you beer, whatever. Seriously," she gloated, "it was an annihilation!"

Mrs. Gardiner returned with Moira in tow and put her hand on Charlotte's arm. "Charlotte," she chuckled, "you're channeling Elizabeth." Charlotte protested that Elizabeth had been eerily quiet and methodical as she dismantled the other team's defense, and Mrs. Gardiner held out a hand to Will. "I'm Elizabeth's aunt, Madeline Gardiner."

Will took her hand, noted her firm grip, and nodded. "Nice to meet you, Mrs. Gardiner."

"Maddy."

"Will."

From his station at the grill, Ed called, "There's no need for first names yet, Maddy."

Maddy chuckled. "My husband is a little protective of his brood, even the ones who can clearly protect themselves."

Will thought that was an odd statement. Georgiana could be a black belt and he'd still feel compelled to protect her. He thought he understood Ed Gardiner perfectly in that sense. His curiosity got the better of him. "Why do you say that? Because she was," he stopped himself, remembering her parting comments, "*is* a Marine?"

Maddy and Charlotte both perked up at this inquiry, their eyes sparkling.

"I thought," Maddy said, "that you were Richard Fitzwilliam's cousin."

"I am." Will had no idea where this was going.

They were joined by a dark-haired young woman wearing a green Montclair State t-shirt and blue jeans. "What are we talking about?" she asked.

"Will, this is Mary, Elizabeth's next youngest sister." Will smiled and nodded at her.

"I believe we were discussing their *explosive* military adventures," said Charlotte with a small grin.

"Do you mean their *fiery* connection?" replied Mrs. Gardiner with a lift of her eyebrow.

Jane chimed in from directly behind Will, making him twist to see her. "Don't you think they are somewhat *volatile*?" She smiled.

Mary caught on to the game. "I don't know, Jane. They seem to have a *blast* when they're together."

There was some giggling before their meaning hit Will, and his face grew hot. *That's* why her last name was familiar. She was the Marine who'd been in De Roos with Richard. He tried to reconcile the Elizabeth Bennet who'd shown up in his office with the bloodied woman he'd seen in the newspaper photo but had a difficult time until he recalled her eyes. There was no mistaking the eyes.

It sounded like her family thought Richard and Elizabeth were together, but Richard had denied it. The whole fraternization issue, Will supposed, but Richard had also said he thought of Bennet as a sister. He didn't have enough time to consider it any further, as the back door swung open and Elizabeth appeared on the deck.

"Aunt Maddy," she said, "Sarah's giving that chocolate cake the eye —she hasn't done anything yet, but I can grab her if you want."

"Just one more," Maddy grumbled at her husband. "'We already have three. How much more trouble would one more cause,' he asked?" She took the stairs, crossed the deck, and disappeared into the kitchen.

Elizabeth grinned as her aunt brushed past her and nodded to Charlotte. "Shower's free if you want it."

"In a minute," Charlotte nodded. "We're busy harassing Will."

"Will, is it?" Elizabeth said flatly.

"Lizzy!" yelled a blonde teen from across the yard, "Jake Long wants to know how many goals you scored!"

"I don't know," she said, glancing at Charlotte.

"Seven, Kit!" Charlotte yelled.

"It wasn't that many, Char," Lizzy's face pinched a bit, as though she was trying to remember.

"It was, too, and it couldn't have happened to a nicer team," Charlotte sang. "They've been blowing us out by ten goals or more for two years and are always gloating. Too bad for them!"

Maddy pointed at the phone and made a circle with her finger. The blonde named Kit nodded and said her goodbyes. Will noticed she went inside and came back out empty-handed. It was impressive. Georgiana had been glued to her phone throughout high school.

Elizabeth looked a little uncomfortable as she joined the group. "I wouldn't have kept going had I realized."

"Where's your killer instinct, Lizzy?" called another blonde Bennet from near the grill.

How many of them are there? Will wondered. This one had a fully-developed figure that made her seem older, but her face revealed her as quite young.

A flash of something crossed Elizabeth's face. "Shut up, Lydia," she said brusquely before turning her attention to Will. "I think we have unfinished business, Mr. Darcy?"

"Will, Lizzy," said Maddy gently. "He's already been the victim of a level-one round-robin, Gardiner style. I think you can use his first name."

"Mr. Darcy," said Elizabeth, motioning with her arm to the house. Will imagined a satisfied gleam in Ed Gardiner's eyes.

"If you survive, you are more than welcome to join us for a burger after, Will," said Maddy with a smile.

"Thanks, Maddy," he said, watching as Elizabeth bounced lightly up the stairs and through the screen door. "We'll see how it goes."

Elizabeth awaited him in the large family room. Two American flags graced either end of the mantle in triangular cases. In between were crowded at least twenty framed photos of all the members of the family. In the center was a wedding photo. Ed and Maddy, he guessed, from his position ten feet away. Elizabeth was looking expectantly at him. *Her eyes are so green. I can't believe I missed that before.* He shook himself and began to speak.

"Ms. Bennet, I came tonight to apologize for my words this morning. It was completely unprofessional and obviously worse than just impolite. I should never have said any of the things I said even were you not in the office, and I'm honestly ashamed of the way I behaved." He paused, drew in a breath. "I was upset with Richard for another reason entirely, and I took it out on you."

"Why is that, Mr. Darcy?" she asked, her arms crossed across her chest, damp hair tumbling down her back.

"Why was I angry?" he asked. She nodded. "Because," he said, softly, realizing the truth of his words only as he spoke them, "you're here and he's not."

She shook her head and he was afraid, for a minute, that he'd made a terrible error in coming here. But then he caught it, the emotion in her eyes he hadn't been able to place earlier in the day. It wasn't anger or hurt or sorrow, precisely, but a little bit of them all. She was feeling exposed in some way, and his statement about Richard had resonated with her. His first response was that he had, thank God, stumbled onto the right explanation. His blunt honesty wasn't always met with this kind of quiet acceptance.

Elizabeth was silent for what seemed like a very long time before she finally spoke. "Very well, Mr. Darcy," she said evenly. "I suspect that was not an easy thing to admit." She paused. "I forgive you."

He nodded. "Thank you," he said, an immense sense of relief coursing through him.

"I suppose you can come have something to eat if it's not all gone by now," she offered, turning to walk to the yard. He trailed along after her. "Aunt Maddy will give me a lecture if you don't."

"I'd like that," he said, watching her hips swing ever so slightly as she exited through the kitchen door to the deck outside. He blinked. *Oh, this is trouble.*

CHAPTER EIGHT

Will was just finishing his burger when the lyrics of Matisyahu's "Live Like a Warrior" came blaring though the screen door.

"That's me," said Elizabeth, who climbed the steps two at a time and dove for the door and her phone inside. Will stood and collected the plates around him, carrying them up to the kitchen behind her. When he entered, Elizabeth was already on the phone speaking in low tones to someone. When she glanced warily at him in the middle of a sentence, he realized it must be Richard. He touched his phone in its holster on his waist and sighed, feeling like he was waiting for the principal to call him into his office for not following the rules. He hated that Richard still tried to boss him around like a younger brother. Yes, he should have checked his calendar this morning, but Richard shouldn't have made the appointment without telling him. He'd been trying to reach the man all weekend—was a quick text too much to ask?

He heard Elizabeth say, "It's your fault too, Richard," and tried not to grin. *Vindicated.*

While he waited, Will glanced around the kitchen. It had traces of the Craftsman aesthetic, too, but it was completely modernized, with polished quartz countertops and glass-tiled backsplashes in muted blues, greens, and browns. White paneled cabinet doors with stainless-steel handles mirrored the light fixtures, and a pot rack was suspended from the ceiling. On the end of the peninsula against the wall was the longest phone charging station he'd ever seen, each slot with its own short power cord and marked with a small bit of masking tape bearing a letter written in black marker. Every slot except one currently held a phone. That spot was marked "EM." *It must be Elizabeth's. What's the M stand for?*

"House rules," Maddy said as she walked in with the children's dishes. Jane and Mary followed behind her holding the barbeque tools and serving platters, which they set near the sink. Maddy put down her load and waved at Elizabeth, gesturing to the deck. When he turned, Elizabeth stepped outside, phone held to her ear.

"When we're in the house," Maddy explained, "the phones stay here."

"Those of us who are out of high school have more privileges," Jane clarified.

Maddy agreed. "However, there are a lot of phones in this house, so we centralize the charging station." She gave Jane a pointed look. "This way there's no searching through a mountain of dirty clothes when someone leaves a phone in her pocket."

Jane threw up her hands. "*One* time, four *years* ago, Aunt Maddy!" she exclaimed plaintively. Charlotte just laughed.

Will didn't know how to respond, so he just nodded uneasily. "Are there other dishes left?" he asked, anxious to be doing something. "I can go get them."

"No, we have everything," Maddy assured him. "Next time we'll leave you to wash up."

Next time? Will wondered. She seemed certain he wasn't about to get pitched out on his backside. He wasn't so sure.

Charlotte seemed to understand. "There *will* be a next time, Will. We were talking it over, and we think Elizabeth likes you."

"Why would you think that?" Will asked doubtfully.

"Lizzy doesn't forgive easily," Jane answered, and made a face. "I love her dearly, but she *is* stubborn about her first impressions. Either you must have made some incredible apology, or she likes you. Most likely both."

"I'm still counting on you for next week," Charlotte said, reaching up to place a hand lightly on his shoulder and looking him full in the face with her eyebrows raised. "You could tell her that women shouldn't be in the military or insult her math skills. I'll make a list. Jane can help me."

"Insult whose math skills?" asked Mary as she waltzed through the crowd to the sink and opened a drawer filled with washcloths.

"I hope you're right," Will said to Charlotte, and saw that she knew what he meant.

"So, what did you do, Will?" Mary asked conspiratorially.

He shrugged. "You'll have to get the story from your sister."

"What story?" asked Kit as she and Lydia stumbled through the door and reached for their phones almost immediately. Maddy held up one finger, and they pulled their hands back.

"Are you finished with everything on your reading lists?"

"Nooo," they moaned in unison. Lydia's shoulders slumped.

"Then there's no point in collecting your phones, is there?"

"But I told Sierra I'd call her tonight," Lydia pleaded. Her aunt just raised an eyebrow.

"I cannot *wait* for senior year," Kit said. The two flounced away dramatically, Kit's golden locks and Lydia's slightly darker ponytail disappearing up the stairs.

Will smiled a little as he recalled similar conversations with Georgiana. He toyed with his own phone. He should call her tonight. He glanced over at Elizabeth. *Should I stay until she's done or should I leave?*

He watched as Elizabeth ended her call. She walked over to the group.

"Can I help with anything, Aunt Maddy?" she asked, shooting Will a look that said *stay here*. He was happy for the clarification.

"No, dear, Will was just offering as well. Next time." She went to the back door to call in her four youngest and was soon deeply involved negotiating a dispute between her two sons and a box of LEGOs.

"Richard wants us to go out to coffee and talk about FORGE," she said reluctantly. "I'm not going to work for you. I've already told him."

Will grabbed the lifeline. "But we should get coffee anyway, so he'll get off your back."

She released a short, pained grunt. "Yeah."

"I'm the younger cousin, so I'm familiar with his edicts. I don't mind, but if you don't want to go . . ."

Elizabeth glanced at her sisters and Charlotte in the kitchen who were making kissing faces at her.

"Like they're twelve," she muttered. "I have to get out of here."

Will grinned, his first genuine smile in days. "So, coffee then?"

"Yeah, all right. It's too late for The Corner." She paused. "Jane, tell Uncle Ed we're going to Tierney's. For coffee."

Jane's blue eyes twinkled with mischief. "Irish coffee?"

"Coffee coffee."

Will dug in his pocket for his keys while Elizabeth went to speak to her aunt.

When she returned, she said, frowning, "It's not far, but you'll have to drive us. My aunt's car is stuffed with some popcorn tins the kids are selling for church choir or something."

"It's okay," he said, trying not to read anything into her desire to take separate cars. He waited for her to precede him outside.

"Wow," she said as he indicated where he was parked. "Nice car."

Will smiled a little. "I love this car," he replied. It was a sleek Audi, something between a sedan and a sports car. It wasn't the latest model, but it was in immaculate condition. He hit the remote to unlock the doors. "It's the first car I bought entirely with my own money, after my second year at FORGE."

She slid into the passenger seat. "Wow," she said, running her hands over the leather seat. She pulled the seat belt across her torso, and he heard the smooth click of the latch.

"So," she asked, "did you never have a car before, or . . ."

He checked his mirrors and pulled the car out onto the street. "Richard's dad is a senator; did he tell you?" he asked.

She frowned, clearly not following the change of subject. "Yes."

"It's not just a job for him, being a politician. It's who he is."

"Okay . . ." The word was drawn out.

Will hit the turn signal and changed lanes. "For my dad, it was being a businessman. Wheeling and dealing. Acquisitions and mergers. He was amazing at it, and it was really how he defined himself. He got so good he had owners in trouble coming to him instead of having to seek them out."

Elizabeth didn't say anything, but he could tell she was listening.

"When he died, I inherited the company. It's a private company, a family company, and it's extremely successful." Elizabeth pointed left. When they had made the turn and pulled up in front of the tavern, Will released his belt but remained in his seat. "It's who my dad was, and I'm proud of it. I'm proud to be his son. But acquisitions and mergers—it's not who I am."

She nodded. "Did you sell it?"

He shrugged. "I hired a CEO whose experience was a better fit and whose age made the advisory board more comfortable. I remain informed of the major decisions and can veto them if I think they're not true to the company's mission and expertise, but fortunately that doesn't often happen." He looked over at her. "I have a sister, so I figured she might be interested in working there when she's out of school, but for now it makes us a good income considering we don't have to invest all that much time in it."

"You'd just hand it over to her?" Elizabeth asked. "I mean, I have no idea how that kind of thing works, but it must be worth a lot of money."

He nodded. "It is, but it's not like I would be *giving* her anything. We both own half. I make the decisions now, but once she graduates, she'll be a more equal partner if she wants." He paused. "It's not quite the same, but Richard would be a partner at FORGE, if he'd ever come home." He shook his head at the bitterness in his words and continued. "So, we have this money," he explained, "but it's the money my parents left us. It's great, don't get me wrong—it's made a lot of things possible. But it's not mine. FORGE is mine. And so is this car."

Elizabeth seemed to mull that over before she released her own belt.

"So, Tierney's?" Will asked as they exited the car.

"It's been here forever. It's Uncle Ed's favorite hangout when the estrogen level in the house gets too high, which is at least once a week." Elizabeth grinned. "The boys are still too young to raise the needle on testosterone much—it's still seven to three. Even the dogs are girls."

They walked in the door, and Will looked around. There was a large bar with a gleaming dark wooden top. The floor was crowded with tables and booths. Elizabeth waved to the man behind the bar and grabbed a booth with a view of the door.

The bartender appeared at the table. "Sam Adams, Liz?" he asked with a smirk. She shook her head.

"Coffee, please, Nathan," she said. He turned to Will.

"And you, sir?"

"Same."

Elizabeth's phone buzzed. She looked at her texts and typed something before she shoved her phone back in her pocket.

Will looked pained. "Richard?"

She scowled. "He's *so* pushy."

Will laughed a little. "He is," he agreed. "Always has been."

She took a picture of him with her phone.

"Really?" he asked, pulling a face.

Elizabeth wasn't fazed. "Evidence," she replied with a shrug.

The coffee arrived, and he picked up the cream. Elizabeth, he saw, drank her coffee black.

Elizabeth stared at him briefly before breaking into a small grin and shaking her head. "Okay, I know I forgave you, and I meant it. But you really were an arrogant ass this morning."

Despite the cheerful tone of her words, Will winced. "Yeah. Sorry." He rubbed the back of his neck. Usually he had full control over his behavior. He had to. But of all people, Richard has the power to provoke him. He wrapped his hands around the warm mug. The coffee smelled delicious, and he took a sip.

Elizabeth was giving him a skeptical look.

"What?" he asked, confused, as he set his cup back on the table. She didn't say anything. "You know," he retorted, "I *have* to be tough. If you're kind in business, you get eaten."

She considered him closely for a few more seconds. "Okay," she said with a chuckle. "You're right—I forgave you, I shouldn't give you a hard time about it. First, call me Elizabeth. I'm used to Staff Sergeant or Bennet, but Ms. Bennet is just weird." She toyed with the saltshaker. "Second, tell me about FORGE so I can get Richard to shut up. All I know is what I learned on your website."

Something was bothering him. "How do they know your order here? I thought you just got back."

That emotion he couldn't place flashed across her face again. She crossed her arms over her chest. "It's what my Uncle Ed drinks. FORGE, please."

"All right, if you don't want to tell me . . ." He hesitated when her face remained stoic, worried that his attempt to tease her back had fallen flat.

He cleared his throat. "FORGE is, for lack of a better term, a venture capital company. We specialize in finding young, innovative companies and funding their projects. We invest in products that are nearly ready to go to market but don't have adequate funding. We help them become more visible, but in a few cases, we've invested more heavily in the development."

She leaned forward. "For example?"

"Most of it is proprietary," Will said, warming to his subject, "but one project was just given the green light by the FDA—it's an improved organic 3-D printer that should be able to grow better organs for transplants. Another is a solar energy collector that's painted directly onto roof tiles, meaning there'd be no need for those heavy, expensive panels."

Elizabeth nodded. "Those are good projects, but I guess I don't see why Richard thought I'd be right for you guys. Seems better suited for an engineer on the design side or an MBA or JD for marketing and clearing regulatory hurdles. Those aren't exactly my forte."

Will shrugged. "I imagine he thought you'd bring a different perspective to the table, and you might help us get an edge on evaluating projects in your area. You know, maybe get your opinion on new AI or technologies being developed in the security field."

Elizabeth shook her head. "At the moment, there's probably more money in infidelity," she said, relaxing a bit. "There are a lot of free apps out there that track phones and so on, but not many would stand up to the kind of scrutiny a court case requires."

"See," Will said with a nod, "that's probably exactly what Richard was thinking about."

"Okay, I *can* see where he was going," Elizabeth said, "but really, the incentive is all on your side here. I know what I can do and how much I can make doing it, and I doubt your company can offer me what I'll have just being my own boss." She took another drink.

Will frowned. "You would have a steady paycheck, good benefits, and the opportunity for substantial bonuses," he said. He was honestly surprised that anyone wouldn't want that.

"Look," Elizabeth said, setting her mug down on the table, "even though we're talking about salary and benefits when I've neither been offered nor accepted a position with your firm, what you are offering is stability. Maybe that's not what I want."

"What *do* you want?" Will asked, truly interested in the answer.

"Think about it," she said with a smile that was almost bashful, "I've been taking orders and working on someone else's schedule for six years." *Longer.* "Stability is nice, in my personal life. But what I want at work," she said, raising one eyebrow as she evaluated him over the rim of her coffee cup, "is independence."

Will took another drink. "So you'd never even consider working for us?"

She paused, considering his question, then said, "Not as a full-time employee, no. But if you ever wanted me to review a good prospect in my field, you could hire me to write up an opinion. Or if you wanted me to test your own system for vulnerabilities, I could do that." She set the cup down. "As a contractor."

Will scratched the side of his jaw. "Okay," he said, "I'll keep that in mind." He felt better already, more awake. Was it the caffeine or the conversation? "One more thing."

She lifted her eyes to his. "Yes?"

Will felt an electric current run through him. He blinked but recovered quickly. "Now that we've resolved that I'm not going to make a job offer and you're not going to accept one, please call me Will."

Elizabeth turned her head a little to hide a grin and raised her coffee cup in agreement. Will touched his own to it softly, thinking that the small clink of the mugs was the start of something. Whether it would turn out to be something good, he couldn't yet say.

CHAPTER NINE

Elizabeth looked at the red brick building and then up and down the street, satisfied. It wasn't a ritzy neighborhood, but it would do. The apartment itself was larger than she thought she'd be able to afford on her budget, and it was close to the parkway.

"Sweetheart," Uncle Ed said carefully, as he stared at a red brick house split into apartments not too far from the Garden Parkway, "I'm not sure I'm comfortable with you living here."

There was nothing wrong with this street. There weren't any plants, and there were a lot of parked cars, but it was fine. "It's a lot better than most places I've lived the past six years, Uncle Ed," she told him with a charming smile, "and it's only a ten-minute drive to your place."

He grimaced. Actually grimaced. "You can afford a better neighborhood." He toed a beer can that had been abandoned in the gutter.

Elizabeth shook her head. "I have a few jobs Abby has sent me, but I'd rather rent low. I don't want to tap into my nest egg, and I can always trade up in a year if I'm earning more." She put a hand on his arm. "You know I can take care of myself, right?"

He was staring across the street. Elizabeth followed his gaze to a group of young people standing around, alternately talking to each other and casting suspicious looks at them. Elizabeth noted them, analyzed their body language, and didn't see a threat.

"Abby," he said in a low voice, "that's another conversation we need to have."

"About Abby?" she asked, a bit surprised. "Why?"

"An issue for another time," he told her, then sighed. "Look, I'd be a fool to doubt your ability to defend yourself, Lizbet," he said, "but I'd rather you didn't have to."

Elizabeth frowned. "Anything I can afford, even here in Bloomfield, is going to look like a dump next to your house. This neighborhood isn't dangerous, Uncle Ed. I've checked the crime stats. It's just blue-collar."

Uncle Ed was quiet for a moment, still assessing. Then he shook his head. "No, honey," he said flatly. "I'd be up at night worrying. And if I'm up, your aunt is up, and if she doesn't get *her* rest . . ."

Elizabeth sighed, frustrated. "I should have just rented a place and then showed you. A black hole is not going to open up and swallow the Gardiner household if I am not living in a crazy-expensive neighborhood."

His expectations were far too high. He'd bought his house in a real-estate downturn for next to nothing when he was still in the service and had friends who'd helped him fix it up even when he was stationed in Maryland. When he'd finally retired from the Marines, he'd taken over the plumbing business. His financial situation was very different from hers.

"We could help you out just to get started . . ." Uncle Ed began, but she cut him off.

"Absolutely not," she informed him. "You didn't use any of my money—I won't take yours." She put her hands on her hips and stared hard at her uncle.

He held up his hands, palms out. "There's no need to stop looking. We can compromise, right? You can go for a little less square footage in a better area for a small increase in rent, right?"

He really wasn't going to budge. Elizabeth knew she'd never rent a place he didn't approve of, but it didn't mean she liked it. "Yes," she said reluctantly. "I suppose. I just want to start putting money away, Uncle Ed."

Uncle Ed smiled. He knew he had won. "I know, and that's commendable," he replied, "but you have to temper that desire with practical concerns." His face relaxed in the manner of a man given a reprieve even as she frowned at him. "Think about inviting Jane over for dinner. Would you want her walking to her car after dark?"

Don't roll your eyes. "Uncle Ed, she works in Newark."

"In the hospital, which is attached to a garage," he retorted, "and she has someone walk her out after dark."

"*I* could walk her out," Elizabeth muttered, but she followed Uncle Ed back to the truck.

Her uncle said nothing.

It's a lost cause. Move on. "Do you think Great-grandpa would have liked your new truck?" Elizabeth joked as she pulled herself into the cab. "Pretty much all I remember about him was that he didn't like to spend money."

"I think you've inherited some of his miserly traits," Uncle Ed responded with a grin. "And once the money was spent, he'd have loved it." He stuck his key into the ignition, but before turning it to start the truck, he gave her a warm look. "You've come so far, Lizbet," he said. "There's no limit for you now."

Elizabeth was embarrassed but grateful. She *had* come a long way. Uncle Ed's phone buzzed, and he pulled it out of his pocket.

It had been hell at Longbourn that last year. Elizabeth was afraid to call her uncle, afraid her mother would make good on her threat to hand her and her sisters over to the county. Fanny Bennet had threatened to file charges against the Gardiners, claiming that Uncle Ed had abused the girls and Aunt Maddy had helped him hide it. Fanny loved Uncle Ed but had never liked Aunt Maddy. Elizabeth often wondered, now that she was an adult, whether Fanny would have followed through on her threat. She'd been pretty convincing to a sixteen-year-old girl, but her mother had been so erratic at the end there was just no way to know.

In the end, her uncle and aunt had come to their rescue when they heard of Fanny's passing. Aunt Maddy had remained with the Bennet girls so they could finish out their school year, despite having two small boys of her own and being pregnant with Moira. Uncle Ed had driven up every weekend.

It had displaced her, but Elizabeth had seen how much better they could care for her sisters.

She'd do anything for them.

"Elizabeth?" she heard Uncle Ed ask, then, "Earth to Elizabeth!"

She looked up at him. "Lost in thought for a second," she said, abashed.

He held up his phone. "I've been texting your aunt. She has an apartment for us to look at on the other side of the Parkway. It's a nicer neighborhood with some trees."

"How much?" Elizabeth asked, feeling skeptical. He told her it was smaller but only about fifty dollars more a month than the one they'd just seen. "Okay," she said, leaning back in her seat. "I trust you."

Major Richard Fitzwilliam had a problem. Taking a page from his cousin Will's book, he had located a yellow legal pad, drawn a line down the middle, and titled the first column "Stay" and the second "Leave." The problem was that there were a dozen reasons to stay but only five to leave, including Georgiana and Will.

"Maybe they should be two different reasons," he said softly, scratching out Will's name and moving it to the line below.

He tossed his pen down and stood, walking to the kitchen and opening his refrigerator. There wasn't much inside. His pantry held some canned soup, and he thought perhaps he could make a sandwich. Once he'd assembled his dinner, he sat down with his phone. He couldn't text Will or Oscar about this, and he'd never discuss it with Georgiana, but he could ask Bennet what she thought. She'd just gone through her own separation, and he could count on her to be logical.

Bennet.

There was a short wait before his phone buzzed. *Hey. Apartment hunting.*

He grinned. *Castle? Show me the moat.*

He waited for the next text and found himself looking at a brown-shingle two-story house with four mailboxes on the porch and then the interior of an apartment with a nice kitchen but not much else. It looked small. *I thought Jersey had more space.*

He could almost hear her indignation. *Do you know how much 850 sf goes for this close to NYC?*

Honestly? No. Why didn't he know that?

Her reply was quick. *You rich kids. What am I going to do with you?*

Dunno. He tapped his pencil on the legal pad.

There was a pause, and then another text. *What's up?*

Trying to make my list.

This was followed by a line of question marks from Bennet.

Stay in or separate.

This time, her text came back immediately. *Hang on.*

His phone rang, and he grinned as he accepted the call. "Hey, Bennet."

"Hey," she said. "So what's the hang-up?"

"I'm trying to be logical about this."

"Tell me." In the background, Richard heard a low voice asking Bennet something. He heard her tell someone, "It'll have to wait," and then she was back with him. "Go," she said.

"I've got lots of reasons to stay," he said, scratching the stubble on his jawline. He hadn't bothered to shave today, knowing he wasn't likely to go outside. "And not so many to leave."

"So why are you calling me?" she asked, sounding annoyed.

"I didn't. You called me," he protested, grinning. Bennet was unintentionally hilarious.

"Oh right, I did. Okay, what are your reasons to stay?" she asked, not stopping to laugh at herself as she normally did.

"Despite the general, the work is easy, there are great benefits, room for career advancement, the travel . . ." He read off his list before she stopped him.

"Okay, I get the idea. What's on the other side?"

"Well, challenge. There's no challenge anymore. More importantly, family. Will, Georgiana, Oscar, even my dad though he'd probably be just as happy for me to stay put."

There was a soft humph on the other end of the line. "I think you already know what you want to do, Richard," Bennet said.

"I don't. That's why I texted you."

"Why me?"

"You're not emotionally involved, so you won't steer me wrong."

She did laugh at that. "Wow, no pressure," she said with a snort. "Look, it's not the quantity of reasons you've got listed there that count. You know that, right?"

Richard felt a smile begin to tug at his lips. "I wasn't thinking about it quite like that."

"Yes, you were. If you were going just on the number of reasons, you wouldn't have texted me. You'd have already decided to sign the extension. You want me to talk you into leaving." She paused. "I can't do that."

"Why is that?" asked Richard, amused now.

She sighed. He could just see her rubbing her forehead. "Because you've already made up your mind to leave."

His eyebrows lifted. "Mind telling me what decision my mind has made?"

"Don't waste my time, Richard," she said with a put-upon sigh. "You want to come home. Your family is here, and there's not one thing on your list of reasons to stay that you can't get in a job stateside. I'm told you even own part of a successful, innovative company in Manhattan. Plenty of challenge there."

Richard chuckled. "I'm not sure where you got that information," he teased.

"Bring me some Nehaus when you come back," she told him. "That's my fee for life advice."

He rolled his eyes. "All right, I suppose you've earned some chocolate. Georgiana likes it, too. Though maybe I should wait to be sure it's the right decision."

"It's not simple, I won't say that," she said, her voice lowered as though she was afraid of being overheard, "but totally, completely worth it." Another brief pause, and then she admitted, "I don't fit in, exactly, and I don't know that I ever will. But it's really great to be here." He heard nothing but her breathing for a few seconds, and then, she added, "Surprisingly great."

CHAPTER TEN

Elizabeth was fast asleep when she felt the sofa bed frame rattle beneath her. She flew up to her feet and into a defensive position before she even opened her eyes. When she did, she realized Lydia and Kit were standing very close to her. Kit took a step back, but Lydia wasn't daunted.

"Moving day!" her youngest sister cried cheerfully and with volume. Elizabeth sat down on the bed heavily and then laid back again, her arms flung wide and her feet still on the floor.

There was another jolt, harder this time. "Go away, Lydia," she said with a groan. "I'm sleeping." Or she would be, when her heart stopped trying to escape her chest.

She didn't hear Lydia leaving. Instead, she heard her youngest sister say, "It's awesome being on the other side of this."

"I wouldn't know," Kit said primly, "*I'm* always up on time."

Lydia snorted. "Liar." Another jolt. "Get up! Geez, Lizzy, I thought you were a Marine! Uncle Ed is always up at five!"

Elizabeth grabbed her pillow and placed it over her face. "I'm a night-shift Marine," she replied flatly. After a moment, she lifted the pillow and stared tiredly up into her tormentor's face. It was covered with pancake foundation and dark eyeliner slathered on thickly.

"Whoa, Lydia, that's a whole lot of monster makeup for"—she fumbled for her phone—"six in the morning." Lydia frowned, and Elizabeth sighed. "I don't have *that* much to move. Why can't we do this later?"

"Unlike you, we all have things to do," Kit replied. "C'mon, Lizzy, Lydia and I want to meet the cute Marines Uncle Ed drafted to help out."

"He doesn't know any young Marines," she grumbled, sitting up and trying to run a hand through her rumpled hair, "but it explains why you two are awake."

"He knows you," Kit pointed out. "He met them through someone at the VFW." Kit twisted her blonde hair back and pinned it up off her neck. It was casually elegant, like Kit herself. "Denny and Saunderson. Please, Lizzy, get up. I need a date for prom. I have the perfect dress planned."

"Prom is nine months away." Elizabeth stretched and then yawned widely.

"But all the best guys are taken in the fall. How amazing would it be to already have a date when school starts?" Kit's expression turned dreamy. "A Marine would be just . . ."

"Deployed?" Elizabeth finished Kit's statement, opening her mouth in a yawn before resting her head in her hands. "If they're active duty, Kit, they have no idea where they'll be in May. And they're too old for you. Better hold off on that."

"Belay that order!" crowed Lydia gaily, her ponytail swishing back and forth.

"That's Navy, Lydia," Elizabeth said sleepily, rubbing her eyes. "Or, no, I guess it *could* be Marines. Coast Guard, too," she added. Her brain wasn't kicking into gear. "Ships are involved."

Kit stuck out her tongue at her younger sister, then turned to Elizabeth. "They're not that much older than I am, Lizzy."

"Are you up?" Lydia demanded, ignoring Kit.

"Yes," Elizabeth said, forcing herself to her feet. She folded the bed into the sofa and shuffled towards the bathroom. She turned back. "Kit, would you make sure they leave me some coffee?" *Lots of coffee.*

"Okay," Kit said, dodging around her, Lydia in her wake. Elizabeth watched them both bounce up the steps.

Fifteen minutes later, Elizabeth appeared upstairs, teeth brushed, face washed, hair brushed out and pinned up. The coffeepot was empty. Sighing, she reached into the cupboard and, with her back to the rest of the kitchen, called out, "Does anyone else want coffee?"

"I'll take a cup," came a low voice from the doorway. Elizabeth jumped a bit before looking up into the handsome face of Will Darcy. He was in jeans and a gray t-shirt, appearing very much at home in the Gardiners' kitchen. She blinked. He'd worn a jacket the night he'd taken her to coffee, but now it was very clear that the man worked out. Regularly.

"Hello," she said after a pause. "What're *you* doing here?"

"Maddy asked if I could help," he said, tilting his head, appraising her with a soft smile. *Great, he's probably one of those early risers.* She stared at him. *He looks really good in that t-shirt.*

He grinned and then walked up to her. "Sorry," he said, "your hair's just a bit . . ." He reached over to tuck a lock behind her ear. His hand was warm, and she froze for a moment when his fingers brushed the side of her face. *Breathe, Bennet.* She pushed herself into action.

"Thanks," she said, grabbing a coffee filter and starting to count out scoops. "Do you like it strong?"

Aunt Maddy had put out the word to the neighbors that she had a niece furnishing her first apartment, and everyone, it seemed, had something they were only too happy to donate. Everything was already piled up in the corner of the Gardiners' garage. Elizabeth suspected that her uncle was paying his recruits to help her move, but he wouldn't admit it. Uncle Ed bluntly pointed out that she was still suffering migraines from the concussion and wore a brace on her knee when she ran and worked out. He didn't want her hauling furniture and boxes up a flight of stairs. Her impulse was to argue, but it was Uncle Ed.

She salvaged some of her pride by carrying her computer equipment up to the new apartment herself and storing it in the second bedroom. She gave in on just about everything else. It made her uncomfortable to watch other people working while she stood aside.

"See?" her uncle said, joining her in the kitchen. "It's not so bad. Pretend you're an officer."

She rolled her eyes. "You are so full of it, Uncle Ed," she told him fondly. "You just miss ordering people around now that Aunt Maddy's in charge."

He waggled his eyebrows. "Happy wife, happy life."

"I suppose it's nice, for once," Elizabeth ventured, "to have other people do the heavy lifting." She glanced over at the door. *After all, it gives me the best view of . . . that,* she thought as she watched Will enter her apartment with a rolled-up carpet tossed over his shoulder. Earlier, she'd followed him up the stairs as he held up the back end of her new mattress. Then he'd hefted the kitchen table over his head and set it in place before returning with all the chairs. In one trip. She opened boxes and began putting things away, trying not to be too obvious in her admiration, lest Uncle Ed call her out. It wasn't easy.

Will Darcy had a lot of experience with women checking him out. Most of them were happy to have him catch them at it. The woman would smile seductively or bat her eyelashes or something else equally ridiculous and expect him to fall at her feet. So he'd become well-versed in ignoring the glances, the hair tosses, the tinny giggles, that weird thing women did when they tilted their heads and exposed their necks. It might have been flattering, in a way, except that he knew from experience that they were attracted less to him and more to his wallet. He had early on become a very careful man. He'd had little choice.

Elizabeth Bennet was the complete antithesis to such women. She'd let him have it when he'd said those stupid things at FORGE, but it was the glimpse he'd had of her at the Gardiners' and Tierney's— intelligent, funny, stubborn, and yes, beautiful, even in soccer shorts— that had made him want to know more about her. After his behavior and apology, though, he figured she would need a reason to spend a little more time with her so she could get to know *him*.

Thus, Will had been very happy to get the call from Maddy Gardiner asking for help with Elizabeth's move. Her uncle was concerned about her knee and the flight of stairs. Will was a little apprehensive about Elizabeth's reaction to his appearance. If she wasn't interested, he didn't want to come across like some creepy stalker. Now, though, she was giving him the eye, and it wasn't the death glare she'd given him at FORGE.

She really did seem to have forgiven him, for which he was grateful. Lots of people over the years had *said* he was forgiven for something stupid he'd said or done only to continue to refer to it. Elizabeth had definitely been surprised to see him this morning, but once she'd had her coffee, she'd been welcoming enough. He made a mental note to always have coffee on hand for her.

Just now, she was attempting to avoid being caught out by her uncle, but she apparently hadn't thought he himself would notice. It amused him no end. If he flexed his arm a little more than necessary when he carried in her rolled-up rug, slowed a little on the stairs so she could watch him from her position a few steps below, brought up four dining chairs at once, or bossed two Marines around to get the sofa in the door, it was all done in the innocent spirit of testing her response.

On his final trip into the apartment, he'd glanced past Saunderson and Denny, who were cramming pizza into their mouths, and met her steady gaze. He gave her a grin. *Caught you.* She turned her back to him, a rosy blush creeping up the nape of her neck as she was suddenly entirely focused on putting her dishes away.

Will Darcy was critically evaluating the neighborhood, his lips curled up disdainfully. Ed Gardiner joined him by his truck and began to check his texts. When he looked up, he chuckled. "You should've seen the place I talked her out of," he said with a smile and a shake of his head. "I nearly tossed her over my shoulder and carried her off like I did when she was six."

"Yeah?" Will asked. He leaned against the tailgate. "What was she like as a girl?"

A wistful expression crossed Ed's face. "Cutest little tornado you've ever seen," he replied. "She was always trying to outdo Jane. Nearly broke her arm trying to do a handstand on the back of a horse." Will grinned, and Ed continued. "Wild hair that would never stay in a braid, and two missing teeth up top." He reached into a wallet thick with pictures and pulled out a small studio photo. "Here," he said, handing it over. "Maddy and I took the girls to get pictures when we could. From the first, Maddy was as crazy about them as I was." He smiled. "It's how I knew for sure she was the one."

Will scrutinized the photo. Elizabeth's hair was done in two neat braids. She wore a jean jacket and a red cowboy hat perched at a jaunty angle. Her green eyes beamed at the camera.

"Are you serious about her?" Ed asked abruptly.

Will handed the photo back and nodded. "It's really up to her at this point," he said. "I can't say it'll work out—we've only just met. But I want to get to know her better, and I'm not a casual dater."

Ed nodded thoughtfully. "All right then." He pulled out another photo, this one of Elizabeth's high school graduation. Elizabeth was holding her cap and gown in one hand, staring into the camera. She was thin, too thin, and there was no smile on her face. He would never have recognized it was the same girl, though he could see the similarities to Elizabeth now. Will's eyebrows pinched together, and he frowned.

"Things went south with her parents, and the care of her sisters was handed over to her," he said. "It meant she wasn't able to do other things, like play soccer or keep her grades as high as she wanted them. Her coach was angry with her. Apparently, she said she had family responsibilities, but Fanny . . ." He paused. "Fanny was my sister and the girls' mother," he explained.

Will nodded.

"Fanny told him there were no problems, so he called Elizabeth a liar and asked if she was doing drugs. Elizabeth wouldn't ever say, but apparently her former teammates turned on her, made her senior year miserable. She was a good player, in line for captain that year, and they were angry she'd left them in the lurch, so to speak."

"Why are you telling me this, Ed?" Will asked, uncomfortable. "It seems like it should be Elizabeth's story to tell."

Ed nodded. "You're right. But she's slow to trust, Will." He shook his head, and laughed a bit at himself. "Sorry if that sounded harsh. I'm not a hit man, and I'm not trying to warn you off. I'm just saying that if you decide to take this further, be someone she can trust." He took the photo back.

Will understood Ed's fears. "I promise to do my best," he said. Ed appeared skeptical. "I have a sister," he explained. "I'm her guardian. I understand what you're saying."

Ed nodded at that and put the photo away.

Will heard voices and saw Elizabeth chatting with an elderly man whose white hair looked like a lion's mane. She shook his hand and gave him a smile before she headed over to the truck.

"Mr. Pizanski," Elizabeth announced as she joined them. "Neighbor down the hall."

"I have to get to the boys' football game," Ed said suddenly. His eyebrows lifted as his phone pinged and he read the message. "Or pick up the girls from ballet," he said with a sigh. "Apparently Sarah's trying to run the class again. I should put *her* on the football team." He looked up. "Lizzy, why don't you take Will out to lunch as a thank you, since the boys ate all the pizza?"

Lizzy struck a pose and put her hands on her hips. "You buying?" she asked impertinently, before the grin broke through.

Ed shrugged, eyes twinkling. "I would, but my niece insists she won't take my money." Her grin stretched into a full smile. "Besides, I've already fed Saunderson and Denny."

She gave a little laugh then and waved him off.

Charming, Will thought, as the word he'd been searching for finally hit him. *She's charming.* Elizabeth Bennet was a host of contradictions, and he wanted to learn more about her.

"Okay," she said, "give me the keys and we can drop the truck back at the rental place."

"Who said you could drive?" Will asked, grinning when her eyes narrowed.

"I did," she said. "It's my truck." She reached for the keys.

He shrugged and held them above his head. "Possession is nine-tenths of the law, I think."

"I am not getting a ladder to climb up the bell tower, Quasimodo," she shot back, moving deftly between him and the driver's door. She folded her arms across her chest. "Give me the keys."

Neither of them heard Ed's laughter as he drove away.

"Did you know *Mishmish* means apricot?" Elizabeth asked as they ate their meals. She had selected a private table away from the large front windows.

He nodded.

"You did?" she asked, lifting her eyebrows. "I'm impressed!"

Will opened the menu and pointed to the top of it. "It says so on the menu, under the name."

She grinned self-consciously. "I missed that." She took a drink of her water. "There was an old Egyptian man in Brussels who used to call me 'mishmisha.'"

"He called you an apricot?" Will asked, crinkling his nose as he dipped a carrot into the hummus.

"Little apricot," she corrected him. She reached for a carrot. "He was a sweet man."

"You sure he wasn't hitting on you?" Will replied, teasing.

She shook her head. "I'm sure. If I really think about it, he was probably just buttering me up so I'd get him his cigarettes." She tucked into her shawarma. "But I liked him anyway. He told great stories."

"Like what?"

"Well, let's see." She speared a cucumber. "His favorite was about

Ahti, the goddess of disorder. I think he made most of it up, but it was colorful. She had the body of a hippo and the head of a wasp."

Will made a face. "I take it back. He wasn't hitting on you."

She shrugged. "I guess you had to be there."

"I'll be honest and say I'm glad I wasn't," he responded with a quiet laugh.

She nodded. Her right leg began to bounce up and down under the table, and she placed a hand on her knee to stop it. "Thanks for helping today. I told Aunt Maddy I was fine moving myself if I had one other person, and I guess she thought of you."

"So *you* didn't think about me?" His voice did not betray any concern. "Because it seemed like you were watching me pretty closely today."

Elizabeth's cheeks felt hot, and her eyes snapped up to Will's. He didn't seem upset. "No," she said bluntly. *Not for moving...*

He raised his eyebrows and gave her a look that was a mixture of amusement and disbelief. "I'm hurt," he said drily. "You didn't think about me at all?"

"You're sitting at a table with me having a conversation," she told him, embarrassed. "I'm thinking about you now."

He eyed her silently for a few seconds before he asked, "Enough to do this again? You know, without the forced labor?" He wasn't smiling now, but his voice was sincere.

She summoned her courage. *He already knows I was watching him today. What do I have to lose? Clearly not my pride.* "Yes," she replied directly. "I'd like that."

When the check came, the waitress handed it directly to her, as she'd been instructed. Will tried to reach for it, but she pushed his hand away. "What is it with you Fitzwilliam boys?" she asked. "You helped me move. I can float you a meal to say thanks."

Will didn't look happy. "I'll get the next one. No arguments."

"Deal," she agreed, and tried not to appear as pleased by that idea as she felt.

Elizabeth stood in her second bedroom, a small, long room with one window covered by a closed blind. Projected on the unadorned white wall were lines of code blown up so that she could look through them without straining her eyes. To a casual visitor, the code would have looked like foreign text, but Elizabeth's attention was focused intently on a small section. She tapped a button on her headset.

"Abby," she said, "it's an XSS vulnerability. Tenth line in—do you see it?"

A high, reedy voice came over the phone line. "Excellent. I've been looking at this section so long I wasn't sure what I was seeing anymore."

Elizabeth smiled. "Happy to help. I appreciate the recommendation you put in over at The Markham. It's a good gig."

"You're welcome, Dutch," Abby replied lightly. "Any time you want to earn some *real* money, all you have to do is call."

Elizabeth winced and cast her eyes up to the ceiling. "Thanks, but no thanks, and please don't call me that."

Abby's disconcerting, evil-faerie laugh filled her ear. "Whyever not, dearie?"

"Stop," Elizabeth nearly pleaded.

"You are really far too straight, Bennet." Abby's teasing voice became businesslike. "Listen, thanks again. I appreciate the confirmation."

Elizabeth relaxed. "Any time. Just keep sending me all those jobs you're too big to take anymore."

Another laugh drifted through the phone line. "Will do. The guys say hi. See you later."

She stared at the lines of code on her wall, heard Abby's voice in her ear, and suddenly the room felt very small. She fumbled for the doorknob and stepped quickly into the living room. She placed one hand on the wall and concentrated on catching her breath. *Damn it.*

Her phone buzzed, and she glanced at the screen. It was Will.

Just finished a meeting in Newark and I'm starving. Join me for dinner?

She had work to do, but clearly she needed a break—she could feel the telltale ache growing behind her eyes. She whipped off her headset and dropped it on a side table before she returned to her phone.

Sure.

"You know," Will said slowly, "there are a lot of really nice restaurants in the area. I offered to treat you. You could have chosen someplace more . . ." He had just assumed she'd pick a fancier place. Even *Mishmish* was quite a bit nicer.

"Expensive?" Elizabeth asked, finishing his sentence. "What's wrong with a good hamburger every now and again?"

Will enjoyed a hamburger as much as the next guy, but a place actually called The Diner wasn't really a *date* kind of restaurant. Then again, he thought, wincing inwardly, he *had* just sort of announced that he *happened* to be passing near her neighborhood and he was hungry. It hadn't actually been a request to go out on a date. "I had a hamburger at the Gardiners' house . . ."

She shook her head and crinkled her nose. "Food snob."

"I'm not, really," he protested.

"They have amazing burgers here," she promised, her eyes scanning the menu. "Oh, and the chili is incredible." She looked up, her eyes dancing. "I have an unhealthy obsession with it. It's painfully spicy, but I can't stop eating it."

He shook his head. "I can take it pretty hot." It was true. He was partial to spicy foods.

"Oh yeah?" she asked, that maddening, challenging eyebrow lifted in an arch. "How hot?"

Will began to reply, but the waitress approached, and he closed his mouth. Elizabeth ordered a salad, but also a burger, medium, with Swiss cheese and mushrooms. He ordered the chili.

She gave him a grin as the waitress walked away. "You are so easy," she taunted him. "You're going to die when you eat that chili. I'm warning you. I like hot food, but this is *really, really* hot."

"Bring it on, Bennet," he said playfully.

Their drinks arrived, and she drank half a glass of water before she put it down and asked, "So what was your meeting about?"

He shrugged. "I volunteer once a month for the Boys and Girls Clubs in the area. I'm on an anti-bullying panel."

"Wow," she said with a nod. "That's great." She squinted at him. "I can't imagine you being bullied in school, though."

"Well," he said uncomfortably, "it's complicated."

She waited a minute, but he didn't offer to continue.

"If you don't want to talk about it, that's okay," she said. "I get it. I do think it's nice that you volunteer your time like that, though. You must be pretty busy."

He nodded, relieved. He might tell her someday, but it wasn't a conversation he wanted to have at a diner in Jersey. It was a topic to discuss in private.

They talked, instead, about what she called her enormously boring work, though he could tell she relished it. Then she told a funny story about her niece Moira choosing a Halloween costume. "She insisted on wearing pink, but refused to go as a princess or a ballerina because 'all the girls do that,'" Elizabeth explained with a laugh. "So Aunt Maddy said she should go as cotton candy."

He shook his head. "How does one find a cotton candy costume?" he asked. "This I have to see."

"You haven't any idea what it means to be a Gardiner, Will," Elizabeth told him, amused. "We *make* things. Well," she clarified, "Uncle Ed and I *fix* things. But most of us make things." She sipped more of her water. "Kit is in charge of all costumes. It broke her heart when my oldest nephew told her he wanted to buy one this year."

"Kit is your youngest sister?"

"Next-to-youngest," Elizabeth corrected him. "She has her heart set on fashion design school, which is why I had to share the basement with a legion of faceless mannequins. Not great when you wake up in the middle of the night." She drank some more water. "Lydia is the youngest."

He chuckled and tried to commit the information to memory. "Lydia's the one who keeps claiming to be the tallest?"

Elizabeth laughed. "Yes. Not sure why that's so important. And it's not remotely true. She has to wear these enormous platform shoes to be taller than me, but she's persistent, I'll give her that."

Their food arrived, and the savory fragrance of the chili was heavenly. His mouth began to water. He dipped his spoon into the bowl and lifted it to his mouth, the flavor of the peppers and the beef exploding against his tongue. He moaned with pleasure.

Elizabeth was grinning widely at him. "I thought that first bite would set your hair on fire, but you seem to like it."

"Is that the reason you brought me here?" he asked, challenging her. "To see what I'm made of?"

She laughed. "No, but when you started bragging, I admit the thought did cross my mind. Shows what I know. You really do like hot foods."

He nodded. "My parents used to travel a lot on business, and they took me with them when I wasn't in school. I was exposed to a lot of cuisines at a young age. I think I got my love of hot food in Thailand." He took several more bites of the chili. "This is really good," he said. It was quite possibly the best chili he'd ever had.

"Right?" she asked, nodding. "I love the stuff."

"Serrano peppers," he said, tapping the side of the bowl with his spoon. "That's why it has more spice—cooks normally use jalapenos. But they also used cocoa and espresso to mellow it out a bit."

She shook her head at him. "That's mellow? I give in." She held up her hands in mock surrender. "Just let the *gringa* eat her burger in peace."

Will took another bite of the chili and sighed. He was definitely getting another order of this to take home.

CHAPTER ELEVEN

Elizabeth took a seat in the bleachers to prepare for her game. She set her boots next to her while she pulled on her socks and slipped her shin guards underneath. As she folded the top of each sock over, she felt the bench bow a little as someone dropped down beside her. She turned her head and was unsurprised to see Will Darcy sitting there. He'd been showing up everywhere the last two weeks—meeting her at the subway to walk her to interviews, showing up at her apartment with coffee, even taking her to the movies once. On moving day, she'd thought he was asking her to date him and it felt a little like they were, but he hadn't ever said the word and he hadn't so much as tried to hold her hand. She was a little disappointed, to be honest.

Will was studying something written on a piece of paper. He scratched his head and said, without preamble, "Charlotte tells me I am required to insult you. I thought she was joking, but she did provide a rather complete list of topics." He looked up at her. "Boy bands?"

Elizabeth grunted. "If I want to listen to falsetto, The Vienna Boys Choir is the way I go. They're amazing. Lip synching, crotch-grabbing, drug-using twelve-year-old boys with bad haircuts and obviously headed for rehab don't appeal." She pulled on one boot and tied the laces.

He leaned forward again. "What do you listen to?"

"Depends on the playlist."

"Okay," he said, lowering the page, "what's in the first spot on your workout playlist?"

She wrinkled her nose at him. "Why?"

He shrugged. "Just wondering. Vienna Boys Choir? Don Ho?"

She frowned and whipped out her phone, holding it out to him. "And yours," she told him, holding out her hand.

The first song on her list was Avery Watts' "A Cut Above the Rest." Will barked out a laugh, and Elizabeth glanced down at his phone. He lifted his eyebrows when he saw her reaction. It was the first song in his playlist, too.

She held out his phone with a smile. "I see you're just as competitive as I am."

He handed her phone back then slid his own into his pocket. He picked up the list and read the next item. "People who name their kids weird things."

"Dillweed," she answered immediately. "That's all I have to say about that." She set her foot down.

He hmphed, pressed his lips together. He glanced up as she yanked the laces taut on her second boot. "Children at weddings?"

Elizabeth shook her head. "Charlotte got that wrong. I think *every* wedding should have kids. The bride and groom should be broken in from day one." She set her other foot down.

"You've got some pretty decided opinions." He scanned the writing. "Halogen headlights?"

"Migraines." She pulled her sweatshirt off.

"You get migraines?" He looked up at her.

"Yeah." She didn't elaborate.

"Mmm," he hummed, returning to the list. "Men who take up two seats on the train because they sit with their legs, um, spread." He met her long-suffering gaze with a roguish grin.

She rolled her eyes. "Nobody's got so much down there that it requires its own seat. If he did, he wouldn't be riding the train."

That earned another snort of laughter. "Is this where I should mention I never take public transit?"

She laughed in return. "No. That's way too much information when you're in soccer shorts."

He shook his head. "Chicken."

Elizabeth tilted her head as if in thought. "You know, I'm fairly sure I'm not."

"Speaking of chicken—cooking?" he asked.

She put her feet down and her head in her hands in mock dismay. "I mean, it's just *chemistry*. Why can't I get it?"

"You seem more despondent than angry."

She responded with a shrug and resumed her preparations. "Charlotte's fault. She should have given you a better list."

Will folded the piece of paper up and stuck it in his bag.

"Charlotte press you into service for co-ed?"

He nodded.

She began to stretch, rolling her shoulders back. "The woman is insatiable. She plays, like, four nights a week."

Will pulled on a sweatshirt. "Are you staying after your game to watch?" he asked her.

I didn't know you'd be here. "Wasn't going to, but if you can tolerate the stink, we could get a sandwich after."

Will checked his watch. "Did you eat before?"

"No, I got caught up with work and forgot." *Don't lecture me, Will.*

His forehead pinched, and she waited. "You shouldn't play on an empty stomach."

And there it is. "Too late now," she explained. "If I eat, I'll get sick when I play."

He shook his head in false consternation. "Careful, or I'll have to call Maddy."

She chuffed at him. "Them's fightin' words, civilian." She stood, gave him a wink, and walked down to the field to stretch.

Will watched appreciatively as Elizabeth bent at the waist to do toe touches, raised her rear in the air to grab her ankles, folded first one long leg up against her chest and held it, then the other. Then she pulled her heel up to her bottom, first the left, then the right. When she started doing hip swings, he had to look away. After a few deep breaths, he composed himself enough to return his gaze to the field, where she skipped from one goal to the other, knees high, then strapped on a knee brace and ran a few gentle laps.

When the players lined up, Elizabeth was positioned on the front line, and he leaned forward in anticipation. The other team had kickoff and passed the ball to their right wing, who ran a few steps forward near the wall before losing it to Charlotte.

As soon as Charlotte had dispossessed the forward, Elizabeth started her run and turned back to meet the pass floating in. She trapped the ball at the top of her chest and forced it down to her feet. Then she made one fluid turn to her right dragging the ball with her, fooling a defender into committing to that side before she stepped on the ball and dragged it back to the left. She took a step forward, taking the defender completely out of the play, and sped down the field with three other players trying to overtake her.

The keeper rushed out to cut off the angle, going into a slide directly in front of Elizabeth, who waited until the woman was halfway to the ground before she lifted the ball on the top of her foot, gave it a little push between the keeper's two flailing legs, deftly stepped around the prone figure, and tapped the ball into the back of the net.

There was no scoring celebration from Elizabeth, though Charlotte was making all kinds of noise, as were their teammates. Elizabeth herself just jogged back up to the center line to restart play. *Workmanlike*, he thought. Charlotte jogged over to exchange a high five, but that was all Elizabeth would do.

The other team restarted, passing the ball back to their midfielder this time, and Elizabeth jogged up to her, stripping the ball away as the woman tried to feint to her right. Elizabeth moved the ball to the left, then right, back to the center of the field, standing with her foot on the ball and her back to the goal, holding off the defender directly behind her while Charlotte began a run down one wing and another woman whose jersey read "Patti" on the back made the run on the other.

Elizabeth waited, waited, and then, just as help was arriving and Will thought she had waited too long, she spun the ball back onto the top of her foot, kicked it straight up about five inches, and as the ball descended, kicked it up and to the right. The ball sailed above the head of the defender, flying over the field, finally falling from the sky at the top of the box. Charlotte was there to head it over the keeper's outstretched fingers, and suddenly, it was 2-0.

This time, Elizabeth slapped Charlotte's hand as she returned to mid-field and gave her a little smile.

And so it went. In short order, Elizabeth had scored a hat trick and moved from her forward position back to defense. Charlotte took over the center, and one of the defenders moved up to the wing. The game played out more evenly then, but Elizabeth's deft handling of the ball at her feet kept the other team from most of their attempts on goal. By halftime, she was subbing herself out on a rotating basis, only subbing back in when it appeared the other team might mount a comeback. The final score was 6-3, and everyone seemed satisfied.

She can't really play her best, Will thought as he stood to get ready for his own match. *She's too good for this division.*

"Charlotte," he called, walking to the player's benches, "when do we start?"

Charlotte waved him onto the field, "You can warm up now if you like." Her phone rang, and he watched her make a face. *It's never a good thing to get a call right before game time.* He watched as she ended the call and then grabbed Elizabeth's arm. Elizabeth listened but shook her head. He walked over.

"What's up?" he asked.

"Two of the girls just called off," Charlotte said, annoyed. "Now we don't have enough women. We need another woman to play, or we'll have to forfeit. *Please*, Lizzy?"

Will turned to Elizabeth. "You should play. It didn't seem like you got much of a workout from the last game."

She turned a cold stare on him, the message clear: *Stay out of it.*

"I don't like to play co-ed," Elizabeth said, frowning. "Nearly all the guys are nice, but there's always one who feels like he needs to mark his territory, you know?"

Charlotte hopped up and down a little. "Please, Lizzy? You can play defense—we just need a body. A female body."

Elizabeth frowned and turned to Will. "List, please."

Will stepped into the players' area to comply while Elizabeth took a pen from her own bag and then wrote something on the paper. Will took it back when she offered it and read aloud, "When Charlotte begs me to play co-ed."

Charlotte just clasped her hands together and begged. "Pleeease?"

"Fine," Elizabeth said, giving in, and then, warningly, "One-time deal."

Charlotte squealed and hugged her before running off to register Lizzy as a guest player.

Will pulled an orange from his bag and tossed it to her. "Eat," he ordered.

Elizabeth looked down at the orange and then up at him. "Do you always carry fruit around with you?" she asked, amused.

"Nature's MRE, baby," he joked, before returning to his warm-up.

"You're cute, Will," he heard her say behind him. "You have no idea what you're talking about, but you're cute."

This game was much faster than the first. Having Elizabeth in the backfield allowed Charlotte and Will to play farther up than they might otherwise, and her passes to them were, for the most part, precise. She did aim a few sharp shots at Charlotte's midsection and one at her head, but settled down after a bit and began to play in earnest.

Will couldn't help but admire her skill, more keenly on display here than in the first game. Elizabeth had no problem maintaining possession of the ball even from the men, though she did not try to hold the ball as long nor did she ever stand in place. She ran faster in this game, he observed, but stamina and skill were her strengths, not speed. A thick man a little older and a lot shorter than Will was always on her, sticking his foot in after she'd already released a pass or frustrated when she maneuvered around him. *There's the one.*

"Martin!" His captain called after the fourth penalty and hooked his thumb back towards their own goal. Will was relieved when the man moved back to play defense on his side and was replaced with a petite Latina woman, an excellent player who challenged Elizabeth without fouling her.

Just before halftime, Elizabeth carried the ball up past midfield, looking to pass, and in what Will recognized as an almost surreal sequence, every player in front of her shifted almost simultaneously to the far right in anticipation, even the goalie. As he was jockeying for position in the box, he glanced her way in time to see her shake her head just a bit and slam the ball into the back of the goal on the wide-open left side. He almost laughed, but squelched it when the keeper looked around, confused as to how the ball had wound up in the net. Instead Will just grinned at her as he trotted back to the middle of the field and applauded, keeping his hands close to his chest so only she would see. She gave him a tiny shrug as if to say *what did they expect?*

After the half, Elizabeth moved up the field a bit with the ball, Charlotte falling back to cover her position. She didn't take any more shots, but she did send in several excellent passes and Will was able to score twice. Finally, near the end of the game, Will motioned that she should make one more play at goal. Elizabeth nodded, sent off a crisp pass to Will, and made her run.

Will sent a perfect slicing pass back into the box, but just as Elizabeth cut in from the wing to take her shot, Martin threw himself into an illegal slide tackle, completely missing the ball but taking both of Elizabeth's feet from beneath her at once. Will could only watch as Elizabeth pitched forward and hurtled headfirst into the wall. It gave a bit, as it was designed to do, but the thud and shake of the collision was sickening.

There was a second of shocked silence before an eruption of movement. Will dropped to one knee next to Elizabeth, who remained face down on the turf, and Charlotte flew up a moment later. Several of the men from his own team dragged Martin off the field as the referee booked him and held up a red card. Will badly wanted a go at him, but it would have to wait. He bent down next to Elizabeth's ear and softly called her name. She started to turn over, but Will put his hand on her back.

"Easy," he said, concerned. "Are you sure your neck and back are all right?" He couldn't help thinking the worst after witnessing the impact. He'd immediately had visions of a backboard and neck brace.

Elizabeth brought her hand up slowly, placed her palm to the ground, and pushed, turning over onto her back. She blinked up at the lights. Will thought her lips might be forming the word "sir" but she made no sound, so he couldn't be sure. Then she squinted directly into his face.

"Charlotte?" she called. Her tone was caustic. Will was relieved to hear it.

Charlotte grimaced. "Yes?"

Elizabeth glared at her. "Ow," she said loudly.

Charlotte was suitably apologetic. "Oh Lizzy, I'm so sorry. I promise, no more co-ed."

Elizabeth held out her arms. "Help me up, please."

"Go slow, Elizabeth," Will said quietly. He wasn't sure she should be getting up at all. He put a hand behind her shoulders and carefully supported her as Charlotte pulled her into a sitting position.

She put her hand to her lower back. "That's going to hurt tomorrow," she said unhappily.

"I imagine it hurts now," said Will drily. "How's your head?"

"Fine."

Both Charlotte and Will gave her skeptical looks.

"As you are both aware," Elizabeth grunted, "it's extraordinarily hard." She held out her arms again and they stood, helping her to her feet.

The referee tapped Charlotte's shoulder. "You have five minutes and a penalty kick left if you want them."

"No," Charlotte said immediately, "we're done here."

The ref nodded and called the game.

A short, slender man trotted up to them. "How 'ya doing, #9?" he asked genially, referring to the number on Elizabeth's jersey.

"How do you *think* she's doing?" Will shot back angrily.

The man held up his hands, palms out. "Just wanted to tell you we escorted Martin to his car, and he won't be playing co-ed anymore—not with us, at least."

"I'll live," Elizabeth said, "but he better not cross my path again, or I'll kick his ass."

The man grinned. "Atta girl," he said approvingly. "Night." He jogged back to his team's bench.

Elizabeth glowered after him. "'Girl,'" she huffed, then turned towards Will, her movements tentative. "I'm going to need that list again."

CHAPTER TWELVE

Will, Charlotte, and Elizabeth gradually made their way to the parking lot. Elizabeth took a few steps towards her car and reached carefully into her bag for her keys.

"What do you think you're doing?" Will asked, incredulous.

"Getting my car keys so I can go home," she replied, enunciating each word as though he had a hearing problem. "Well, Jane's car keys."

"You're *not* driving yourself home," he said firmly.

"That's not a good idea, Lizzy," Charlotte chimed in.

"What were you expecting?" Elizabeth asked, irritated. She removed her hand without the keys.

"You should let me drive you to the ER, actually," Charlotte said. "Jane's working tonight. She can meet us."

Elizabeth rolled her eyes. "I am not going to sit in the ER for six hours so they can tell me to use a heating pad on my back when I could be at home with a heating pad on my back. And Jane does not need to know about this. You've seen her in nursing mode, Char. It's not pretty."

While her attention was on Charlotte, Will reached into Elizabeth's bag and plucked out her keys. He tucked them into his pocket.

"Hey, give me those," Elizabeth cried angrily. "Seriously, you two, I'll go see the doctor in the morning if you're that concerned about it."

Charlotte shook her head. "Tonight," she said firmly. "I can call my dad. He's at a party, but he'll probably insist on an MRI to be safe, so we should meet him at the hospital."

"For crying out loud, Char," Elizabeth huffed, "don't be ridiculous. I'm fine."

Will cut Elizabeth off. "Why would he insist on an MRI?" he asked worriedly.

Charlotte met her friend's glare with one of her own. She crossed her arms across her chest and said, "Because Elizabeth just recovered from a concussion a few months ago. Secondary concussions can be serious, Lizzy. Even I know that."

"Almost *four* months ago, Char. I do not have another concussion. I know what one feels like, and I don't feel like that now." She shifted uncomfortably. "I'm *fine*."

"From Brussels?" Will asked, his voice hard.

Elizabeth didn't respond, but Charlotte gave him a nod. Will took out his phone and began to type.

"You have a few choices here, Elizabeth Bennet," Charlotte said, her eyebrows raised. "You can get a ride with me and go see Jane, you can get a ride with me and see my dad, or . . ."

"Or she can ride into the city with me and see my doctor," Will said, shoving the phone back into his pocket. "He's on his way to the office. He'll be there before we are." He saw the two women in a face-off. Charlotte's hands were on her hips, and Elizabeth's arms were crossed over her chest. Will noticed the little grimace that flitted across Elizabeth's face as she shifted.

"I also have a Jacuzzi at my place," he added.

Charlotte made a face at him. "Jacuzzi?"

"Jacuzzi," he repeated, and turned to Elizabeth. "I'm guessing your back could use a little more than a heating pad, am I right?"

Elizabeth's posture relaxed just a little. "Maybe," she said reluctantly, shifting her eyes to the car and away from his. She uncrossed her arms. "How did you get your doctor to open his office this late?"

Will took the bag from Lizzy's shoulder and slung it over his own. "He's been our doctor for a long time."

Elizabeth thought about that for a minute. *Must be nice to have been in one place that long,* she thought, before sighing and rubbing her forehead. Giving in to Will was better than going to someone she knew and getting a lecture about how she shouldn't have been playing co-ed, but it wasn't exactly how she'd imagined seeing his home for the first time. "How do we get Jane's car back to her, Char?"

Charlotte's arms dropped to her sides. "My dad will drive me out here, and I'll take it to her. She won't need it until tomorrow morning, right?"

Elizabeth nodded. "Right. And not a word to anyone."

"*If* you get a clean bill of health. But you should still tell Ed and Maddy."

"I'll think about it."

Charlotte uncrossed her arms. "That's a mistake, but since I talked you into playing, I won't say anything."

Elizabeth could feel the muscles in her low back stiffening and sighed. *I just want to get out of here.* She nodded at Will. "Okay, let's go."

Will tossed their bags into the trunk before unlocking the doors and helping her in. "Do you want the seat to recline a bit?" he asked, crouching beside her to tinker with the controls. She nodded, feeling ridiculous.

"You know, I'm really okay. You don't have to make such a big deal."

"Sure," he said teasingly, "I know you planned all this just so you could get a ride into the city with me. Let me at least show off a bit."

"Well, don't fuss, dear; get on with it," she quipped as she tried to find a comfortable position.

Will's face brightened. "Hey, that's Audrey Hepburn," he said with a grin, still working on the seat. The back began to recline, but the seat tipped up too, taking some of the pressure off her lower back.

"You recognized that?" Elizabeth asked. *Nobody ever knows what I'm talking about.*

He nodded. "My mother loved the classics."

She nodded. "A woman of taste." She leaned back uncomfortably. "As my friend, I think you should know that I am completely in love with Audrey Hepburn."

Will chuckled. "So I'm too late to ask you to go steady?"

"Funny," Elizabeth retorted. Will gently shut the door and walked around the driver's side, got behind the wheel, and punched a button on the dash. Elizabeth felt her seat warming up, the tendrils of heat wrapping around her back and easing the tension from her aching muscles.

"Is the seat supposed to heat like this, or is the car about to burst into flames?" she asked cheekily. "Just so I know to prepare."

He started the car and carefully backed out of his spot. "My sister Georgiana is always cold, so I got a car with seat warmers. I didn't think you'd mind."

Finally, Elizabeth had to relent. "I don't. Thank you."

His eyes crinkled a bit at the corners. "You're welcome."

Will watched the road as he pulled out, but there was comparatively little traffic. He glanced at Elizabeth and saw her eyes closing. He wasn't sure that she should sleep until he got her to the doctor, so he asked, "You like Hepburn, then?"

"Mmm," she said tiredly. "Both of them."

"They weren't related, you know," he said, trying to make small talk.

She chuckled. "I know. Audrey lived through the Nazi occupation. One of the reasons I like her. She was a survivor."

"Which movie's your favorite?"

"I have to be a traditionalist here and say *Roman Holiday*. I like *The Nun's Story*, too, though. You?"

"Hard to choose," he replied, glancing at traffic and moving into the middle lane as they passed the border into New York. "Maybe *Charade?*"

"Ah," she agreed, "good one. Hidden treasure."

He kept up their conversation about old movies, touching on her dislike of *Sabrina*—which, despite her fondness for Bogie, she found "disturbing"—his interest in *The Treasure of Sierra Madre,* hers in *The African Queen.*

"Your most quotable movie ever?" Elizabeth asked.

"Modern or classic?" Will pulled up next to a tall, skinny office building just off Central Park and maneuvered into the last available parking space.

She thought for a second. "Classic."

Without hesitation, he said, "Has to be *Casablanca.*"

She nodded. "Okay, I'll give you that one."

He shut off the engine. "Hang on, I'll help you out."

Elizabeth would have reached for the door, but the way the seat was positioned, she felt like a bug on its back, so she waited patiently. She had not been lying to Charlotte before. She did feel fine other than her back, and she was embarrassed by all the attention. "You'd think I was the Queen of England," she muttered. In no time at all, Will had the seat up and had taken both of her arms in his to help her stand.

"Will," she protested, "I'm not ninety."

"It's not you, Elizabeth," he deadpanned, "I'm afraid of your uncle. Humor me."

"Only if you *do* take me out to eat after this," she said, as her stomach growled. "I'm starving, and since we're in the city, we can get food around the clock."

"I've got food at my place, if you don't mind that. It'll be more comfortable, and you can use the Jacuzzi, too."

"You cook?" Elizabeth asked, surprised.

"Don't sound so shocked," he replied, pretending to be affronted.

Elizabeth lifted her eyebrows.

"Okay, Mrs. Summers cooks for me and leaves meals in the freezer. I just heat things up. But I happen to very good at it."

She smiled. "I see you share my talent for the art."

"I can cook a little if I need to, but it's nothing fancy. I prefer to leave it to the experts and actually eat well."

"I can cook eggs eight different ways and just about nothing else." She paused. "They're good with salsa and tortillas."

Will shook his head as he guided her to the entrance. "You eat like a college student. I don't even want to think about what your diet looks like."

"It's my job to keep the Gardiner/Bennet computer network up and running," she replied, "and it's quite a complicated endeavor. You cannot believe what Kit and Lydia do to their laptops. Since I'm there, I eat with everyone, and then Aunt Maddy sends me home with more food than I can possibly finish." She smiled. "I have a Mrs. Summers, too."

They reached the door and Will pressed the intercom for Dr. Garcia, who buzzed them into the building. Elizabeth eyed the stairs warily, but fortunately the doctor's office was on the first floor. The pair entered the brightly lit office.

"Will," greeted the doctor, "good evening."

"Dr. Garcia," Will said with a nod, "thanks for meeting us. My friend here had a disagreement with a wall."

Dr. Garcia smiled. "Drinking?" he joked.

"Hit and run," she said with a smirk, and the doctor laughed.

Elizabeth liked him immediately. Dr. Garcia was a square man of medium height, probably in his sixties, with a full head of wavy gray hair and a pleasantly lined face. She was put at ease by how graciously he responded to being rousted from home long after business hours.

"Let's take you in the back then, Elizabeth," he said, waving her ahead.

Will stood awkwardly in the waiting room. "Should I stay here?"

The doctor answered immediately, "Yes. We'll be out shortly."

Elizabeth followed Dr. Garcia into an examination room where he had her sit.

He checked his phone. "So, Will said in his text that you went into the wall headfirst."

"Yes. It's an indoor arena, though, so the wall does give a bit."

"Okay. And you've had a concussion before?"

"Yes. Almost four months ago."

"Did you lose consciousness with the first injury?" He put the phone down and picked up a small light.

"I don't think so." She expected him to chastise her for not knowing, as they had done in Brussels, but he just moved on, checking her pupils for reactivity. She'd been through these tests before. He finished and put the light down.

"And you still have migraines?"

She nodded. "When I get stressed or work too long."

"Okay." He had her rotate her head while focusing on something else in the room, change focus quickly between two objects, and track the movement of his finger before he performed a few other tests. Elizabeth was surprised that the little office was so well equipped. *This guy must cost a fortune.* The doctor reached up to feel the top of her head where she'd hit the wall and seemed satisfied when she didn't flinch.

"So," Dr. Garcia said at the end of his examination, "it doesn't seem as though you have another concussion."

"I tried to tell them," she began, but he cut her off.

"That doesn't mean it wasn't very important to have this exam, Elizabeth." He waited until she nodded. "How did you sustain the concussion?"

This wasn't something she wanted to discuss, but at least Will wasn't in the room. She sighed. "Bomb blast. I dove into a bunch of tables. Can't really say whether it was one or the other or both." She waited for the inevitable emotional response, the one where people didn't know what to say and either said too much or nothing at all.

Dr. Garcia nodded, unperturbed, and made a note in his phone. "Military or law enforcement?"

"Military."

"Were you medically retired?"

She shook her head. "No."

He grunted a little. "So it wasn't severe. That's good."

The doctor was so matter-of-fact about the whole thing that Elizabeth began to feel easier speaking to him, and she did have a question.

"I wanted to ask something," she said cautiously.

"What's that?"

"This is confidential?"

He nodded. "Of course."

Elizabeth bit her bottom lip. "Well, after I hit the wall tonight, just for a second, I thought I was somewhere else."

"Where?" still the calm, no-nonsense voice.

"In the bombing. Where I was hurt. I thought Will was his cousin." She waited for a flash of recognition, but either the doctor didn't make the connection, or he didn't show it. Elizabeth was relieved. "Just for a second, you know, but it was weird."

"This hasn't happened before?" His brown eyes sought hers out.

Elizabeth shook her head.

He wrote something down. "Are you having nightmares?"

She shrugged. "I've had a few."

Dr. Garcia leaned back, contemplative. "Well, I wouldn't worry about it too much. You're bound to have some residual response from the experience. If the nightmares become more frequent or you have another episode, with or without the physical trigger, you might want to talk to a therapist. I've got a good recommendation for you if you want it."

That'll never happen, she thought. *I don't need a therapist.* "Okay," she said.

"All right then," he replied, "let's look at your back."

CHAPTER THIRTEEN

Back in the car, Elizabeth finished texting Charlotte and dropped her hands in her lap, a satisfied smile on her face. Will shook his head.

"Go ahead and say it," he told her, feigning defeat. "You know you're dying to."

"I would never say 'I told you so,'" she said smugly. "But I did."

"This is you *not* saying 'I told you so'?" Will asked, his eyebrows raised.

She smirked. "Okay, so I said it. It happens to be true."

Will paused for a second. "If you'd seen the flight pattern you took, you'd have insisted, too."

"I *felt* that flight pattern *and* its abrupt termination." She cocked her head at him. "I know how I feel, Will. I was and am fine, just a little sore. I believe Dr. Garcia's exact words were 'take some ibuprofen and use a heating pad if you have one.'"

Will couldn't help but laugh a little. She was irritated and self-righteous, but he felt reassured. "The offer of the Jacuzzi still holds."

"Oh, I'm definitely using the Jacuzzi," she informed him. "That's what got me in the car."

He shrugged. "Is that all it took? I should have offered sooner."

She looked at her feet and shook her head slightly. "Well, now you know." She raised her head, and he could see her eyes light up.

"We should text Richard."

"What? Now?" *Why is she thinking about Richard?*

"Oh Will," she rolled her eyes. "You really do have so much to learn."

"It's only about five in the morning there."

"Sounds about right." She appeared so pleased he thought she might begin rubbing her hands together in glee. It made him smile. It made him *feel* the smile.

"What are you planning, woman?"

"Nothing," she said innocently. Will caught a glimpse of her eyes sparkling as she turned to face him, and he felt his heart begin to beat a little harder.

"Elizabeth . . ." he said warningly.

"I just thought Richard might like to wake up to a message that I'm at your place. Close to midnight," she said liltingly, her smile lighting up her face, "in your Jacuzzi."

Will started to laugh. "And then we turn off our phones?"

"Now you're getting it." Elizabeth drew in a quick breath, as though another thought had just occurred to her. "I think we need to send pictures."

Having a prank to play helped Elizabeth not to overreact to the splendor of Will's home. First, they pulled into a parking garage attached to an old Art Deco building only five minutes away from Dr. Garcia's office. Will had access to three parking spots. Three. Those tiny slices of real estate alone were probably worth two years of rent for her. More. His building had a doorman who wore white gloves, and there were signs for a pool and gym.

"You'll like this," he said with a grin, "I've had the apartment converted so everything's controlled remotely. You need my phone to open the door."

"Smart apartment?" she asked. "Is that a good idea?"

Will appeared a little surprised. "I'd have thought you would be on board with it."

"Just a little neurotic," she replied with a shrug. "What's online can always be hacked. I should know."

"My security is very tight," he assured her.

"I believe you," she responded, and they dropped the subject.

The door to his apartment opened to a foyer with inlaid marble flooring and white walls. There was a line of silver coat hooks and a blue and white chinoiserie umbrella holder to the left. On the right was a hall table with a small blue and green mosaic bowl perched in the center and a large mirror in a thin gilded frame hanging just above. Will tossed his keys in the bowl and dropped his bag beneath the coat hooks.

Elizabeth stood still for a moment, drinking it all in. Will's apartment was on the top floor of a building across the street from Central Park. She realized that the interior was huge—she was sure it took up the entire floor. It was a small building, to be sure, but still—in Manhattan, where apartments in a far less prestigious neighborhood often sold for more than fifteen hundred dollars a square foot, the sheer size of the place was breathtaking.

"The bedrooms are all on the first floor," he said, moving into what looked like a formal living room with sleek leather couches that Elizabeth thought looked uncomfortable. "The stairs are there," he said, pointing to his left, "but given the state of your back, I thought you'd rather take the lift down." She took in the art on the walls, the high ceilings, the large windows that faced the park. He glanced behind him and then turned to wait for her.

Elizabeth met his gaze. "You have an elevator inside the apartment?" she asked. "I'm impressed."

"Well, it's pretty small," he explained with a small grin and a shrug. "It's only good for two people. My parents had it put in for my grandmother when she was no longer able to take the stairs."

"How long has your family owned this place?" she asked. "It's stunning."

"My great-grandparents bought into this building just after they married in the early 1920s," he said quietly. "When the apartment next door came on the market in the '30s, they bought it and expanded. My grandfather lived here his entire life—when he married my grandmother, they just used his room until his parents passed. When my grandfather eventually passed away, my parents moved us back in to take care of Grandmother. My parents were offered a chance to purchase one of the apartments below us, and they entertained a lot. So the main floor, where we entered, became the entertainment space, and the bedrooms are all downstairs."

"Your great-grandparents were buying property in the '30s?" Elizabeth asked, curious. "They didn't lose a lot of money in the stock market crash?"

Will shook his head. "No, they were smart *and* lucky. My grandfather always said my great-grandfather felt that because they had been spared, they should put money back out into the community whenever possible. The neighbors had lost everything and needed to sell. He could've bought the place for pennies on the dollar, but he paid the full asking price, enough to get them reestablished somewhere outside the city. Then he put some folks to work remodeling the space. When they finished, a friend of his needed to sell his apartment, so he bought that property and sent the men to work there. He just kept buying properties and putting the crew to work. After the war, he had a real estate empire and could have cashed out, but he carried most of his holdings for years and just rented them out. A few of the workers remained on the payroll until they retired in the '50s." He paused. "Managing and maintaining the properties was also a kind of therapy for my grandfather when he returned from the war. He waited a long time to get married, though my grandmother was much younger."

"Not Bogart and Hepburn difference, I hope?" Elizabeth asked jokingly.

He shook his head and smiled. "Twenty years."

"Wow," Elizabeth replied, enthralled. She loved stories like this. "Your family history is amazing."

Will nodded, his expression just a bit grim. "Big shoes to fill."

She fell silent for a moment, just watching Will's face. "Family tradition, then," she said after the quiet grew awkward. "FORGE, I mean."

His forehead furrowed. "You know," he said, punching the button for the lift and turning to look at her, "I don't think I've ever really thought about FORGE as a humanitarian enterprise before. I mean, we are in business to make profits."

"Your great-grandfather made profits too, eventually. And so do your clients."

Will grunted a little in assent. When the door opened, he tried not to wince at the horrible groaning noise. He turned to usher Elizabeth in, but her expression told him that she was far away.

"You okay?" he asked.

"Fine," she responded, "I was just thinking about where I grew up." She stepped into the lift which was barely big enough for the two of them. "Your grandmother must have been smaller than we are," she said, pressing up against his arm.

"She was," he agreed. "This was top of the line when it was built, but I almost never use it except to be sure it's working."

"Well, I'm glad to give you an excuse to run an equipment check."

He chuckled. "Yes, it's very considerate of you."

The door opened with a loud creak, and this time Elizabeth held in a laugh. Will shook his head. "I'll have to have that looked at."

They stepped out, and Will opened a door to the room across the hall. "So where did you grow up? I guess I just assumed it was in Montclair."

"Upstate New York, in Meryton. Jane moved in with Uncle Ed and Aunt Maddy when she started college, and the rest of us joined her after I graduated."

"Any particular reason?" Will opened Georgiana's dresser.

Elizabeth's lips pressed into a thin line. "My mother died."

He straightened up to look at her. "I'm sorry to hear that."

"It's all right," she assured him. "It was a long time ago."

"Still, it's hard to lose a parent, especially so young."

Elizabeth made a noncommittal noise and sat down on the bed.

Finding a swimsuit wasn't too difficult. Georgiana had left some of her clothes in her room so that she wouldn't have to check luggage when she flew home. It took him no time at all to locate both a bikini and a one-piece, which he tossed on the bed after bringing Elizabeth to a guest room. He took a quick shower and then walked upstairs to put something in the oven. He poured over the contents of the refrigerator and decided that the lasagna Mrs. Summers had left him would be the best choice. He threw a salad together, and the preheat setting had just beeped when the lift door screeched and Elizabeth reappeared in the one-piece, damp hair hanging down her back. *It curls more when it's wet.*

He glanced at the suit, a little disappointed, and she clucked her tongue at him.

"Now, now, Mr. Darcy," Elizabeth scolded, "there's no need to make that face."

Did I make a face? I could swear I didn't.

"I did try on the bikini, as it would be better for our purposes," she told him teasingly, "but pictures last forever, and I think you sister might be a little less, um . . ." She paused to make a circle with her hand at chest level and finished lamely, "...than me." She ducked her head, embarrassed. "As much as I want to harass Richard, I wouldn't want anything out there I'd be ashamed for my family to see."

Will could not tear his eyes away from her. This glimpse of modesty and respect for her family was both sweet and enticing, and despite his initial reaction, he could not be sorry she'd chosen as she had. The suit was black with turquoise panels along the sides. It was meant for swimming, not just reclining on a lounge and tanning, and it fit both her personality and her figure well. The suit was cut high on the hip, making her legs appear even longer than they were. Her waist was trim, her abdomen flat, and although she wasn't busty, she was indeed more fully endowed than he had thought. She'd looked sexy in her soccer shorts, but this . . . When his gaze reached her face, she was arching an eyebrow at him, but he took another second to evaluate her features.

Her eyebrows were a bit uneven, and her eyes were perhaps a little larger than they ought to be for her face, but they were an arresting shade of green that darkened when she was irritated with him. They shone with intelligence and good humor and were framed by long, thick black lashes. Her nose was straight and perfectly proportioned, her smile wide and genuine. Her skin was clear and creamy. *She and Jane have the same complexion*, he thought, *but Jane looks more like a runway model and Elizabeth the girl next door*. While he'd dated many women who could have been models, and one who actually was, he had to admit a decided preference for the unadorned beauty of the woman who stood before him. *Who knew?*

He turned to slide the lasagna into the oven, giving himself a moment to recover. He stood and set the timer before moving his gaze back to her face. "Looks like it fits," he said curtly.

She snorted, looked him over. "Now you," she said.

He moved his eyes back to her legs. "Now me what?"

"Oh, for the love of . . . your suit, Mr. Darcy. And please tell me you don't wear one of those bikini-bottom Speedos." She gave him an appraising look, briefer than the one he'd given her. "Even *you* can't pull that off."

"Oh. Right." After pointing to the timer, Will made a hasty retreat to his room to put on his trunks.

He returned upstairs ten minutes later in his suit and a robe only to find an empty kitchen. He checked on their meal and then went in search of Elizabeth. He noticed the door to the terrace was open and walked out. She had tossed a large sweatshirt on over the suit and was standing against the wrought iron fence gazing out on Central Park Lake. It was dark, but even with the city lights, the stars were bright and reflected on the water. She turned her head a little as he approached.

"Will," she said in a low voice, "this is incredible. If I had a terrace like this, I think I'd never go inside again."

"You wouldn't say that when there's a foot of snow out here," he replied.

"I'd live in an igloo," came the quick reply.

"You know," he said, some regret in his voice, "I don't think I've been out here all summer."

"Are you kidding me?" Elizabeth asked, incredulous. "You missed the whole summer? That may be an actual crime, Will. I mean, an on-the-books, going-to-prison, Bubba-for-your-cellmate crime."

He laughed lightly. "I just get so busy that I'm hardly home. When Georgiana was finishing high school, I wanted to be here when she was out of school, so I worked from the apartment more often. Now that she's in California, there's no need."

"Poor Will," Elizabeth murmured. "I feel so sorry for you, all alone in your palace."

Will cleared his throat. "Careful, or I'll have to send pictures to Ed, too."

"Oooh, that's a really bad idea," Elizabeth replied, shaking her head. "I won't be the only one in his crosshairs."

She's right. Miscalculation. "You never said what he did in the Marines."

"He could tell you, but then he'd have to kill you."

Will was unconvinced. "Really?"

"No," she said with a laugh. "He was a gunnery sergeant, that's all I really know." She grew serious. "He doesn't like to talk about it."

"Okay," Elizabeth said, laying her fork down on an empty plate and placing them in the sink. "Jacuzzi time."

"Take the lead," he said. "Let me know how you want to do this." He checked the time. "It's nearly six there now, he should be up."

She grinned. "We need to hurry then. I'm hoping for full-on coffee-spray."

Although she was making jokes, her movements were tentative. Her back was clearly troubling her. They walked back out onto the terrace where she cautiously sat on the edge of the hot tub, placed her hands behind her, and swung both legs over into the water at the same time. He turned the jets on as she lowered herself into the hot water and sighed.

"This feels so good," she told him. "Would you take a picture? Make sure to get enough detail in it so he knows where we are."

Will shook his head. "I'm not so sure about this now," he said, but he took a few pictures with his phone.

"Okay, now set the timer and get in here for another one."

"You are truly evil, you know that?"

She grinned wickedly. "Oh, this is child's play, Mr. Darcy. He set us both up. He deserves it."

Will piled the lounge cushions on top of one another until they were high enough to take the shot, set up the angle and the timer, then clambered into the hot tub next to Elizabeth. He tossed his arm around her shoulders but held his arm taut so as not to put any weight on her.

"Very good, Mr. Darcy," she said, eyes twinkling up at him, "you make a fine practical joker, but if you stick with me, I'll take you to the World Cup."

Will had promised himself he wouldn't try anything with Elizabeth tonight. She was hurt, and he'd essentially forced her to drive to the city with him. But she was here in his home, eating in his kitchen, relaxing in his Jacuzzi, wearing that swimsuit, snuggled up against him. His expression softened as he searched her face. She was smiling up at him, and he just couldn't hold back any longer. His somber eyes caught her merry ones, and he leaned in for a kiss. Their lips touched just as the flash went off.

CHAPTER FOURTEEN

W ill's lips lingered on Elizabeth's for a moment before pulling back. His heart was pounding even harder than before, and his lips were still tingling. *That was the sweetest kiss I think I've ever tasted.* He waited anxiously for her response. *Did she feel it too?*

Elizabeth opened her eyes and looked up at Will. She appeared bewildered for a moment, but then broke their connection.

"Will," she said, feigning exasperation, "the idea is to make Richard wonder what's going on. A kiss is too much information. We just want to send a picture of us together, so he'll go nuts trying to figure it out."

Will frowned. *He's not the only one.*

Elizabeth started to get out of the water, but Will held out his hand.

"No, you stay in. I'll get it. Do you want to try again, or should we just send the ones we have?"

"Again," she said, and glanced away.

Will levered himself out of the Jacuzzi and walked over to the phone, his trunks dripping water behind him. He sighed as he reset the camera. *Nothing ventured, I guess.* He started the timer and returned to the hot water. This time they took the photo without the kiss. He retrieved his phone and shared the pictures with Elizabeth, who typed a message.

"Should I pretend I was sending to Jane?" she asked but answered herself. "No, he'll see through that."

Will shrugged, his good mood broken. He'd been so sure she felt something for him the day of the move. *Maybe I waited too long.* He couldn't deny he was disappointed. She didn't seem to notice as she decided on a message thanking Richard for introducing them and sent it off. Then she made a dramatic show of turning off her phone.

"There. I bet there will be a voicemail on my phone within an hour."

She glanced at Will surreptitiously and let out a shaky breath. "Okay, so I have to ask you a question."

Will smiled faintly. "What's that?"

She closed her eyes. "Nothing ventured," she whispered. Will heard it, and his heart leapt.

"You are a very handsome man," she said, swallowing hard and refusing to look at him. "I thought that from the beginning, you know, before you opened your mouth and spoke."

Will winced a little, but his smile was growing more genuine. *She's attracted to me. I knew it.* "That's not a question," he replied playfully.

She frowned. "I knew you were well off, but tonight you bring me to this truly magnificent home. Obviously, you are far wealthier than I thought when you were bumming a hamburger off my Aunt Maddy."

Will started to laugh gently. "Maddy *invited* me."

Elizabeth rolled her eyes. "Don't get a swelled head. She invites everyone."

"You and Richard are a pair," Will retorted. He gave her a smile. "He's always telling me I'm too apt to believe my own press."

She sniffed. "I would guess you need that from time to time. Too many minions willing to do your bidding."

He just shook his head at her and fiddled with his phone.

"In short, you are what my mother would have called a *catch*."

Will shuddered. "Makes me sound like a fish."

She grinned. "Well, I didn't want to say anything, but after the game, you did have a sort of smell . . . "

"Elizabeth," he growled, "you had something to ask me."

She nodded and shoved both her hands under the warm water. "Okay. So, you are who you are, and I'm a Marine—an inactive, *enlisted* Marine—living in an 850-square-foot apartment in a blue-collar neighborhood in Bloomfield. I'm starting from near zero, and my business, while it's likely to be lucrative"—she held her hand out to indicate the terrace—"well, it would take me generations . . ." Her voice trailed away, but after a moment, she shook her head and continued. "Not that I *need* to be rich like this, of course, it's just . . . even when I lived at Longbourn and we had money, it wasn't like this."

As always, Will was listening intently. *They had money. What happened to it?* He couldn't think about it long, though, as she was about to ask the question he desperately wanted to hear.

"So, I guess I was just wondering . . ." Her voice trailed off.

Say it, Elizabeth. Ask me.

Elizabeth took a deep breath and said in a rush, "Was that kiss for Richard or for me?"

Will was elated, but he forcibly restrained himself. *Don't scare her off.* "Elizabeth," he said evenly, "I love my cousin, but I don't want to kiss him. Ever."

She huffed, embarrassed. "You know what I mean, Will Darcy."

Will put his hand under her chin and very gently raised her face to meet his. Slowly, slowly, he lowered his lips to hers, and this time, he didn't pull away. Elizabeth moaned, a small, soft sound that encouraged him to part her lips and take the kiss deeper. His hand moved to her cheek and one of hers made its way to the back of his head. When at last they came up for air, they stared at each other until Elizabeth spoke.

"You're right," she said softly, her eyes lingering on his lips. "I don't think Richard would like that at all."

In Brussels, Major Richard Fitzwilliam was standing in his kitchen sipping his first cup of coffee when his phone buzzed. He picked it up, hoping it wasn't the general. When he saw that it was Bennet's number, he opened the text. There, in full color and sharp focus, was Bennet. And Will. In Will's Jacuzzi.

He coughed, dribbling coffee on the front of his uniform, and cursed. "Damn you, Bennet," he sputtered, trying to get the stain out. *No good*, he thought. *Now I'll have to change, and I'll probably be late.* He gazed at the photo. *You clean up nice, Bennet.* Then he set both his phone and the mug down next to the sink and allowed himself to grin.

Quick work, Will. I knew you had it in you.

———

"In the spirit of the evening," Elizabeth said, finally, "I'll be blunt."

"Careful," Will warned playfully. "Any more of your bluntness might just kill me."

She touched his arm. "Not that this isn't incredible, because it is."

"But. . ." he said warily.

"But being with someone . . . I've never . . . I'm not good at it. You'll have to be patient with me." She pursed her lips and tipped her head to one side. "I might say or do things wrong."

Will nodded. He'd noticed she was skittish and was relieved it was inexperience rather than an aversion to him. "I'm happy to go at whatever speed makes you comfortable, Elizabeth," he said sincerely. He gave her a skeptical look. "Though I thought you Marines were all gung-ho, jumping out of airplanes and so on."

Elizabeth rolled her eyes. "That's Special Forces, doofus. HALO and HAHO. I'm a Marine, but I'm not crazy." She grinned. "Well, maybe a little crazy."

He laughed. "Doofus?"

She grinned. "I stand by the insult."

"Richard told me about HALO and HAHO," Will chuckled. "He didn't want to do it either."

"Jumping out of airplanes," Elizabeth muttered, and bumped him gently with her hip.

"What I *would* like to know," he said seriously, "is more about you, your family, why you chose to leave the Marines . . . whatever you want to tell me."

She thought about that. "Let's get out. I want to get some water and change."

"Georgiana should have something you can wear."

"I have a set of clean clothes in my bag."

"Okay." He stepped to the terrace and held his hands out for Elizabeth, who seemed to have an easier time swinging her legs over the side.

"Feeling better?" he asked.

"Much." She gave him a wicked grin. "Must be the ibuprofen."

They dried off and went back downstairs. Once in the guest room, her curiosity got the better of her and she turned on her phone. She already had a voicemail. She smiled mischievously and tapped play.

Richard's droll voice came on the line. "Well done, Bennet. I'll send you the dry cleaning bill." Elizabeth grinned and pumped her fist in victory, but the message continued. "Listen, not to get all brotherly on you, but you should know that Will is probably the most uptight, overprotective, grumpy ass I've ever met. For the CEO of a company, he's remarkably anti-social, and he doesn't understand the phrase *stand down*. But for the few people he truly cares about, he's also the most trustworthy, loyal man I've ever met. If you're joining that very exclusive club, my friend, count yourself lucky."

Elizabeth turned off the phone's display. Despite having achieved her goal, the message left her unsatisfied. Richard hadn't seemed very surprised. She started to change her clothes and then it hit her. *I've been had. He* wanted *me to meet Will; he just thought I'd have to go to work at FORGE to do it.* Try as she might, though, she couldn't muster any anger. Not after Will's kiss. *Kisses,* she thought with a smile, touching her lips.

She typed a one-word reply to Richard: *Loki!*

When Elizabeth and Will met back upstairs, she dragged him back out on the terrace. Will asked if she wanted some wine, but Elizabeth shook her head. He then moved two of the long lounge chairs over near the railing where Elizabeth had been standing before, then straightened the cushions and tossed a few blankets on a small table between them. Elizabeth set her bottle of water down, and for a while, they just stood at the railing and gazed out at the lake across the street in Central Park.

Elizabeth relaxed into the companionable silence. Though she hadn't taken the time to examine the terrace itself in her rush to see the lake view, the light from the house illuminated it enough to see that it was lush with greenery. There were several trees in large stone planters casting nighttime shadows, and flowers lined the walls in pots and boxes. Ivy grew up several trellises, and there was a small vegetable garden in several raised planters. *Garden behind us, lake across the street— it's a bit of country in the city*. She was contented in a way she couldn't ever recall feeling.

"So," she said, speaking into the darkness, "Richard told me you have a sister at Stanford."

She could just make out his smile. "Georgiana," he said. "She's much younger than me, obviously," he added. "A little more than ten years. Kind of a surprise baby, but my parents were thrilled." He grunted. "I was *not* thrilled."

Elizabeth chuckled. "I don't remember, but Jane assures me I was not happy to be replaced as the youngest. I was five when my sister Mary was born."

"Exactly," Will agreed. "I was an only child for ten years."

"Spoiled," Elizabeth jibed.

"Probably," he replied easily. "If they were going to spring a new kid on me, I thought they should at least do the right thing and give me a brother." He arched his back and crossed his hands behind his head as he stretched. "I wasn't interested in her at all until she started walking and talking."

"And then?" Elizabeth prompted. She walked over to a chaise and perched on the end of one.

"When she was three," he said slowly, moving to join her, "she had this yellow stuffed duck she dragged around with her. She was never without it. It was filthy and tattered, and I think Mom was afraid it would dissolve completely if she put it in the washer. And one day Georgiana couldn't find it. My mother and father were going crazy looking for it because she wouldn't stop crying."

"So you found it for her?" Elizabeth guessed.

"No," he answered. "I hated the racket she was making and resented the attention she was getting. But then I looked—really looked—at that little grubby, tear-streaked face, and I was just a goner."

He shook his head ruefully and Elizabeth laughed.

"Yeah," he admitted, "it didn't really do my reputation with the boys any good." He leaned back in the chair and put his feet up. "I convinced her that her duck had become real, like that rabbit in the story she liked. I told her real ducks didn't like to be dragged around, but that we could go across the street to the park and visit her duck anytime she wanted. Her eyes got really big and she demanded we go see her duck right away."

"Quick thinker," Elizabeth said. "I approve. What did you do?"

"What else?" he said, tossing up his hands. "I took her to see her duck. We went every day for a month before she gave me a break."

"Did her duck have a name?" she asked, smiling.

"Yes," he responded drolly. "Duck."

Elizabeth found this very funny. She would never have guessed that Will Darcy, surly CEO, was such a soft touch. "You're a good big brother," she declared, charmed by the story. "She's lucky."

He laughed softly. "Not *so* good. She hates when I tell that story." He shrugged. "But she's not here to stop me." He sighed so gently Elizabeth almost missed it. "She's all grown up now and doesn't need me."

"Wrong," Elizabeth corrected him, taking a drink of her water. "She just doesn't want you to *know* she needs you. She wants to prove herself to you. And to herself."

"You don't even know my sister," Will replied, amused.

It was Elizabeth's turn to shrug. "She's eighteen, right? Never been away from home?"

"Right," Will confirmed.

"Trust me," she said firmly. "I've actually been an eighteen-year-old girl. I know these things."

He nodded, and Elizabeth could see that he hoped she was right.

"Your turn," he said. "What about your sisters? Have I met them all now or are there more?"

Elizabeth set down her water. "No, you've met them all, thank goodness. The order is Jane, me, Mary, Kit, and Lydia." She sat up, pulling her knees to her chest. "Mary was twelve when I left, so she remembers more, but I'm not sure how well Kit and Lydia even remember me. I've not been home a whole lot over the past six years. Lydia was barely nine when I left."

Will waited, eager for Elizabeth to tell him more about her family. He wasn't sure why he wanted to know, really, other than learning about her family would help him learn about her.

"When we were all still at Longbourn," she said finally, "I used to call Kit and Lydia our Irish twins. Their hair was the same color then, and Lydia was the same height as Kit even though she was two years younger." He turned to watch her face and saw that her eyes were closed.

"I still remember when they only wore footed pajamas and needed their hands to climb up and down the stairs. Kit loved Paddington Bear, so I had to read the book to her every night. Lydia couldn't ever share anything, so she demanded Pooh Bear stories—always more than one—before she'd go to sleep. They constantly argued about which was the better bear. Mary called it the Great Bear War." She opened her eyes and grinned at Will. "There were quite a few skirmishes involved. Lots of threats and hair pulling."

Will nodded solemnly. "Fortunately, I just had the one sister, and she couldn't reach my hair."

"Well, you *are* excessively tall," Elizabeth agreed, deadpan. She paused before picking up the story again. "Jane was the one who figured out how to end it, of course. She's the peacemaker."

"What'd she do?" Will asked.

"She bought Lydia a Tigger costume. Bye-bye bears, hello tiger. Kit thought she'd won; Lydia was certain she had."

He laughed.

"Lydia wore that costume everywhere—even when she grew and the hems were at her shins. She'd bounce around singing 'I'm the only one,'" and she'd cry when it had to go in the wash. Jane had to start doing the laundry when Lydia was asleep."

Will watched the soft smile playing on Elizabeth's lips and felt a rush of affection for her. He noticed that she'd not mentioned her parents, who would normally be doing these things, but he didn't want to push her into confidences if she wasn't ready to share them.

"You know," she said quietly, "I grumbled about it, but I loved taking Lydia places in that stupid costume. She got lots of attention in it, which was all she wanted, really. She loved it so much Kit wanted one, so I bought her red boots and a yellow slicker with a hat for her birthday. Kit wore them every day in the hopes it would rain."

"Did she wait long?" Will inquired, thinking it was something Georgiana would have done at that age.

"Well," Elizabeth said with a drawl, "her birthday's in July, so . . ."

They both laughed.

"I've missed a lot," Elizabeth said, her voice wistful. "They probably don't remember this stuff. They're practically grown now."

"They seem pretty happy," Will offered. "They probably remember more than you think."

She nodded. Under her breath, she mumbled, "Hope not." Will knew he wasn't supposed to hear it, so he didn't ask her to repeat or explain it. He just filed it away for later. For Elizabeth Bennet, he was willing to wait.

CHAPTER FIFTEEN

Elizabeth's phone rang in her ear. "Bennet," she said in a sleepy voice.

"Liiizzzy," Jane whined, "where's my car?"

"It's not there?" Elizabeth asked, befuddled. She sat up but didn't open her eyes.

This set Jane off into a panic. "Did you drop it off last night?" she asked hurriedly. "Should I call the cops?"

"No, no," Elizabeth said, more awake now. "Charlotte was supposed to drop it off for me."

"Well, I'm awake now," Jane replied. "Thanks for the shock to my system." She paused. "Why would Charlotte drop it off? Lizzy, what's going on?"

Elizabeth knew Jane must be exhausted to be so impatient. Charlotte would need to be dealt with. "Jane, let me call Char. If it's not there in ten minutes, call a cab. I'll pay for it. I'm really sorry."

"That's like a thirty-dollar fare, Lizzy, are you sure?"

That sounded more like the Jane she knew. *Charlotte had better have a good reason for not taking Jane's car back last night.* "Yes. I'll make Charlotte pay me back."

Jane harrumphed. "Are you home?"

"Yes," Elizabeth replied. She felt terrible about stranding her sister. "You've got to be dead on your feet, Janie. I'll call Charlotte and call you right back."

Jane agreed, but added, "When I'm not feeling like a zombie, you are going to tell me what happened. I'm not kidding, Elizabeth."

Elizabeth grunted, irritated. *Charlotte's a dead woman.* "Fine."

She heard Jane say someone's name and then a few words. It sounded like someone was asking if she still lived in Montclair with her twenty-seven cousins.

"I am," she heard Jane say. "Old woman who lived in a shoe, that's me."

Then Jane returned to the line. "Elizabeth," she said flatly, "I'll call you back."

Elizabeth rubbed her eyes. She'd only had about two hours of sleep before Jane's call. Quickly she found Charlotte's number and tapped the screen of her phone. She counted the rings—*four, five*—before Charlotte answered.

"Good morning, Lizzy," came Charlotte's sunny greeting. "Where *are* you this fine day?"

"I'm home, Charlotte. And the question," Elizabeth said in a clipped voice, "is where are *you?* Where is Jane's car?"

Charlotte giggled. "First, that's a little disappointing. Second, that's two questions."

Elizabeth was not amused. "And your answers would be?"

"Oh," chirruped the musical voice on the other end of the call, "Dad was delayed this morning. I'm just driving into the staff lot now."

Elizabeth groaned and put a hand over her eyes to block out the light. "You promised, Char. Jane just left work and couldn't find it. Now she's grumpy and she'll never let me borrow it again. *And* she wants to know why I didn't return it. You *promised.*"

"Oops," Charlotte replied without a hint of remorse. Elizabeth frowned. Her hand tightened involuntarily around her phone.

"What do you mean, 'oops'?" Elizabeth asked, irritated. *I'm definitely buying a motorcycle. Maybe even a car. Argh, insurance, gas, repairs . . .* "This was all your fault to begin with, begging me to play co-ed." Her eyes felt gritty, and she rubbed absently at them. Staying up all night trading life stories with a handsome man was fine if you didn't have to function the following day.

"Sorry, Lizzy," Charlotte nearly sang. "I did uphold my end. I didn't tell Jane a thing, and I'll never ask you to play co-ed again. How was the hot tub?"

Elizabeth bent over, holding her head in one hand. "I don't get it, Char. You were all protective last night, and now . . . "

"That's when I thought you were hurt. But you weren't," Charlotte informed her.

"You are a prime-grade rat, Charlotte Lucas," Elizabeth replied menacingly, "and you had better watch your back."

Charlotte laughed, entirely at ease. "I'm not afraid of you. Jane won't let you do anything to me, and even if she did, Maddy wouldn't."

"Call Jane and tell her where you are," Elizabeth said coolly and terminated the call. "All right, Lucas," she said quietly, "gauntlet thrown." She tossed her phone on the side table and dropped back onto her bed, rolling over and falling asleep almost instantly.

Will Darcy felt like he was on his last legs. He'd come into work late, a first for him in the five years since he had started his company, but it hadn't been late enough. He'd managed to grab only a few hours of sleep after driving Elizabeth back to New Jersey, making an appearance around ten. Fortunately, FORGE was in a rare lull, with the final work on several large projects just completed and the new cycles not yet begun. After the holidays, they'd have more work than they could handle, but fortunately Charles would be back from South America by then and could shoulder some of the load.

Charles, Will thought as he organized his computer's desktop and stopped at some of his friend's presentation files. *What to do with Charles?*

Will had met Charles Bingley when he was looking to hire someone to do business analytics. A former Harvard professor had recommended three graduating students he might wish to interview, and it had been clear from the moment Bingley began speaking that he was the right candidate. By the end of the first year of his employment, it was just as clear that the man belonged on the executive team.

Charles was a wizard with both data analysis and projections, but more than that, he could rally the troops almost effortlessly. His affable nature, coupled with his business acumen, had been a valuable addition to FORGE, and he and Will had eventually become friends. Their backgrounds were somewhat similar, which helped. Charles's family had the same sort of expectations of their son that the Darcys had had for theirs.

Will opened a bottle of water and took several long gulps while loosening his tie. Even with the risk of losing Charles to another company, there was something holding him back from inviting Charles to invest in the company. Charles was more actively involved in the business than Will's own family had been to date, but in his personal life, his friend still behaved, well, like a stereotypical frat boy.

Will had been mulling this over since Charles's latest break-up had resulted in a suddenly "urgent" need to get out of the city. The man's love life was negatively affecting his ability to do his work, work that then was added to Will's plate. He'd agreed to Charles's trip, but not with terribly good grace. *Maybe Charles doesn't want a place here long term anyway*, he told himself, then grunted softly. He was too tired to be in the office today. He should forget about this and just go home.

"Mr. Darcy?" Wanda was at the door, holding a cup of coffee. She was grinning at him as though she knew a secret, though he couldn't imagine what it might be.

"Bless you, Wanda," he said with a sigh. *I'm sure she'll tell me eventually. It's probably something embarrassing.*

"Did your team go out for beers after the game?" she asked, trying to appear as though the question was innocent.

Ah, that's it. She thinks I'm hungover. "No, one of the players was injured, and I took her to the doctor. It was late when we got back."

For a moment, Wanda's face fell, but then her eyebrows lifted. "Her?"

"Oh, for pity's sake, Wanda, I'm tired," he groaned. "It's a co-ed team, so yes, it was a woman. How much more coffee is there?"

"An entire pot. I was hoping maybe you'd actually gone out on a weeknight." Her dangling earrings today were in the shape of a treble clef, reminding Will of his sister.

He grinned at Wanda, and for the first time, noticed that her short gray hair had been coaxed into small spikes. *That's new. It sounded horrible when G wanted to try it, but it looks good on Wanda.* "Thank you. I need the caffeine." He motioned at her head. "I like the hair."

She shook her head and gave him a little cluck. "When you think before you speak, you can be a very charming man, Mr. Darcy—a very good man. Just don't be *too* good, or your young lady will die of boredom."

Will thought about Elizabeth and tried not to smile. He'd never be bored with Elizabeth in his life. He hoped she felt the same way.

Elizabeth was lying on the asphalt beneath the front of Charlotte's car, her head and arms the only part of her visible, when her phone rang. She touched a button on her earpiece and whispered, "Hello?"

Why am I whispering? she asked herself, rolling her eyes. *They'll never hear me out here.*

"Why are you whispering?" came a deep voice. *Will,* she thought happily.

"Because I'm up to no good," she replied, with an impish grin. "Charlotte totally railroaded me this morning by not returning Jane's car on time. Now Jane knows why I needed Charlotte to return it, and she's both worried because I didn't get an MRI and mad at me for not calling. Something about trusting a stranger over her and Dr. Lucas, and I sure wasn't going to tell her about the Jacuzzi. Ergo, Charlotte has to pay."

"I'm almost afraid to ask," he responded.

She reached up with the screwdriver to replace the grill. "Then don't," she said, vigorously twisting the screws back in place. "Charlotte told me she was sleeping over at Aunt Maddy's tonight, so I took an Uber and made the guy drop me off a block away. I'm sure you'll hear the tale when she starts crying about how her classic 1960s station wagon is falling apart."

"Elizabeth," Will said warningly, "you can't mess with her car. It's dangerous."

"Settle down, boy scout," she chuckled. "I'm not messing with the mechanics."

"Then what are you doing?"

Elizabeth finished screwing the grill back in place before she said cheerfully, "Wouldn't you like to know?"

"I believe that's why I asked." His voice was muffled, and then she heard a dresser drawer open. She thought about him changing and smiled.

"Never mind," she replied. "You'll hear about it later. Can I call you back in about five minutes?"

Will made an impatient growling sound, and Elizabeth snickered. "Yes," he said with a sigh, and the call ended.

When the phone rang four minutes and thirty seconds later, he picked it up immediately. "Elizabeth?"

"It's me, Will." He could hear her sisters in the background. "What're you up to?"

"I slept this afternoon, and now I'm wide awake. Do you want to come into the city tonight?"

"I have no car, genius, and now I'm unlikely to be allowed to borrow Jane's ever again." She paused for a minute, "Let me find the train schedule." Will could hear the rattling of objects being displaced as Elizabeth began to sort through a junk drawer.

"Stop, Bennet," Will said decisively. *What is she thinking, taking the train into the city after dark?*

"Hey, is that your CEO voice?" she teased.

Will smirked. "Yes, and it's worked on tougher cases than you, so listen up. Are you in Montclair?"

"Yes. Charlotte's here." There was the squeak of a refrigerator door opening. "I thought I'd torture her all night with what I'm going to do, but she won't even look at me. She's going to spend the night here before driving to Philly in the morning for a gallery opening." Will could hear the clinking sound of ice cubes being dropped in a glass.

"You know," he mused, distracted, "I never asked what Charlotte does for a living. Does she work with artists?"

"She *is* an artist. She paints mostly, but does some sculpture, too. She's pretty good. Even starting to make a living wage at it."

Will considered that. *Fits her.* "Did you have other plans tonight?"

Elizabeth lowered her voice and replied, "You mean other than wiring my friend's car to shoot whipped cream in the air when it starts?"

He snorted. "How about Tierney's? Or do you want to go somewhere else to eat?"

"I did miss dinner," she mused. "Aunt Maddy offered me leftovers."

Will chuckled. "Well, as good as I suspect her cooking is, there are plenty of people in that house to make sure they don't go to waste. I'll call my driver and he can take us to dinner. You know," he said, laying emphasis on the word, "a *date*."

Elizabeth set her glass down and looked around. Life was going on around her. Jane had slept through dinner but had been called back to the hospital to cover a shift, so she was eating a quick meal. Mary was lounging on the loveseat with her textbooks and a highlighter. Kit was engaging in a math study group via video chat while Lydia listened in and asked questions about their teacher. Because Aunt Maddy sat only a few feet away conversing with Charlotte, the math conversation remained mostly on topic. The two youngest Gardiners were already getting ready for bed with Uncle Ed while the older two were sitting at the kitchen table, doing homework on their tablets.

She glared at Charlotte, who appeared entirely unconcerned about any retaliation for her treacherous behavior. Everyone was busy. Her own work, providing evidence of off-shore bank accounts for what was a relatively straightforward divorce case, had been less than challenging and was complete. She smiled as she thought about how her own bank account was steadily growing. *Everything is falling into place,* she thought.

After another moment, she realized that Will was formally asking her out on a date, that he had even said the word. *First date,* she thought, a strange but pleasant warmth suffusing her body.

"Elizabeth?" Will asked. He sounded a little nervous.

"Sure," she said when she realized she'd taken too long to reply. "I'd like that."

CHAPTER SIXTEEN

For a moment after she ended the call, Elizabeth stood still, moving only to reach for her glass and drink the remaining water in four long gulps. *I have to change my clothes. They're all dirty from the road.*

She took another surreptitious glance around the crowded great room and realized that nobody had taken any notice of her call. Relieved, she washed her glass, put it in the drying rack, and sauntered upstairs. She entered Jane and Mary's room and began to go through their closet. Both sisters wore clothing her size, but Mary was several inches shorter and her chest was smaller while Jane was nearly the same height and her chest was larger. Mary's coloring was darker, but she wore mostly black, whereas Jane's complexion was fair, so she wore pastels. Mary's style was conservative, and Jane's more sophisticated. *What to choose?* Her arm dropped as she stared blankly at the closet stuffed full of clothing.

Footsteps in the hall made Elizabeth whirl to face the newcomer. She let out a relieved sigh when it was Jane, coming up to change for work. The eldest Bennet was in the middle of pulling her long, golden hair up into a bun, but she stopped midway into the room to stare at her sister.

"What are you doing, Lizzy?" Jane asked. Elizabeth was grateful that there was only curiosity in her tone.

"Will is going to pick me up for dinner," she said, embarrassed. "But my clothes are at home."

"Honestly, Lizzy," Jane said, "I've seen your clothes. I think you're better off here."

Elizabeth frowned at that, waiting pensively as Jane looked her up and down carefully. Her sister then walked directly to the closet, pushed a few things aside, and reached deep into the back to remove a red halter dress from the very back. Elizabeth noted that the tags were still on it.

"It was a gift," Jane said with a little eye roll. "I tried to give it back, but he wouldn't take it."

"Yes, I can see that men giving you things is a problem," Elizabeth said with a grin.

"It's what they want in return for the gifts that's the issue," Jane replied.

"Ah."

"I'd rather have a guy wash my car," Jane replied acerbically, and Elizabeth laughed. She scrutinized Elizabeth's figure. "It's pretty, but red is definitely not a good color with my complexion. It'll look great on you, Lizzy." She turned the hanger and pointed to a clasp at the back, tucked away so it was invisible when the dress was worn. "The neck here is adjustable."

Elizabeth worried her bottom lip a bit and evaluated it. The neckline reminded her a bit of the famous white dress Marilyn Monroe had worn in *The Seven Year Itch*, though thankfully it wasn't nearly as daring. She reached out to take the hanger from her sister and walked to their full-length mirror to hold it up to herself. The color of the dress brought out the red highlights in her hair.

"Perfect!" she exclaimed and ran into the bathroom to quickly shower and change. When she walked back into the room, barefoot, wearing the dress, she watched Jane take a deep breath.

"Close your mouth, Jane," Elizabeth joked. "You'll catch a lightning bug." She twirled in front of the mirror. "I like it," she announced. The straps of the dress curved around Elizabeth's neck, exposing the lean muscle of her shoulders and arms. The cut of the bodice and the built-in brassiere accentuated Elizabeth's chest, and the skirt flared slightly at the hips, dropping in soft pleats to her knees.

Jane stepped back to give her sister the once over from head to toe and then walked all the way around her sister as Elizabeth waited nervously for a verdict. Jane gave a short, delighted laugh and shook her head. "You look incredible, Lizzy. Are you sure Will deserves you?"

Elizabeth grinned, "I'm sure he doesn't, but I'll let him buy me a meal anyway."

Jane winked at her. "That's my girl."

Elizabeth took Jane by the hand. She didn't mind when *Jane* called her a girl; they had, after all, been girls together. "Only *you* could just pull something like this out of your closet without even looking, Jane," Elizabeth said with a pleased sigh. "You're never getting this dress back."

"Oh, Kit has me well-trained," Jane said with a small laugh. "It's yours. I will need the shoes back, though." She held out a pair of black, strappy heels, and Elizabeth made a face at the stilettos.

"Try them on," Jane said firmly. "You can't wear Mary's flats. Her foot is too small, and they'd look awful with this dress. Your man is tall, and you've got great legs, Lizzy. Show them off."

"Really?" Elizabeth asked, bending over to look at them, scrubbing one finger along the small slick scar near her left knee. "You think I have great legs?"

"You're kidding, right?" Jane scoffed. "You run every morning. Any moron can see that you have great legs. It doesn't hurt that they're so long, either."

"I don't run *every* morning," Elizabeth said slowly, slipping on the shoes and looking herself over in the mirror. *I love this dress. The shoes may be hazardous.*

"False modesty," Jane said, shaking her head.

"No, I'll gladly take your word for it, Janie," Elizabeth said, then laughed. "I just never really thought about it before." She picked up her phone and opened the camera. "I have to show Will."

"No!" Jane cried, grabbing the cell from her sister's hand. "Lizzy, you don't spoil a reveal. You wait until he's here in person and then come down the stairs. Slowly."

Elizabeth laughed, abruptly self-conscious. "I do?"

"Oh, little sister," Jane pretended to moan. She opened Lizzy's contact list and found Will's number.

"What are you doing?" Elizabeth asked when Will's name came up on the screen. She reached for the phone. "You just said not to show him!"

"I'm going to text him," Jane said, turning away and lifting her index finger in the air to stop her sister. "Back off, Lizard. You owe me for almost giving me a heart attack this morning. Stanley wanted to give me a ride home."

Elizabeth winced and asked, apologetically, "Do you like him?"

"As a colleague, he's fine, but I don't want him as a boyfriend and he hasn't been able to take the hint," Jane said.

Elizabeth grimaced. "Sorry."

Jane waved her hand dismissively. "I think I have the gist of it. Charlotte wanted to tell me but promised not to, so she resorted to trickery. She just didn't consider how panicked I'd be when my car wasn't in the lot." She found Will's number and began typing. "You are both lucky she showed up in time to save me from Stanley."

"What are you doing?"

"Telling Will to dress up." She pushed the "send" button and did something else before handing the phone back. "I presume a retaliatory strike against Charlotte is being planned?" Elizabeth only grinned in response. "Never mind," Jane said, gathering her shower things and her phone before heading for the bathroom. "I don't want to know."

When Elizabeth tried to pull up Jane's text to read it, it had been deleted. A moment later, Kit came in with a curling iron, saying Jane had sent her.

Will was standing in front of a mirror in his bedroom. *Tie? No tie?* He fidgeted uncomfortably. *Jacket or sweater? Damn, I should have asked her where she wanted to go before I hung up.*

He was still holding a tie, figuring he could just bring one and put it on if Elizabeth appeared in something other than jeans, when his phone buzzed. *I hope she's not canceling,* he thought, as he picked it up and saw her number.

This is Jane, it said. *Dress up. It's a first date and she's excited. Sports coat and tie.*

He grinned. "Bless you, Jane," he said, tossing the tie around his neck, choosing a sports coat and pulling it on. "Tie it is."

When he arrived at the Gardiners' house less than an hour later, he had made reservations at a restaurant in Montclair called Laboratorio and was carrying a bouquet of flowers in his hand. If there was one thing he was good at, he thought wryly, it was *first* dates. He'd been on too many of those to count. Before his parents were killed, he'd dated lots of painfully thin models, senator's daughters or nieces, debutantes living off their trust funds, every one of whom forced him to loiter in living rooms or foyers as they made their sometimes *very* belated grand entrances. They'd been set-ups, mostly. His mother wasn't a matchmaker, Richard's mother was—or had been, before she fell ill.

Will had never thought about it much before. This was just what women did, at least the women his family would consider suitable. He suspected Elizabeth was different. *I know she's different.*

He had never talked through the night with another woman, not even in college, and he felt an almost overpowering need to see Elizabeth again right away. He straightened his tie, took a deep breath, and rang the bell, feeling for all the world like an eighth-grader. He muttered a quiet prayer that Ed Gardiner wouldn't be the one who opened the door.

That prayer was answered when Jane appeared and invited him inside. She was dressed for work, her hair up, wearing scrubs and bright blue Nikes. Will had to admit that even without trying, Jane was a beautiful woman. But there was only one woman he was interested in tonight.

"Hi, Jane. Is Elizabeth ready?" he asked quietly.

"I'll get her," Jane said, looking him over approvingly before disappearing upstairs.

It was only a moment before he heard movement in the hallway. *No pointless delays or cooling my heels with this one*, he thought gratefully.

"Hello, Will," Elizabeth said cheerfully from the top of the stairs. He grinned at the difference between the phony sultry tones of his former dates and the unabashed cheerfulness of Elizabeth's.

He looked up, and his eyes widened at the halter dress and how it drew attention to her breasts, but he managed to smile and reply. What exactly he said was a mystery to him. He did see that her smile grew wider at his words, and she began to pick her way carefully down the stairs.

Will thought his heart just might leave his chest, hard as it was beating. He had seen Elizabeth in less clothing; after all, the bathing suit she'd worn left little to the imagination. Perhaps that was it. This dress left something to the imagination, and his fantasies were already forming. He recalled the green business suit, how her eyes had shone like emeralds, but in red, she glowed. It picked up the flush in her cheeks and the bit of red in her hair, which had been gently curled. A shimmery black shawl was draped over the crook of each arm. He swallowed hard and told himself to stand still, to let her come to him, and then he noted that she was careful on the stairs, not because she was trying to keep his attention with a prolonged entrance, but because she wasn't used to the height of the heels. The thought made him smile.

Then she was standing before him, the heels making her only slightly shorter than he, and he offered her the flowers. She thanked him, touched them gently with a strange expression on her face, and Will, learning to read her, thought it might be wonder. *Has no one ever given her flowers?*

Elizabeth excused herself for a minute to take them to the kitchen and put them in water. He turned to watch her go before he realized he had an audience. Mrs. Gardiner, Charlotte, and Lydia were gathered at the end of the hall, the one that led from the family room, and they were all smiling, though Lydia's smile was more of a smirk. He glanced at Lydia's feet and tried not to laugh at the wedges she was wearing. Instead, he just said hello, and Maddy beamed at him. He started to ask Charlotte about her show, but then Elizabeth was back, telling Maddy she'd have Will's driver return her home to Bloomfield and that she'd call the next day. They said their goodnights.

Then they were outside, and Will released a deep breath he hadn't known he was holding. The cold air helped clear his mind, and he gathered his wits enough to say, "You look beautiful, Elizabeth."

"Thank you," she said, tilting her face up to his, "but you've said that already."

"It bears repeating," he said, grateful that at least his mangled appreciation had been appropriate.

"You look great, too," she said. "I like you in a sports coat. It suits you."

"Better than my soccer kit?" he asked teasingly.

"Oh, I wouldn't say *that*," she shot back, one eyebrow raised in an arch.

He laughed. "Fair enough. I don't mind you in shorts either."

As they approached the car, Jerry got out to open the back door.

"No Audi tonight?" she whispered to Will.

"I thought we might have some wine," he replied, placing one hand on her lower back. When they reached the car, she stopped short, and he stepped to the side to avoid running into her.

"Elizabeth, this is Jerry Kardasian. He'll be our driver tonight," Will said.

"Hello, Jerry," Elizabeth said with a smile and held out her hand.

Jerry glanced at her hand, then at Will, before saying, "Yes, miss."

"Oh, I'm just Elizabeth," she said with a laugh, lowering her hand.

Jerry nodded. "Yes, miss."

She glanced up at Will. "I see I'm going to have some trouble with Jerry," she joked.

"Not at all," Will replied, with a wink at his driver. "He's a consummate professional."

Elizabeth laughed. "That's the problem."

Will helped her into the back of the car and shook his head as she automatically pulled the shoulder belt across her dress. No woman he took out did that. They would rather die in a crash than wrinkle their gown.

"What?" she demanded.

"Nothing," he said affectionately. "I'm just really glad you're here."

This earned him a stunning smile as she reached out to squeeze his hand. "I'm glad I'm here, too." She blushed and shook her head. "I mean, here with you."

CHAPTER SEVENTEEN

Will had never been to this restaurant, but the modern décor and the menu were promising. He looked through the entrees and quickly decided he wanted a steak. When he glanced up at Elizabeth, she was perusing her own menu a little too carefully, her eyebrows pinched together as she read. When he asked, she told him she would order the chicken, but something about the way she said it made him ask, "Are you sure that's what you want?"

She smiled a little and nodded but didn't say anything.

Will frowned and picked up the menu again. When he reviewed the entrees, he realized she'd ordered the least expensive meal.

"Elizabeth," he said quietly, "why are you ordering the chicken?"

She lowered her head a little, pretending to reread the menu. "I know you do this all the time, Will, and I'm impressed by Jerry and all, but the prices are really high here."

He tried not to laugh, only partially succeeding. If she knew what he paid at a typical business dinner, her eyes would pop out of her head. He'd chosen this place in part because he knew she'd want to reciprocate at some point and the prices had seemed moderate. "The restaurant was my choice, Elizabeth. I knew what the prices were when I made the reservation." She glanced up at him, and Will thought she looked worried. *Does she think I'm upset with her?* He met her gaze and asked, "What do you really want to order?"

She met his gaze shyly. He hadn't realized she had it in her to be shy about anything, but he found it charming. "Scallops," she said softly.

"Then scallops it is," he replied, eyes alight with humor. *She's watching my pennies.* "Do me a favor, and don't make me work so hard just to order the food next time, okay?"

Elizabeth brought her chin up, then said, "You're very sure of yourself. How do you know there will *be* a next time?"

"Touché," he replied with a smile. "I guess we'll have to wait and see."

The waiter arrived to take their order, and Will ordered salads and wine as well as the entrees, giving her a wink before requesting the additional items. She shook her head at him.

When the order was in, they settled back and contemplated one another for a minute before Elizabeth said, "I'm going to ask you a question."

Will narrowed his eyes, mildly alarmed. "Okay . . ."

She rolled her eyes. "Relax. Like first-date questions. I ask one, and then you get to ask one."

He chuckled. "Fair enough. What's your first question?"

She hummed a little as she reached for a piece of bread. "How did you first decide what your company would do? It's very different from what your father did."

Will took a sip of his wine and watched her butter the bread in two precise passes with her knife. "I wasn't very old at all before I knew I didn't want to break failing companies up and sell off the parts. But I didn't know exactly what I *did* want to do until I started my MBA program. My mother and I had a long conversation about it, and she asked what I planned to do to make the world a better place."

This caught Elizabeth's attention. "Your mother's idea?"

Will laughed a little and shook his head, "No, just her nagging." His voice softened. "She was the captain of our ship. Even my dad admitted it. She was just unassuming about it." He took a bite of his food. When he swallowed, he continued. "She told me that we'd been very blessed, that we ought to try to pass that on. She worked hard for the Darcy Foundation, the family charity. She told me that while my father would be proud to hand his company to me when he retired, she didn't think it would make me happy." He picked up his glass. "She was right, of course."

The salads arrived, and Will noticed that Elizabeth's didn't have any dressing.

"Do you not like it?" he asked, motioning to the saucière.

"No," she replied with a shake of her head. "I always get it on the side so I can go light. I actually like the taste of the lettuce."

"For a second there, I thought you were on some sort of diet." He grinned as her eyes widened in mock horror.

"Not a chance," she replied, tucking an errant lock of hair behind her ear and meeting his gaze. "I love to eat." She grinned. "If I overdo it, I just run another mile." She swallowed a bite and asked, "So how did you decide what you wanted to do for this company that wasn't your dad's and was meant to make you happy?"

Will speared some of the lettuce on his fork and ate, chewing while he gathered his thoughts. He swallowed and said, "That's more than one question."

Elizabeth rolled her eyes. "Same topic. You can ask follow-ups too."

He nodded, then cleared his throat and said, "My dad thought it was just an exercise, making a list of all the things I wanted to do and then trying to form a company around that, so he and I talked a lot about it." His eyes looked faraway as he remembered. "In the end, I realized that good products sometimes take thirty or forty years to get noticed and become mainstream. What would happen if I could help speed up the process?"

"Digital revolution?" Elizabeth asked archly.

"Not just digital, but yes, that's the idea," Will said warmly. He took another bite of the salad. "My turn," he said suddenly. She glanced up and shrugged, and for a moment he was mesmerized by what that did to both the dress and what was in it. Then he blinked and asked, "Why the Marines?"

She froze for a second, and Will silently kicked himself. He'd thought this would be an easy one.

"No one else would have me," she joked. Will was silent, just watching her. On the terrace she'd seemed detached from the story she told, but now she just looked embarrassed. Sad? *Good work, Will*, he berated himself.

Elizabeth cleared her throat. "I told you my mom died." He nodded. "There wasn't any money for college, and no time left to make any, so I enlisted." He waited and she sighed. "The truth is I sort of lost myself for a while when we all moved to Montclair. I'd overseen the girls and my mother and the house and the bills—you know, *everything*—for so long. But after my mother died and Aunt Maddy came, nobody needed me anymore." She lifted her water glass and took a sip. "So I did what any self-respecting seventeen-year-old would do. I packed an entire adolescence into a few weeks right after graduation." She sighed. "Uncle Ed thought that wasn't such a great idea and became my personal drill sergeant. He figured if I was too tired to sneak out, he'd done his job."

Will frowned. "Where was your dad?"

"Oh," she said. "I guess I missed that part. He left us about a year before my mother died."

Will felt his stomach twist. "I'm so sorry."

She shifted in her seat, and the light caught a line of uneven skin on her left shoulder. His eyes lingered there until she spoke.

"It happened a long time ago," she told him easily. "We're all better off without him, honestly. Uncle Ed is a better father than he ever was."

"So, you chose the Marines because Ed was one?"

She nodded. "That, and my father was anti-military. Bonus."

The expression on her face was enigmatic. Will thought it might be both pride and defiance, but before he could decide, the meals arrived.

He took a good deal of satisfaction in watching Elizabeth take a bite of her scallops and scoop up the butternut squash puree that accompanied it. Her eyes closed involuntarily, and a tiny smile appeared on her lips. He heard her shoes tapping the hard floor and assumed it was a good sign. Only after she opened her eyes and he lifted his eyebrows in a mute question did she nod and say, "Okay, you were right."

He held one hand up to an ear. "I'm sorry, I don't think I heard that correctly. Can you repeat that, please?"

She laughed, shaking her head at him. "Here, you have to try this." Her hand stilled. "You don't have any allergies or anything, right?"

He shook his head as she offered him a bite without releasing the fork.

"Mmm," he said as he chewed, "that was amazing." He gestured to his own plate. "Would you like to try some of the steak?"

"Dude," she said affectedly, making him grin, "it's steak."

He cut her a piece and offered his fork to her. As she slid her mouth over the tines, Will thought of their kiss and how much he'd love to catch her lips with his own. She swallowed and began to sit back, but he cupped her cheek and leaned forward until they were only inches apart. She looked up and met his gaze, all humor melting into desire. Their lips touched.

A flash of light brought the kiss to an abrupt end.

"What the hell?" sputtered Will, jumping up but catching only the blue jacket of a figure retreating through the entrance. He cursed under his breath. "I'm not even safe in New Jersey."

"Who was that?" Elizabeth asked, scowling. "I have something I'd like to show him."

Will glanced at her, surprised, but also curious. "What?"

She held up one of her shoes, her eyes shooting fire. "How far the heel of this shoe could be shoved up his . . ." Her voice trailed off as the manager appeared at their table, apologizing for the disruption and offering them a free dessert. Her shoe disappeared back under the table.

Will was mortified and angry that their date had been ambushed. He knew Elizabeth wouldn't be happy to have her picture in the paper, unlike most of the other women he'd dated, and he hadn't talked to her about it yet. He hadn't thought it necessary. This was only their first date, after all, and it wasn't as though he was a movie star.

He wasn't angry with the manager. He knew all too well how difficult it was to keep the photographers away, and outside the city, very few places had experience with them. Still, he was too angry to speak. He sat down without responding.

Elizabeth glanced at Will, apparently waiting for him to answer the manager, but as the awkward silence stretched out, she smiled at the man and made their reply. "I think we'll finish our meal if you think you can keep any other photographers out, and then we'll take the dessert to go."

The manager nodded, relieved, and asked, "Which dessert would you like?"

"Oh," Elizabeth said airily, "surprise us. Something with dark chocolate, if you have it."

When the man was gone, she reached out and placed a hand over Will's fist where it was resting on the table.

"Hey," she said quietly. "You okay?"

He nodded. "I hate this," he replied quietly. "It doesn't happen whenever I'm out. Half the time the woman even calls the paper herself to make sure she gets a photo in the society pages." He opened his fist and took her hand in his. "But the Darcys have been in the city a long time, and when our parents died, Georgiana and I became good copy. She was the tragic orphan heiress, and I was the struggling heir. They seemed disappointed when I didn't even try to run my father's business." He rubbed his thumb over the back of her hand. "They were probably rooting for me to fail."

Elizabeth pursed her lips. "Bottom-feeders."

He chuckled, but it rang hollow. "Yeah, that's just it—I live in a bit of a fishbowl." He sighed. "I don't even know why. It's not like I'm Jeff Bezos. Other than the name and the money, my life is really dull." He traced the pattern on the tablecloth with his eyes.

"Will," he heard her say, "please look at me."

He met her eyes and saw compassion there.

"I want you to repeat after me . . ."

He stared at her, almost flinching when she reached up to touch his cheek. Her face was so perfectly heart-shaped, her skin so clear, her eyes so verdantly green. She was everything lovely. Then she spoke to him in a voice that was deadly serious.

"Screw 'em." He startled a bit, and she shook her head. "Say it."

"Screw them," he said hoarsely.

"Once more, with feeling," she said, her lips bowing in a little pout he was anxious to kiss away.

He drew a deep breath, let it out. "Screw 'em," he said, a grin beginning to make its way back to his face. Elizabeth returned to her meal and nodded at his. The tightness in his chest eased. She was tough, Elizabeth. Tougher than most men he knew. Maybe tough enough to stick it out with him. He picked up his fork and knife and attacked his steak with energy.

Later, as Elizabeth watched Will place his credit card in the folder, it struck her that while she was difficult to intimidate, the idea of his wealth and especially his high profile did concern her a bit. His life, his problems, weren't remotely the same as hers, and although he'd seen her modest little apartment, he might soon begin to view her differently if he saw her budget or the balance in her checking account. She didn't like the feeling. She wanted to get him on some common ground. An idea occurred to her, making her lips stretch into a wide smile.

"Uh oh," she heard him say, "that's a rather diabolical smile."

She looked him over and said, "I just thought of something we can do this weekend, but before I tell you, I have to see whether there's still room available."

The waiter arrived to clear the dishes and deliver two boxes.

Will opened one of the boxes to investigate and showed it to Elizabeth. Dark chocolate cake and raspberries. "Will I like it?"

She glanced longingly at the sweet. "The dessert or our event?"

Will gave her a look, and she chuckled. "It's dirty," she warned, and then smiled. "Really dirty."

Will's face lit up. "Bring it on."

On his way back to the city, Will's phone rang. He checked the display and saw it was Richard, so he answered it.

"Will?" he heard on the other end. There was a lot of background noise.

"Richard? Where are you?" Will closed the partition between Jerry and himself to block out any additional sound.

"At the Embassy, in the lobby. Sorry, there's a whole delegation passing through."

They waited for a minute for the line to clear, and then Richard continued, "Three weeks," he said.

"What do you mean, three weeks?"

There was a laugh on the other end. "You'll need to pick me up at the airport in three weeks. I put in my resignation and finally got a separation date. You still have a job for me, right?"

"Yes!" Will cried enthusiastically. "In fact, things are going to start getting really busy around the end of January. I've been thinking about taking some vacation time while we're slow."

"Will Darcy is taking a vacation?" Richard asked, incredulous. "What momentous occasion has prompted this unprecedented action?"

"Shut up, Richard," Will replied, not honestly upset but unwilling to let his cousin know it. He ignored the question. "This is fantastic!"

"Don't get too excited—sometimes they decide with no notice that they need you to stay a bit longer. But for now, three weeks from today. Any chance Georgiana can get out to see me?"

Will sorted through his calendar. "That's right around Thanksgiving, Richard. It'd be amazing to have you both here for that. I'll ask Georgiana what her schedule looks like."

"Hey, ask Bennet to come, too. I owe her a beer. Two."

Will smiled at the thought. "I will. Why do you owe her?"

"Well, the trip to De Roos was a thank you for a favor with helping me with my computer. She only got a few sips of her beer before things kicked off. The second beer is for talking me through what she called *separation anxiety*," he said with a short laugh.

Will ran a hand through his hair as he thought about Elizabeth taking off her high heels and sprinting up the stairs to her apartment, about how comfortable it was to sit next to her on her secondhand couch eating their dessert and drinking coffee. She had a brand-new coffee maker she wanted to break in, she said, scoffing at the fancy espresso machine he had in his apartment. She liked her coffee strong and black. *I should take her somewhere to try Turkish coffee*, he thought, and then absorbed Richard's words. "She talked you into coming home?"

"Not exactly. She harangued me into doing what I wanted to do. Turns out that was to come home to my annoying younger cousins and a job I still have trouble imagining."

Will sighed. A tension he didn't even realize he had been carrying around with him melted from his body, leaving him more relaxed than he had been in years. *God bless that woman.*

CHAPTER EIGHTEEN

For the second morning in a row, Elizabeth awoke to blaring music from her phone. She moaned and reached out for it, checking the display to see that it was only seven in the morning and the caller was Charlotte. She laughed into her pillow and turned the phone off, rolling over and returning to sleep.

Around nine, she turned her cell back on and saw that Charlotte had left three messages. Between her feeling that justice had been served and her amazing date the night before, she felt almost giddy. She shoved her feet into some thick socks and padded into her kitchen to make breakfast, scrolling through the phone numbers. The dessert containers were still on the counter, and she swept them into the trash while noting that there were quite a few more voicemails than Charlotte's. She sighed, wondering where the photo had wound up; she thought about checking online but decided against it. Presumably she'd see it sooner or later. Lydia and Kit read the gossip rags. They'd tell her if they saw anything. She set the phone up on speaker and let them all run.

The first message had come in near midnight, just after Will left for home. *I must have been in the shower*, she thought with a grin and started to hum, remembering the kissing. It was so much better than at the restaurant where they'd had a table between them. At home, he'd pressed the side of his leg against hers, his hand moving to touch her face. He'd held her upper arms gently as they kissed, tentatively at first and then more urgently. One of his hands had slid around her back . . . she thought dreamily about how the other had plunged into her hair and how smooth his face was as her fingertips traced his jaw.

Making out on my couch. She smiled. *Now that's something I definitely missed out on as a teenager.* She stared out the window into the bare branches of an oak. *His lips are so soft.* Her attention was yanked back to the phone as Charlotte's volume increased to a yell. "Harmonicas under the grill? Two hundred miles, Elizabeth Bennet. Two. Hundred. Miles. A little overkill, don't you think? I thought my car was dying. I never pegged you as a sadist."

"Oh Char," she chuckled, pulling out a saucepan and setting it on the stove. "That was such a tiny little baby prank. Who do you think you're dealing with?"

Her wistful state was reinstated with a brief message from Will, saying he'd arrived home safely and was "looking forward to getting dirty with you." *Such a sexy voice.* She shook her head. *Dirty. He has no idea.*

As she was measuring out her oatmeal, the other messages played. There were a few offers of work, a call from Jane asking to meet for coffee on her lunch hour, and surprisingly, a message from Kit asking her something about volunteering at the high school. Elizabeth made a "humph" sound and conceded that she might enjoy that, provided it didn't involve putting on a sweaty mascot costume. She added milk to the oatmeal and stirred it, distracted.

As she drew closer to the messages from the early morning hours, the tone began to change. A few reporters called to see whether she'd agree to an interview about dating Will Darcy. They were offering a lot of money. *Disgusting.* "Nope," she said before she deleted each request.

The oatmeal was ready, and she paused the messages while she poured it out into a bowl, adding slivered almonds and a handful of blueberries. She ate silently as her cheerfulness settled into a kind of wary anxiety. She needed a run to sort things through. *Everything is falling into place*, she reminded herself. *Everything I've wanted. Why can't I trust it?* She turned off the ringer and shoved her phone into a pocket without bothering to listen to the rest of the messages.

"Pick up your damn phone, Elizabeth," Will ground out, jaw clenched, his elbow propped on the surface of his desk. With one hand, he held his cell to his ear. His head was resting in the other.

He'd made it to work early this morning, planning to make up for the hours he'd missed the day before and to finish up any loose ends so he could take the vacation he'd been pondering. He was pouring himself a cup of coffee in the break room as the rest of the staff began arriving. As they passed by, he noticed some grins sent his way, a few raised eyebrows, and one wink. His stomach sank. He'd been afraid of this. A vacation was starting to look extremely appealing.

His fears were confirmed when he returned to his office and Wanda, wearing long, gold bride and groom earrings and light green eyeshadow, slipped the *New York Post* under his nose. "Oh God," he groaned. "Front page." The headline screamed *Brussels Hero Turned New Jersey Princess*. He read the first few lines.

Our favorite gorgeous former Marine Sgt. and terrorist fighter Elizabeth Bennet looked like a modern-day princess in a hot red dress and stilettos last night, but she sure isn't kissing any frogs. Accompanying her to Montclair's Laboratorio was none other than NYC's own bachelor prince, billionaire Will Darcy, owner of Darcy Enterprises and CEO/Founder of FORGE, NYC's cutting-edge venture capital company.

"This isn't happening," he said, rubbing the back of his neck. The photo was sharp and in full color. There they were, clearly kissing. It was probably all over the internet, too.

"At least it's below the fold," replied Wanda, catching her bottom lip in her teeth and glancing up at him, trying to look optimistic. "You both look great," she added after a moment, her lips turning up at the corners. "And it was a work night. Extra points."

"You're the one who told me not to be boring," he grumbled.

"I didn't say to advertise it to the entire city," she responded, a bit sarcastically, arms crossing over her chest.

"One date," he said, "in *New Jersey*. I leave the state, and they still can't let me just have one uninterrupted date."

"Oh, I beg to differ," snorted Wanda. Will glared at her. "I know you have this happen from time to time, Mr. Darcy, but has anyone followed you out of the city before? A pap in Montclair, New Jersey? Boss, it wasn't *you* this guy was following. It was *her*." She paused. "I mean, from what you've said, the Gardiners don't exactly hide that she's their niece, and she's still big news here. Any pap worth his salt. . . "

Will's eyes widened as that sank in. He'd had Jerry drive them right to her apartment, assuming the photographer was already on his way back to a New York office. Jerry hadn't waited, but he'd returned later. *Arrogant idiot*, he told himself. *You didn't think.*

He'd led them right to her.

Damn. He grabbed his phone and called her number, but it went straight to voicemail. He tried again. Voicemail. He didn't have Ed's number, and after a quick search, he realized it wasn't listed.

Will checked the time. 8:45 am. No chance he'd get to New Jersey in less than two hours with traffic. He tapped the edge of his phone lightly on the desk. Jane Bennet—Jane would know how to get in touch with her uncle, even if she couldn't reach Elizabeth. Which hospital did Jane work for again? Newark? He quickly went online and scanned the names of the hospitals. University Hospital. That sounded right. He tapped the numbers into his phone.

"Emergency Department, please," he told the hospital operator. He waited, drumming his fingers on the desk until after what seemed an hour long wait and was probably about a minute, a nurse answered. He asked for Jane Bennet.

"Is this hospital business?" a female voice asked.

"No," he replied tersely, palm to his forehead.

"I'm sorry, sir," she responded mechanically. "I'm afraid she's not available at the moment."

"Look, this is important. Can you please ask her to come to the phone? It'll take less than a minute."

"I'm sorry, sir," she said again. "I can take your number and have her call back."

The hand holding his phone dropped from his ear and he came perilously close to throwing his cell against the wall. But that, he knew, would cause even more talk among his staff. *Calm down, Will*, he told himself. *Doesn't do anyone any good.* He lifted his arm and forced himself to say, "Thank you." He left his number and the message for Jane to call him back. He had a feeling it would be hours before Jane was flagged down.

"Wait!" he exclaimed. "Bingley!"

Charles had flown into Philadelphia yesterday afternoon and spent the night with a friend in Old City. He might be making his way back now. Will hit the speed dial.

"Bingley," came Charles's voice immediately. Will almost sagged with relief.

"Charles," he bit out, "not a moment too soon."

Elizabeth was about a mile into her run when she realized she'd picked up a tail. Her adrenaline soared. *Who is that?* He was in brand-new jogging clothes right down to his shoes. She thought about where she'd seen him before and realized it was at the very beginning of her run, near her apartment. Carefully, she changed direction, first taking a long left out of the park and then a winding right. He stayed about the same distance behind her. She picked up her pace a bit, and he matched it. Her arms erupted with goose bumps as she fled into the neighborhood, trying to keep her wits about her. *He's faster than you are with your gimp knee, Bennet. Focus. What's at hand?* As she ran, she opened her eyes and glanced around. It was garbage day, and cans lined the street. *Excellent.* She kept running, eyeing the plastic lids. *C'mon,* she chanted under her breath, *c'mon . . .*

Finally, she spied the telltale glint of an old, rusty, beat-up metal can. There was a second man joining the first now, and they were closing the distance a bit. She grabbed the handle on the lid as she went by. It came off with a short tug, and she took another left onto Broughton Avenue, glancing quickly behind her as she turned. *Better than nothing,* she thought. As she passed an open can, its lid tossed back and hanging on hinges, she stuck her hand inside and came away with a white plastic kitchen bag of foul-smelling . . . she gagged. Diapers? *Perfect.*

Once around the corner, she sprinted for her destination. Bloomfield's VFW was just ahead.

She slowed, listened for the footfall, and turned. For an instant, she was looking at two dark men in winter clothing, one wearing a backpack, both running at her and pointing guns. Her heart began to thrum like a hummingbird's.

Elizabeth pulled on the seam of the plastic to create a slit. She held it by the hole as she hefted the bag and raised the metal lid to her chest. She had just reached the lawn and turned back for a look when the two men stopped about ten feet away and lifted their hands simultaneously. She held the lid to shield her face, swinging the bag once, twice, and releasing it. A trail of dirty diapers arced in the sky, several hitting the men and exploding like little poop bombs, covering the lenses of their cameras. They cursed and jumped away.

The sun reflected off glass, and Elizabeth's vision cleared. Suddenly, they were just two guys in soiled running suits trying to take photos. Elizabeth heard them calling her name, pleading with her, as she burst through the door of the VFW building and shut it firmly behind her. Her hands were shaking, her chest hurt, and she was still clutching the metal lid. *Have to return that later*, she thought distractedly as she gazed down and willed herself to calm.

She bent over at the waist, one hand over her chest where her heart was still hammering painfully. When she glanced up, five or six men from about sixty to eighty years of age were staring down at her. One man with a tattoo on each dark, burly forearm began to wag a finger at her as he said, "I know you. Bennet, right?"

Here we go, she thought, but nodded slightly, her face ashen.

He nodded his head more vigorously. "Yeah, yeah. You're Ed Gardiner's niece." He looked approvingly at the logo on her sweats. "The Marine." He jerked a thumb at his chest. "Lopez."

Elizabeth nodded again and barked out a laugh edged with hysteria. *Ed Gardiner's niece. That's the nicest thing anyone could say to me right now.* She gulped for air, put her back to the wall, and let herself slide to the ground, dropping the garbage can lid next to her with a clatter, laughing until she couldn't stop, trying to choke out an explanation of what had happened. Three of the men stepped outside immediately, and she just wrapped her arms over her head and tried to breathe.

There's the other shoe, she thought grimly, her body shaking and her lungs burning. *It always drops.*

She heard a round of cursing outside and turned her head to peek out the window. Lopez and two other vets who had to be in their seventies were confronting the photographers.

"You don't chase a veteran through the streets!" one of them hollered, poking the man in the shoulder. This was followed by another round of curses. "What's the matter with you?"

Her breath eased when the three men pointed at the scattered garbage and the younger men reluctantly bent to pick it all up. They trudged over to the cans on the street several times under the watchful gaze of the two older men. Lopez walked around the side of the building where she couldn't see him.

Suddenly, the two vets stepped away, and a powerful stream of water hit the photographers, including their cameras. They shouted and protested, but Lopez appeared around the front of the building. He was holding a hose and spraying them down.

"You stink!" he yelled cheerfully. "Hit the showers!"

Elizabeth dropped her phone between her feet and again buried her head in her arms. She wasn't shaking anymore, and she could breathe again, but she just wanted to curl up and disappear for a while. Around her, the men went on with their activities, though as they passed by, she'd feel a rough pat on the shoulder or a hand resting briefly on her head. It felt good, to be somewhere she didn't have to explain. She asked them not to call her uncle, and they agreed. She was a vet, and they respected her wishes. Lopez told her in a surprisingly soft tenor that she ought to think about confiding in him, though.

"No one steadier than Ed," he had said, and she nodded. She just needed a little time.

You're tougher than this, Bennet. Get it together.

It was nearly two hours later, a bit past noon, before she felt able to call her uncle. When he arrived, he just offered her an arm up, which she took with relief, and they walked back to his car.

"Hope you don't mind," he said, "but there's some friend of Will's sitting in the living room. Will called him this morning as he was driving back to the city from Philly, and when you weren't at your apartment, he drove around a bit looking for you. Wound up at our place when you called." He checked his mirrors before pulling out onto the street. "Will's been calling you all morning. He was hiding it well, but I think he was starting to panic when you didn't call back. I told him I'd heard from you, but I think he's still worried."

Elizabeth closed her eyes and leaned back against the headrest. "I'll call him soon, Uncle Ed. I promise." She felt drained, exhausted. "Just not right now."

They drove in silence for a few minutes before Ed spoke again. "So," he began, his lips twitching suspiciously and his voice full of pride, "diapers."

Elizabeth turned her head without raising it to look at her uncle. His head was bobbing slightly in amusement, and he was smiling from ear to ear.

"Yeah," she said, taking a deep breath and letting it out slowly. "Nasty, dirty ones." She chuckled softly then, beginning to feel the smallest bit better. "And Lopez made them clean it up."

Ed Gardiner laughed all the way home.

CHAPTER NINETEEN

Elizabeth gazed out her window as they drove past the maple trees lining Gracechurch Street. Sunlight filtered through the nearly bare branches, casting dappled shadows that reminded her of flickering celluloid film. The neighborhood was quiet this time of day, no kids on bikes or playing basketball, nobody shouting to call their kids to dinner or slamming front doors. As they approached the Gardiners' house and pulled into the driveway, Ed opened the garage door and parked the car inside. It wasn't lost on Elizabeth that her uncle usually left the car outside this time of year. She stared at the wall for a minute, willing the throbbing that was starting behind her left eye to ease before she released her seat belt and shuffled into the house. Behind her, the door rolled shut with a squeal.

Maddy was waiting inside to hug her niece. She pulled Elizabeth's head down to kiss her on the cheek before pushing her back to look her straight in the eyes. Elizabeth shook her head.

"I'm fine, Aunt Maddy. More embarrassed than anything."

Maddy placed her hands on either side of Elizabeth's face and held it there. "You have no reason to be embarrassed. Those men should know better than to try to chase you in the streets. They're just lucky I wasn't there. I'd have ripped them limb from limb."

Elizabeth looked down at her diminutive aunt and grinned. "That would have been something."

"I'd have done it," Maddy growled, shaking her fist. "Taken them out right at the knees."

Elizabeth laughed quietly and gave her a squeeze. "Thanks."

Maddy gave her another quick, hard hug, and then grabbed her niece's hand. "Come meet Charles."

"Who?" Elizabeth rubbed one eye tiredly.

"Will's friend," said Maddy, bustling back into the kitchen and grabbing a tray with sandwiches and carrot sticks. "Didn't your uncle tell you?"

Elizabeth tucked a few strands of loose hair behind her ears. "Oh, right. I didn't get a name." *Charles,* she wondered. *Not Charlie? Chuck? Chaz?*

She rolled her head from one side to the other, shook out her shoulders, and then followed her aunt to the living room. Sitting on one of the couches with a photo album in front of him on the coffee table was a man, dirty blond hair just below his collar, light blue eyes, about Jane's age. He was handsome in a soft kind of way, though he was certainly fit. No, there was just something easygoing, almost lax about him. *Not like Will.* He sat comfortably, dressed in chinos, a blue button-down shirt, and a dark gray sports jacket, left ankle resting on his right knee displaying an expensive-looking black leather shoe polished to a high gleam. As soon as they entered the room, he stood and moved to take the tray from Maddy. *Not as tall as Will.*

Maddy scooped the photos out of the way, and Charles set the tray on the table before he straightened and turned back to Elizabeth and held out his hand.

"I heard Maddy say my name," he said with a smile, "so I won't offer it again. My mother wouldn't let anyone call me anything but Charles, and I've just gotten used to it."

Nice smile, she thought, giving him a half-grin and shook his hand. "I admit I did wonder."

He flashed another toothy grin. "I imagine everyone does." He was about to say something else when the doorbell rang.

"It's probably Will," Ed called from the kitchen.

Charles narrowed his eyes in a friendly way, half-apologetic, half-satisfied. "I called him before your uncle left to pick you up."

Elizabeth turned without a word and walked to the door, her speed increasing with each step until she was almost running. She peered through the peephole and saw him standing on the porch wiping his shoes on the welcome mat. She cracked the door open and nearly fell into his chest. He quickly wrapped his arms around her, and she allowed herself to relax for the first time since she'd spotted someone following her. She wrapped her arms around him. *Everything's okay.*

"I was worried," he said quietly. "I saw the paper this morning and tried to call, but you weren't answering your phone, and nobody had heard from you. Charles said you weren't at your apartment and your uncle and aunt didn't know where you were, either." He moved her gently backwards into the house and closed the door. "There don't seem to be any photographers out there now, but inside is better." He closed the door behind them with his foot and reached back to lock it. "I know you can handle yourself," he said. "I know it seems stupid to panic, but one of their vans nearly ran Georgiana down when she was fifteen, and she knew they were there. If you aren't expecting them . . ."

"All they did was follow me and try to get pictures, but in my experience, being followed is generally a bad thing," she said, her voice muffled in his shirt.

She felt the vibration of his deep, rumbling voice as he replied, "It's okay," he said. His arms relaxed around her. "You're okay."

At last, Elizabeth pulled away and took Will's hand to lead him into the living room. Everyone else was eating. Ed winked at her as they entered.

"I figured you'd be awhile, and we were hungry," he said with a grin, the skin at the corners of his eyes crinkling. "Did you tell him, Lizzy?" Ed asked her. She shook her head.

"Not yet," she said. Will sat on the loveseat and pulled her down next to him. He took her hand and held it tightly.

"It's all right," he murmured, just loud enough for her to hear. "I can wait."

She shook her head again. "It's fine." She opened her mouth to begin when she heard a key in the front door and her sister's voice in the hall.

"Elizabeth?" Jane's voice drifted down the hall. "Are you here?"

"We're all in the living room, Jane," called Maddy. "Come have something to eat."

Elizabeth moved the cuff of Will's sleeve to check his watch. It made her smile that he still wore one, and not a smart watch, either, but a heavy gold one with arms and roman numerals. He grinned at her, a little embarrassed.

"It's my dad's." He shrugged. "You can't always have your phone out in meetings," he said. "My interns think it's retro."

Lizzy laughed softly and looked up at her sister. *It's half past. Jane must be on her lunch break. She'll barely have time to get back.*

Jane strode into the room and gazed with exasperation at the assembled party. "What in the world is happening?" she asked with a huff. "I got a call from Aunt Maddy, and then when I was leaving for lunch, I was handed a note that Will called, and nobody was answering my calls!" She stood in the middle of the room, hands on hips, glaring at everyone. "You can't just leave messages and then not pick up your phones!" She stared pointedly at Elizabeth. "Especially you."

Elizabeth winced. "Sorry."

Will was sympathetic. "Sorry, Jane," he added. "I left that message early this morning. I honestly didn't think you'd ever get it."

Jane rubbed her forehead. "Okay, at least Lizzy is all right. What happened?"

Ed clapped his hands and rubbed them together. "Lizzy was just about to tell us."

"Introductions first, Ed," scolded Maddy. Ed sat back and folded his arms over his chest. "Jane, this is Charles Bingley, Will's friend and colleague. He was on his way to the city, but Will asked him to detour here this morning."

Charles stood and offered his hand, but there was no easy smile or polite banter. He just blinked. Maddy sucked her lips in, and Elizabeth snorted softly. *Men and Jane. Some things never change.*

Jane shook Charles's hand and said hello, smiling at him warmly before turning to her sister. "I want to hear the story, and it better be fast. I've got thirty minutes left, and it takes twenty to get back." Maddy rose to press a sandwich in Jane's hand, and then the eldest Bennet sister found a place to sit while she ate.

Elizabeth quietly cleared her throat, trying not to laugh at Charles who was only now realizing he ought to reclaim his seat. She was suddenly overwhelmed with an intense gratitude that Will seemed to prefer her. *He's never been anything more than polite to Jane.* She clasped his hand where it was resting on her leg, and launched into her story, leaving out the worst parts but describing in detail how she'd hidden her face, how the white, tucked-up diapers had hit the photographers, how they were still begging her for a photo as she ducked inside. She added the part about them being ordered around and the soaking Lopez had given them.

By the time she got to the end, Ed was nearly rocking out of his chair with silent laughter. "No matter how often I picture it," he crowed, "it just keeps getting funnier." Maddy rolled her eyes at him.

Jane nodded vigorously, her blonde ponytail springing up and down. "Excellent, Lizzy. I know everyone needs to earn a living, but chasing you like that was wrong. They completely deserved it."

Elizabeth shot a look at Charles, who was grinning at Jane. She felt Will's hand tighten around hers as the others laughed. He wasn't laughing, just smiling a little, and she instinctively knew he'd want to hear the story again when they were alone. *It's not normal to know someone as well as this after a month. We've only been on one real date. It can't be normal*, she thought, a whirl of anxiety beginning in her stomach. She took a deep breath and, for the first time, smelled herself. She was still in her sweats and badly needed a shower.

"I should probably go home," she said, releasing Will's hand and preparing to stand.

The room burst into sound so suddenly that it startled her. Even Charles was shaking his head. She stiffened, and Will drew her hand back. "It's okay," he assured her. "It's just that there may be more of them staking out your apartment. Let me send someone to get your clothes, and you can shower here."

Elizabeth shook her head. "The girls will be home from school in a couple of hours, and I don't want them putting this mess out on social media. They've got accounts on sites even I've never heard of. Besides, I need my computers, my equipment."

Uncle Ed scowled, but nodded at Will.

"Why don't you just come back to the city with me?" Will asked her softly. "You can use Georgiana's clothes until we can send someone for your things, and you know there's plenty of room." She heard the laughter in his voice. "You can even sit out on the terrace." He leaned over as though he was relating some great secret to her. "Should I tell your uncle you'll have your own room?"

"Let him sweat a bit," she grinned. "He deserves it after laughing at me."

"He's just proud of you," said Will. Elizabeth knew he was just trying to be fair—she suspected Uncle Ed had gotten on *his* nerves too. When she didn't reply immediately, he added, in a more serious voice, "I'm used to this sort of thing, so my security is quite thorough. I really think you're better off there for now."

Charles walked them out. He waited while Will handed Elizabeth into the car and then pulled him aside.

"Will I see you at the office in the morning?" he asked. "If you're taking a few weeks, I need a complete update on what's happening, and I still need to debrief you on the final leg of the trip."

"I'll be there," Will replied. Charles nodded but did not move to his own car. Instead, he pursed his lips and sighed.

Will glared at him. "What?"

"Sorry," Charles said, shaking his head. "I've just never seen you act this way. Are you sure . . .?"

Will crossed his arms across his chest. "You've never seen me hold a woman's hand?"

Charles ran a hand through his hair. "Not in front of her family. Did you see the grin on Maddy Gardiner's face?" He lifted both eyebrows. "I leave for six weeks, and when I get back, you're acting like you're me. Frankly, it's more than a little disconcerting."

Will frowned, annoyed, but then considered what Charles had said. "Stop right there," he said with a disbelieving laugh. "You're worried because I'm acting too much like *you*?" He linked his hands behind his neck and stretched his back. "That's rich. Do I get to take a six-week business trip to South America if I experience a sudden romantic breakdown and need to quickly leave the country?"

Charles blushed. "Will, I'm just saying she's gotten serious really fast—maybe too fast?"

"She's gotten too serious? No," Will replied firmly. "We're not having this conversation in the middle of the street." He glanced at the car and saw Elizabeth watching them closely. "In fact, we're not having this conversation at all. If I need your advice, I'll ask for it."

"You always give me advice," Charles pointed out.

Will pinched the bridge of his nose. "That's because you ask for it, Charles. And I've stopped giving you advice on your personal life because you never listen anyway." The last time, he had told Charles his latest angel was after his money; it was the predictable end of that relationship that had sent Charles to the other side of the world.

"Okay, Will," he said, acquiescing with a shrug. "I'll see you in the morning."

"Don't be late," Will growled. He turned without another word, opened the driver's door, and dropped himself into the seat.

"Mr. Bingley does not approve of me, I'm guessing?" Elizabeth asked archly as he reached for his seatbelt.

"Mr. Bingley has nothing to say about my private life," Will snapped, "and he can damn well keep his hypocritical insinuations to himself."

"Okay, then," Elizabeth responded with a grimace, "got it in one. Let me guess, I'm after your money? I want my picture in the paper?"

His lips pressed together and he stared out through the windshield. She put her hand on Will's arm. "Worse than that?"

He didn't answer.

"Aw, relax, cowboy," she told him in a gentle voice, "I doubt he said anything more than I said myself that night on the terrace." She paused. "Was that only the night before last?" She tipped her head to the side. "It feels so long ago now."

Will was still working himself up. "He questions *me* when his love life is . . . Begged me for a way out of the city," he grumbled. "*Begged* me." His hands were gripping the wheel of the car so hard his knuckles were white. "Insinuations against you. Last thing I needed today."

Elizabeth leaned over and elbowed him softly in the ribs. "You're already forgetting our mantra," she complained.

Will sighed a little and carefully elbowed her back. "Mantra?" he asked.

"I believe we established it last night. Starts with an 's' and ends with a 'them'?"

He laughed a bit at that, then started the car and pulled out onto the road. "Let's just go home. I can spike his coffee with Tabasco in the morning."

Elizabeth smiled widely. "Well played, Will. I'll drag you over to the dark side yet."

Will saw her rub her ear against her shoulder as he was checking his rearview mirror. "You okay?" he asked.

"Just a bit of a headache," she sighed. "I'll take something for it when we get to your place."

A few minutes into the trip, Elizabeth reclined the seat a bit and closed her eyes. He drove all the way back to the city, into the garage, and parked the car without her waking.

Will watched her sleep for a moment, then pulled out his phone to make some calls. After the final one, he checked his watch. *She's a deep sleeper*, he thought, watching her until she began to mumble and become agitated. He touched her arm and her eyelids fluttered open.

"I made three calls while you were sleeping," he informed her, "but

I think we should probably go inside at some point." He touched her cheek. "There's more room in there. And a bed if you're still tired."

She looked around. "Thanks," she said, pushing her door open.

In a few minutes, they'd made it through the lobby and the elevator and back into Will's stunning apartment. She punched the button for the lift, mostly to reassure herself that there was at least one thing in this house that wasn't perfect, though the grinding gears made her headache a little worse. She stepped out into the hall and wandered into the bathroom. Fortunately, there was a new bottle of acetaminophen in the medicine cabinet. She shook out three tablets and swallowed them with water. *The sleep helped. Maybe I can stop it before it gets too bad. It'd be a shame to waste my time here alone in a dark room.* She stared at herself in the glass. *It's a good thing Will likes me. I look like I did after the first day of boot.* She grimaced. *Or maybe the last day.*

She sighed. "Stand down, Bennet," she said to the mirror. "Just take your shower."

Will was making notes on his tablet when Elizabeth reappeared in a long white skirt and black cropped top, her long hair loose and damp. He couldn't help but stare at the strip of skin showing between the bottom of her shirt and the top of the skirt. He thought he might be able to see her belly button.

She shrugged uncomfortably. "The only things that really fit," she said by way of explanation. She looked around the room.

"Sorry," Will said sympathetically, "your stuff won't be here for a while, but I threw your sweats in the washer." He tossed the file he was holding onto a smaller stack and held out an arm. "Thanks for not arguing too much about the bivouac."

She snorted. "Right, because this is *just* like pitching a tent." She took his hand, and he guided her to his lap.

He laughed lightly, close to her ear. "I've always thought so."

"I *am* a little confused as to why you are working on paper files." She raised her eyebrow. "Between that and your watch, it's like time travel."

"Some clients don't want their things online," he explained with a smirk. He pulled her in a little closer.

"I thought you had to work," she said teasingly.

"Do you not *like* this location?" he asked, kissing the nape of her neck.

Elizabeth shivered.

"Are you cold?" he murmured, pressing his lips to a spot behind her ear. She felt herself melting into his body, her head thrown back as she rested against his shoulder.

"Mmm," he said softly, trailing kisses along the exposed skin of her throat, lightly tracing her jawline with the pad of his thumb.

He stopped there and pressed a kiss on her forehead. "Do you want to nap a little more?" he asked. "You can lay here and sleep while I work."

"I think I'm okay," she assured him, "but I can just stretch out and relax. I can go over some programming in my head until my computers get here."

"What kind of programming?" Will asked, curious.

Elizabeth folded her arms behind her head and laid back on the couch, her arms and head propped up on a pillow, her legs still draped over Will's lap. "You know, going line by line to find infiltrations is spectacularly inefficient. There's artificial intelligence being developed that can determine the normal workings unique to a specific network and then pinpoint any deviations. It's all about devising the algorithms in such a way that the AI doesn't miss anything."

Will looked incredulous. "You're developing a program like that?"

Elizabeth looked at him fondly. "Sort of, but it's not all that fancy. I wrote a program to help me locate vulnerabilities more quickly, but it belongs to the Marines." She glowered. "Actually, my commanding officer took credit for it. But I wrote it, and I know it's not perfect. I'm working on a better version to use in my own work now."

Will shook his head. "Wow," was all he could say, and then, "You need funding for that?"

She laughed. "Right," she replied. "Because there's absolutely no conflict of interest there." How purple would Charles's face turn if Will informed him about such an investment? She wasn't sure, but her speculations were highly entertaining.

He took a deep breath. "You really are a marvel, you know?"

"Like the comics?" she shot back merrily, trying the change the subject. Her eyes sought out the ceiling as she rambled on, "I could have a costume with AI on the front in red—oh, wait, maybe too close to the scarlet letter? Or does anyone even read Nathaniel Hawthorne anymore?"

Will didn't reply. He just continued to stare at her, but the gaze suddenly softened. "Elizabeth," he said quietly, "you really scared me today."

Elizabeth didn't know how to respond to the sudden change in topic. Ultimately, she decided on an apology. "I'm sorry, Will. If I'd just waited and listened to all my messages before I went out for my run, none of this would have happened." His expression was still pinched, so she sat up. "This can't be just about a couple of photographers following me."

He rubbed the back of his head roughly. "It's just . . . Things happen, Elizabeth, but I would appreciate it if you called me after. Even texted me. Just let me know you're all right before you go off the grid, okay?"

She nodded. "I promise. You too, right?"

He nodded. "I'm sorry to bring it up," he said apologetically. "I mean, we've not been going out that long and I don't want to sound possessive. It's not about that." He took her hand. "You didn't do it to worry me and you were dealing with the situation." He met her gaze. "It's just that my parents went out one night and never came back, and it's, you know, it's still a problem for me."

"Oh Will," Elizabeth whispered guiltily. "I should have thought . . ."

He shook his head at her. "It's a problem for me when I can't find the people I love," he continued. "I'm better than I was, but I still worry, and you were out of touch for hours."

Elizabeth let the word "love" pass. He cared for her, she knew, but he didn't seem aware he'd used that word, and it wasn't a good time to press the point. "I promise not to do it again, Will. I had no idea anyone was aware I was even out there." She pressed his hand. "Other than Lopez, of course."

"By the way," Will said softly, "I owe that entire VFW membership a steak dinner. And Lopez gets a case of beer if he wants it. Scotch, whatever."

She chuckled and kissed his cheek. "You'll be the most popular man at Post 711."

CHAPTER TWENTY

The light was beginning to fade as Elizabeth opened her eyes. She silently watched Will sleep. His face, bathed in weakening sunlight, was unguarded, almost boyish in its repose. It made her wonder what he'd been like as a child. Had he always been so solemn, she wondered, or was that a result of his parents' accident? Had he always been wound so tight, or was that due to the heavy expectations he must have faced from his family? It was difficult, at times, to think of Will as ever having been young.

She propped herself up on one elbow. He was lying atop the covers on his side, his long legs bent, one hand under his cheek. She'd wanted to sleep a bit more, uncharacteristically exhausted from the day's events. Will had accompanied her downstairs, and they'd been talking when she fell asleep. He must have dozed off not long after. She smiled at the shadow on his jawline, his carefully trimmed but now entirely mussed dark hair, how his lips were slightly parted, the way he took two soft breaths and then paused before taking another. She wriggled her bare toes against the soft white sheets and lowered her head to curl into his chest. When he threw an arm over her and pulled her close, she sighed contentedly.

"Elizabeth," came a deep, sleepy voice, "are you awake?"

"Mmm hmm," she replied lazily, pulling her head back to meet his gaze.

There was a short silence while he looked at her and rubbed her back under the cropped t-shirt. Then his stare intensified, and he said, in a quiet voice, "If you don't want to talk about what happened with the photographers, I'll understand, but I think you might have left something out of your story."

Elizabeth closed her eyes. If she'd just told him that she didn't want to talk about it, he'd accept it. *But he won't forget. He'll just wait until I'm ready.*

She swallowed hard and then spoke. "I wasn't thinking cameras." Elizabeth glanced away from Will, replying softly. He bent closer to hear her. "When they stopped and reached . . . I thought they had weapons. I was absolutely sure of it."

Will's arms tightened around her. "No wonder you reacted the way you did."

"What does that mean?" Elizabeth asked defensively. "I didn't overreact. They deserved what they got." She struggled to sit up.

Will released her and let her settle before he sat up next to her. "Of course they did," he said soothingly. "I meant your reaction afterwards. Your uncle told me you sat in the VFW for nearly two hours before calling him."

She could hear the worry in his voice. She pulled her knees up to her chest and rested her arms on them. "It's hard to get out of your system, you know?" she replied flatly, laying her forehead on her arms. "De Roos wasn't so long ago. It'll pass." *It will.*

Will stroked her hair. "I know I can't really understand what you're going through, but sometimes it can help to just talk. If you ever need someone to listen, I'm here."

Elizabeth leaned into his hand, his touch easing her tension. *Could he be any sweeter?* "Thanks." Her stomach rumbled, a very loud sound in an otherwise quiet room.

Will chuckled. "When did you eat last?"

"Umm," she said, brows pinching together as she thought about her day. "Breakfast," she concluded sheepishly.

"Didn't you eat at your aunt's?" he asked before he recalled he hadn't seen her take any food.

She shook her head.

"No wonder your stomach sounds like a leviathan," he said jokingly. "For pity's sake, Elizabeth, you're one of the smartest women I know—you should be able to remember to eat." He kissed the top of her head.

"Leviathan?" she snorted, nearly humming with the pleasure of such a casually loving gesture. "Have you had many opportunities for comparison?"

He laughed. "My sister loved dragons until very recently," he replied. He paused for a moment, and his forehead furrowed. "In fact, she might still, but doesn't want me to make fun of her." He swung his feet over the side of the bed.

Elizabeth smiled. "My sister loves them, too, but a leviathan is a sea creature, not a dragon."

"Oh yeah?" Will asked, opening the second drawer on his dresser. "You think there can't be sea dragons?"

Elizabeth laughed. "I concede the point."

"Which sister?" he asked while he rummaged through some clothes.

"Mary," she replied, thinking about her shyest sister. Mary had read *How to Train Your Dragon* when she was around eight and had become enthralled with dragons of all kinds, toting home stacks of books from the library, drawing them, dreaming about them, playing elaborate games in the woods near the house where she designed an entire dragon kingdom, complete with rudimentary social rules, class systems, and languages. She'd even asked Elizabeth to help her build a lair. No dragons had lived in it, but Mary had spent a lot of time there when the weather was good.

She'd sent Mary to bed one night and turned to the dishes when she heard her mother yelling. Upstairs, she found Fanny towering over Mary, berating her for "being a baby." Everyone knew that dragons didn't exist, she'd barked, and Mary had better get used to living in the real world. For every point she made, Fanny gave Mary's braid a sharp tug. Elizabeth reached them near the end of the tirade, quickly removing her sister's hair from her mother's hand and earning herself a sharp slap to the back of her head. When their mother had at last stormed away, Mary blinked twice, then silently followed Elizabeth to Jane's room, her dark eyes wide with fright behind her thick glasses, one hand in her sister's, the other clutching her green and purple stuffed dragon to her chest.

Jane was scribbling in a notebook with her earbuds in and her chemistry book open on the desk in front of her. She'd taken one look at their faces before she tossed her pencil down and turned off the music.

The three had cuddled in bed together, whispering sisterly secrets until Mary had asked, in a small, tremulous voice, "Are dragons *really* for babies?"

"Dragons are for everyone," Jane had assured her.

"I *love* dragons," Elizabeth had declared.

Jane had begun to spin a fairy tale about a blue dragon, and when she finished, Elizabeth took over. They wove story after story of kind dragons and smart dragons and evil dragons and a knight named Mary who, through acts of selfless bravery and deft dragon-handling, had saved everyone in town. "And that is why," Jane had concluded, in the wee hours of the morning, "we live in MARY-ton."

Mary had giggled and dropped off to sleep.

Elizabeth had fallen asleep shortly after, the sound of Jane's quiet crying into her pillow unable to keep her awake. She had long ago learned not to bother crying about anything her mother said or did. There was no point. Instead, she threw her arms over both Mary and Jane as if that could magically protect them. When Elizabeth woke again sometime before dawn, Jane was back at work, her task lamp lowered over her textbook, her eyes bloodshot, her pencil moving relentlessly across the paper.

Elizabeth was jolted from her reverie by the sound of a drawer being opened and closed. Will was getting dressed. He pulled out a sweater and stuck his arms in before flipping the rest of it over his head.

He caught her steady gaze and stepped back to the bed. "I'll heat up some dinner while you get dressed," he said, placing a chaste kiss on her lips. "Come on up when you're ready."

Elizabeth reached out to grab her toes, slowly stretching her back out. Her phone buzzed and vibrated on the side table, and she rolled over to grab it.

Princess?

She groaned. Abby. *Not my fault.*

Had a one-off job for you but the guy doesn't want to work with royalty.

Funny. This princess thing *was* annoying, but if someone wouldn't hire her over it, he was crazy. She knew she was good.

Serious. This is not good for your image.

Elizabeth could just see Abby saying this with that expression that always made her feel a little stupid. *What do you want me to do?* she typed. She couldn't control the newspapers, after all, and she wasn't going to stay cooped up in Will's apartment forever.

You know you can always work for us. The boys are good with it. Let things cool down a bit, make some real money.

She sighed. Abby was working as a civilian contractor for the military. It required a lot of last-minute travel and wasn't always conducted in safe locations, but the pay was incredible. However, she'd made up her mind. Whereas Abby left the Marines so she could make more money, Elizabeth had left because it was time she returned home. Now there was Will to think about, too.

Elizabeth hadn't even really wanted to apply to officer training, but she'd thought she ought to do so, given all the time and money the Marines had invested in her education. When her request was summarily denied by Captain Carter, she'd been annoyed, but also relieved. When he'd passed off her software as his own, she'd been angry. Cool in the face of her indignation, he'd transferred her. It had all made the decision to separate easier. Yet here Abby was, trying to draw her back in.

She rubbed her ear. *No, thanks. I'm good here.*

The offer stands. Just get rid of the tiara or it'll be tough to get you gigs.
I'll do my best. She pulled out a glass and filled it with water.
You always do.

Will arrived at work early, but he knew Wanda would still beat him, so he wasn't surprised to hear her voice as he walked up the empty hall to his office. What did surprise him was hearing Charles's. He could hear everything being said in the outer office, but he was still too far away to be seen. Something—he couldn't say what—made him stop and listen.

"Welcome back, Mr. Bingley," Wanda said pleasantly. "How was your trip?"

"Productive," Charles replied warmly. "In the end, I met with fourteen potential clients. I think there are three projects we'll want to be involved in, and another that's a possibility."

"Good news, then," Wanda said breezily. "Do you have a meeting with the boss this morning?"

He thought Charles probably grinned at that. "In other words," his friend said, "I'm in the way?"

"Not you, sir, never," Wanda replied blandly. Will frowned. Wanda generally wasn't rude, but that had sounded almost insolent. He picked up his bag.

"I was a little surprised to learn that Will has a girlfriend," Charles said, and Will put his bag back down.

"I wouldn't know anything about that, Mr. Bingley," Wanda replied. "Mr. Darcy doesn't discuss his private life with me."

"So that's a yes," Charles responded. "Do you know her?"

Wanda sighed. Will could imagine her removing her reading glasses from their perch on the end of her nose. She only did that when she was irritated with him about something, and she seemed to be displeased with Charles. He wished he could see them, but if he moved any closer, they'd spy him right away.

"Mr. Bingley," Wanda said in a long-suffering tone, "forgive me for not entertaining you, but I have work to do. Over the past six weeks, I've wasted a good deal of time explaining to your sister that you were not in the country and that no, Mr. Darcy would not like to speak with her in your stead."

Will hadn't known that. He'd have to buy Wanda some flowers.

"Now that you are back from walkabout," she continued, and Will grinned at the gibe, "Mr. Darcy is going on his first vacation in five years, and he has given me exactly thirty hours' warning." She cleared her throat. "I suggest that if you have questions about his personal life, you pose them to him when you meet."

Forget the flowers. The woman was going to get a big holiday bonus and a raise.

There was silence for a moment, but Will waited it out. As he had suspected, Wanda was processing what Charles had told her, but she had more to say.

"You *did* ask him, didn't you? And he wouldn't tell you?"

Will nodded. He had refused to discuss it. It wasn't any of Charles's business.

"I'm worried about him, Wanda," Charles said. He sounded genuine, but Will chafed at the notion that he required a keeper. "Don't you think he's getting serious too quickly?"

Unbelievable, Will thought. He tried to school his expression as he leaned down to collect his briefcase again. He clutched the handle so tightly his knuckles were white. Before he could charge into the office, he heard Wanda huff indignantly.

"You think the *boss* is getting serious too quickly?" she cried. "Out. Get out. I'll call you when he's ready for your meeting." There was a scuffing sound. "And take your ridiculous bribe with you."

Bribe?

When Charles rounded the corner out of the office, he was carrying two cups of coffee. Will snorted. Wanda didn't even drink coffee. Green tea was her drink. It made him grimace even thinking about it.

"Morning, Charles," he said agreeably, as though he'd just arrived. "Meeting this morning?"

He was gratified that Charles seemed embarrassed.

"Yes," Bingley stated firmly, and held out one hand. "Coffee?"

Wanda's polished nails were clicking against the keyboard at a punishing rate when Will stepped in.

"Good morning, Wanda," he greeted her.

Her head flew up. "Good morning, boss," she replied with a smile. She indicated the desk. "I'm almost ready for your flight from responsibility."

He grinned at her, suddenly feeling like a schoolboy on the brink of summer break, and her eyebrows lifted in surprise.

"You're the one who pushed me to have some fun, Wanda," he teased her. "You can't complain now that I've taken your advice."

She stared at him. "Holy frijoles, boss, turn down the wattage on that smile. The facial recognition photo won't match, and you'll put security into a panic."

He smirked.

"Mr. Bingley was in here earlier to ask about Ms. Bennet," she said.

"Was he?" Will asked as though he were curious.

Wanda's expression soured. "I chased him out. Just wanted to give you a heads up in case he mentions it later."

She really was worth every penny. Will shook his head and moved past her desk to his office. He dropped his briefcase on his desk and settled in. Without being told, Wanda knew when he was ready for her, and she entered his office to brief him about his schedule for the day. He'd had her do that ever since he'd disastrously insulted Elizabeth. He made mistakes, lots of them—but he hoped never to make the same one twice.

"You know," Wanda said when they were wrapping up, "you wouldn't have been half as interested in Ms. Bennet if she hadn't called you on your behavior. You need a woman who won't let you have your way all the time."

He scratched the back of his head. *She knows me a little too well, I think*. "Thank you for the insight into my character, Ms. Soames," he said, shaking his head. "I think I have it handled."

Wanda laughed gaily. "Oh yeah, boss. You've got her handled. I'm sure you're right."

He just shook his head at her while she wagged her eyebrows at him. Then she stopped, serious again. "You've done yeoman's work, Mr. Darcy," she told him. "You've taken care of your sister, your business, your father's business, your cousins' money, your employees—you've even taken care of Mr. Bingley's difficulties." She gazed at him approvingly, and he felt the tips of his ears growing warm. He always flushed there first. "It's your turn."

Will met Charles with a cool gaze.

"Morning again, Will," Charles said cheerfully, as he entered Darcy's office. "I have some great prospects to discuss."

"No more attempts to gain information about Elizabeth?" Will asked coldly.

Charles grimaced and cast him a penitent look. "Nope. I confess I sent her information to our regular sources this morning, but a quick search online didn't turn anything up. I'm here to apologize and say that I hope this works out, Will. And I'll never try to wheedle information out of Wanda Soames again. I'm hopelessly outclassed." He shrugged.

"What do you mean, you sent her information to our regular sources?" Will asked, incredulous. "Who asked you to do that?"

Charles raised his eyebrows. "I didn't think I needed permission. It's SOP, isn't it?"

"Charles," Will said with a sigh, "it's only SOP when the person you're dating works for a competitor. You know, like all of *your* girlfriends." He felt a headache coming on.

His words were greeted with skepticism. "Well, you know what the board would say, and it's against my better judgment, but I can call them back and cancel." Charles leveled a cool gaze at Will.

Will stared at him for a moment, then shook his head. "I'll take care of it."

There was a moment of silence. "Presentation?" Charles asked.

Will nodded. "Presentation."

They spent most of the morning discussing possibilities, further research, and next steps before digging into the duties Charles would be handling while Will was away.

"You can call me each morning if you want to check in," Will said finally, but Charles shook his head.

"I will call you if there's a need," he replied. "I know you're good about answering your cell, and I can handle what's here." He clapped Will on the shoulder. "Just enjoy yourself." He stretched his arms out wide, shaking out his muscles after sitting in one posture for so long. "Any plans?"

Will stared at Charles across the desk. He was unsure why Charles didn't see how far over the line he had crossed. "Yes."

Charles laughed, then asked, "Are they secret?"

Will shrugged. "Whatever she wants to do. Those are my plans."

"She's a fortunate woman, Will." Suddenly, Charles grinned, rubbing his hands together and sitting on the corner of Will's desk. "Now, tell me about her sister."

CHAPTER TWENTY-ONE

"Wait, what?" Elizabeth asked, suddenly on alert. She listened intently.

She and Will were getting ready to return to the city after spending the day together in Montclair. They'd headed downtown and toured the shops, stepping into Nest and Company, the antique store where the Gardiners had found many of the Craftsman items for the house, before going for a stroll in Edgemont Park and walking around the art museum. She'd shown him how she sent music to her sisters' various accounts on their birthdays, even when she was far away, and added a few songs to his. "They're all girl singers," he'd teased her. *Pop. Not my thing, but okay.*

Will had thoroughly enjoyed himself, though truthfully, he didn't much care what they did. What he would remember from the day was watching Elizabeth's cheeks turn ruddy with the cold, rubbing her hands in his to warm them up, her eyes lighting up as he stole a kiss, the feel of her body leaning into his as he put his arm around her shoulder. She'd suggested that they spend the evening compiling a list of the things they wanted to do in the city over the rest of his days off and then work up a schedule. She suspected that her jobs would slow over the holidays, though her full-time clients would still pay her retainer. "Not that we won't stop and do something else if we feel like it," she'd added, and he'd just nodded.

"Do you know who did it?" Elizabeth asked, drawing Will's attention to her phone conversation. "Who? Are you sure it wasn't . . . okay, okay."

It was Jane on the other end, which was odd enough in itself because she was supposed to be at work. He had figured she must be on her break. Elizabeth's lips flattened and her eyes narrowed.

He signaled for the check.

They had just been finishing dinner at a restaurant called Escape, because when Elizabeth spied the sign, she couldn't resist. "Serendipity," she'd stated, and asked him to park the car. Will thought fondly of her clucking at the prices on the menu, but he hadn't had to convince her to order what she wanted. *It's progress.*

"Really?" Elizabeth said disbelievingly into the phone. She paused, the teasing glint that nearly always visible in her eyes transforming into something hard. "Okay, ask him to stick around. We'll be there shortly." She hit a button and immediately made another call.

"Char?" she asked, her voice clipped and professional. "Is your dad around?" She stood, motioning to Will that she was going to step outside. He nodded, certain that his evening had just become more complicated. When he signed the check and left a tip a few minutes later, he stepped outside to see Elizabeth shoving her phone in her pocket. She glanced up at him and gave him a steely glare that made him very glad that he was on her side, whatever this was.

"We need to make a stop at the hospital on our way back," she said in an eerily calm voice.

"I feel responsible for this," Elizabeth said, shaking her head as they got into the car.

"I don't think I can comment until I know what's happening," Will replied.

Elizabeth shot him an exasperated glance. "You remember when you and Charlotte made me leave Jane's car at the soccer park?"

Will didn't see what that had to do with anything. "Yes?"

"Well, Charlotte returned it just late enough for Jane to think she didn't have a ride home." Elizabeth was positively glowering, so he kept his reply brief.

"Okay . . ."

"That gave this guy Stanley the opening to offer Jane a ride home. She declined, and apparently my sister hasn't wanted to tell anyone that he's been relentless ever since."

Now Will was frowning. "Why doesn't she report him?"

Elizabeth huffed. "You know as well as I do, Will, that there are ways to harass someone without appearing to break any of the rules. Tonight, he asked her out again and nearly called her a . . ." Elizabeth grunted in frustration. "I'm not allowed to say it, but it starts with the letter b. Still, she cut him off before he got there, so there's nothing to take to Human Resources."

Will rolled his eyes. *Great. Another shining example of manhood for the rest of us to live down.* "And he thought that would be the best way to get a woman to go out with him?"

Elizabeth shook her head. "Apparently he thinks she's just playing hard to get."

"Was that it?" he asked, knowing there had to be more but not sure he wanted to know the answer. "I'm not minimizing it," he assured her quickly. "I just figured there's something specific that's sending you on this mission."

"Her lunch was missing, so she looked in the garbage, and sure enough, someone had dumped it and her containers into the trash." She frowned. "She thinks it was Stanley. I don't like that this is escalating. It's time he felt some push back."

Will thought maybe he'd have a few words with the man—or what was left of him—after Elizabeth was through. "Do you want to pick up something for Jane to eat?"

Elizabeth raised an eyebrow. "No. She's already eaten."

"How?"

She looked out the window. "Charles was there, though Jane didn't say she'd expected him. He'd brought them dinner."

Over the rest of the short ride, Elizabeth explained that Dr. Lucas had told her she should remove the refrigerator from the staff lounge, and Charlotte, furious at the slight to Jane, had said she'd meet them there with appliance sliders. Elizabeth told him that he and Charles would be on moving detail. Evidently, she had something else to do.

Will glanced at Elizabeth a few times as she gave him directions. There were no jokes now, no teasing, not even an explanation of her plan. She was no longer relaxed or mischievous. Instead, she was focused on her plan, almost to the exclusion of anything else, her eyes staring straight ahead, her body tensed, almost . . . coiled to spring. *This is the Marine in her*, he thought, impressed.

Charlotte was holding four brown plastic disks when she met them at the door to the staff room. Charles held up a hand in greeting as Will entered, and they quickly rocked the refrigerator first one way and then the other while Char slipped the sliders under each foot. Then Charles walked backward, steering, while Will pushed. With two men and the sliders, it wasn't a difficult job.

Char opened the door to her father's office to reveal Elizabeth already sitting at the computer.

"I think it'll fit in the corner here," Charlotte said, pointing, as Will and Charles guided it over the small threshold and shoved it against the far wall.

"Do you have it, Char?" Elizabeth asked, her eyes gleaming with a wicked fire. Charles looked at Will, who shrugged.

"I do," Charlotte said with a smile. "It's a bit rushed, but it'll do the job." She reached into a cardboard cylinder leaning against the desk and removed a rolled-up sheet.

Elizabeth didn't return the smile. "You ready to help me hang it?"

"I am. Do you have the video done now?"

"Yep. Thank your dad for getting permission to pull it." Charlotte nodded, and Elizabeth returned her attention to the computer. A sly smile began to creep across her face. She tapped something on the keyboard with a flourish, grabbed the sheet as Charlotte held it out to her, and disappeared into the hall. Will and Charles looked to Charlotte for an explanation. She shrugged.

"Dad was pissed. He's been warning the entire staff for close to a year to stop acting like they're in middle school, and he loves Jane. He even said she should file a harassment complaint, but I doubt she will. So he gave Lizzy permission."

"For . . .?" Will asked. Charles stood watching the entire proceeding with his arms across his chest and a crooked grin on his face. Whatever was happening, he seemed pleased to be a part of it.

"Oh, this you just have to see," Charlotte chirruped, following Elizabeth's quiet, determined steps out of the room. "She's in full-on protection mode. It took her thirty seconds to devise her evil plan of revenge, and Dad was happy to help. C'mon."

There was one doctor in the room, short and slight, hands in the pockets of his white coat, turning around in a tight circle as though the refrigerator might suddenly reappear if he looked hard enough. In the corner where the appliance had previously been located, Elizabeth was already standing on a chair and attaching one edge of the sheet to the wall as high up as she could reach. Charlotte moved over to help her get it straight.

"Will," called Elizabeth, "you're tall. Can you help us here?"

He held the other side up on the wall until it was secured.

"Ready?" Charlotte asked Elizabeth.

"Let it go," Elizabeth said, still business-like.

Charlotte released the sign. It unrolled rapidly, a piece of blotting paper floating away and onto the ground, and the women got to work securing the sides and bottom. Will heard Charlotte tell Elizabeth, "I'm glad it's not me this time."

Elizabeth grabbed a Sharpie from Charlotte's pocket and wrote out a web address in bright blue ink on the sheet.

The doctor who'd been in the room when they entered stopped his search to read the message and look something up on his phone. "Gibbons," he muttered. He turned to Charlotte. "Is there any way to get the food we had in there?"

"You just have to sign in at the desk," Charlotte explained, "then you can go into my father's office and get your stuff, but don't forget to sign out."

"What a pain," he said. He held up his phone, displaying a video. "Jane's food?"

"Yes," Elizabeth replied.

He nodded. "He's a spoiled brat," the resident said. "Tell Jane we're on her side." He exited.

Will watched him go, then stepped back to read the sign himself.

Charlotte stood back to admire her work for a moment. "It's amazing what a couple of fabric markers can do," she said, pleased.

Above the web address Elizabeth had added was an artistic rendering of one-foot high black and gold letters, reading:

THIS IS WHY WE CAN'T HAVE NICE THINGS.

Elizabeth wasn't finished yet. She stepped back, took a photo with her phone, typed a quick message, and sent it.

Will took her phone to examine the video. A man in a white coat held Jane's bento box upside down as her food fell into the trash can. Although it was upside down and a little fuzzy, BENNET was written in marker on the side of the container.

"Talk about caught red-handed," Charles said, looking over Will's shoulder. "How could he miss that thing?" He gestured to the camera positioned in the corner.

Jane ran into the room. "I told Dr. Heller I had to use the restroom," she panted. "He almost nailed me for the phone, but I told him I forgot about it after my break. What did you do?" She looked at the sign, checked her phone, and smiled. She did not laugh like Will, Charles, and Charlotte had, but she was clearly relieved. Elizabeth gave her the resident's message.

"I'm so glad you're home," Jane whispered, throwing her arms around Elizabeth's waist and leaning her head on Elizabeth's shoulder. Elizabeth stopped glowering as she pulled her sister in for a hug.

"I've got you, Janie," she said softly.

"I know," Jane said with a tiny sniffle, "and I have you." She kissed Elizabeth's cheek, and with a quick wave and a round of thanks to everyone, went running back to work.

"What did you text her?" Charlotte asked, holding out her hand. Elizabeth wordlessly handed her phone over.

"Give the enemy no quarter," she read aloud. She shook her head, handed the phone back, and shouldered her purse. "I'd have rushed over too, if I were Jane. She probably thought you were staging Waterloo in here."

Elizabeth's entire face lit up.

"Oh no," Will interrupted with a groan, moving to stand behind her and wrap his arms around her. "I see those cogs turning." Elizabeth turned her face up to gaze up at him through her lashes. "No," Will said with a chuckle. "I am impervious to your charms, and I am not bailing you out of jail. You've made your point. Let's go home."

Elizabeth moved her gaze to his arms. "Don't think I don't know this is more a restraining hold than a hug, Will," she said sourly.

"Trouble in paradise, Will?" Bingley asked. "There's always my sister." He grinned.

Will steered Elizabeth out of the room after tossing Charles a dirty look.

"Have a nice vacation," Charles called after him.

When they were finally back on the road, Will checked his mirrors and asked, "Are you feeling any better now?"

Elizabeth leaned back in her seat and cracked her window open just a bit. Taking a big breath of cold air, she nodded. "I'm feeling a tad less murder-y, yes."

"Murder-y?" Will asked carefully, trying to keep the laughter out of his voice. He didn't think Elizabeth would appreciate it at the moment.

"It's not funny, Will," Elizabeth ground out between clenched teeth.

Apparently, he hadn't hidden his amusement well enough.

"I wanted to strangle that man. *Jane*, of all people. Kindest, nicest . . . she was practically crying when she told me." Elizabeth rolled her shoulders and leaned forward, stretching her back. "I don't mind saying, though," she told him crisply, "that when Jane was telling me the story, I thought for a second it might be Charles who had dumped her food."

Will was all attention. "Charles? Why would you think that?"

"Gee, I don't know," Elizabeth replied sarcastically. "Her dinner winds up in the trash, and suddenly he's there as the hero with a replacement meal in hand."

"Ah." Will was silent for a moment. "Okay, I can see that makes a warped kind of logic. But while Charles isn't perfect, he's not a misogynist."

Elizabeth's shoulders lifted a bit. "Look, I know he doesn't like me —at least, he doesn't *want* to like me, but you say he's your friend, and I respect that. Just be glad I didn't condemn the guy without solid evidence," she replied. "Before the Marines, I would have. Believe it or not, you are dealing with the older and wiser version of Lizzy Bennet."

Will tapped his hands on the wheel. "Here's the thing," he explained, "Charles *likes* women—I mean, genuinely likes them. He wouldn't pull that kind of scam."

"He likes women," Elizabeth repeated slowly. "Just not me."

"He doesn't know you. Give him time." Will's eyes scanned the road ahead. "Charles's problem is that he likes women too *much*. He gets too serious too fast and then can't get out. He raises expectations he doesn't fulfill."

Elizabeth's face clouded over. "*We've* gotten serious very fast." She paused. "I mean, we *are* serious, right?"

"Yes, Elizabeth, we're serious." Will shook his head and gently insisted, "You know I'm not like Charles."

"No," she replied, somewhat mollified, fingering the hem of her sweater. "You are not."

Will shifted into a higher gear and changed lanes to get around a semi. "What did Dr. Lucas tell you when you asked permission to view the security film?"

A wicked grin formed on her face. "'Go to it,'" she said proudly.

He cast his mind back to review the whole event. "You really sprang into action there, marshalled your forces," he said admiringly. "It was . . . impressive."

Elizabeth turned her intense gaze on him. "I have always been the one who protected my sisters," she explained. "That extends to all my family. And you'd better get used to it, because that covers you and the major now, too."

"I doubt Richard will need your services," Will joked, "but Georgiana might."

She shrugged. "I don't know," she suggested waggishly, "he was a diplomat for a long time . . ." She wriggled in place. "When will I meet your sister?"

Will flipped on the turn indicator and turned to check traffic before changing lanes. "Thanksgiving, I hope. She said she'd make the trip because of Richard, even though she's coming back at Christmas, too."

Elizabeth grabbed her phone when she heard a text notification.

York CU looking for an eval of their website. Interested? They're looking at Jan.

The York Credit Union was local, but they were fairly large. It could be a good account and she might be able to score some recommendations.

Send the details. Thanks.

CHAPTER TWENTY-TWO

A few days later, Will entered his apartment to a pleasant aroma, like fresh bread and . . . fish? He dropped his keys in the bowl before heading for the kitchen. When he arrived, Elizabeth was walking in circles around the island muttering to herself and shaking a spatula for emphasis. Her hair was swept back into a ponytail that bobbed a little each time she took a step. He felt his lips stretch into a smile as he stood there. He was just about to announce that she couldn't have been much of a Marine if she still wasn't aware of his presence when she addressed him without breaking her stride.

"Stop laughing at me, Will," she all but snarled. "I'm counting."

"Counting what?" he asked, amused, but trying not to show it.

"Sheep," she shot back, irritated, then stopped, looked directly at him, and groaned. "Now you've messed me up," she complained. "I was nearly there."

"Why didn't you just set a timer?" he asked, leaning against the doorframe and loosening his tie as he watched her pace. He wasn't supposed to be working, but a client had insisted on speaking with him.

Elizabeth was wearing Mrs. Summers's hideous purple apron with a ragged hem over a green sweater and chinos, slim black boots with sturdy square heels on her feet. He noted that they were an expensive brand and not yet broken in.

"When I set a timer, I feel free to get involved in something else," she replied, running a forearm across her sweaty forehead. "And then I miss the alarm." She placed the spatula on a clean plate. "When I have to concentrate on numbers, I remember." She reached out and opened the oven, peering inside. "Yes!" she cried excitedly. "I think it's done."

She searched a few drawers before she found the oven mitts and moved to lift a casserole pan out of the oven. She set it down on the stovetop triumphantly.

"I did it!" she crowed, tossing her arms up in the air in an exaggerated victory dance. Will could see she was laughing at herself. "I actually made an incredibly easy dish and didn't burn it. We can eat in tonight!" She spun around, stopped, and directed a smile his way.

She had a loaf of warm French bread from the bakery down the block already sitting on the island. When she moved her casserole dish to set it down beside everything else, he saw that it was salmon with some sort of mustard sauce. He smelled lemon and dill, too. It looked and smelled wonderful.

"Did you make a vegetable?" he asked, looking around. She made a noise that might have been a curse had it not been strangled in her throat, and a little laugh escaped him.

"I knew I forgot something," she huffed. "I have salad stuff in the fridge. Go clean up and change while I make it."

He returned in khakis and a dark v-neck sweater. He moved to the wine refrigerator and was in the process of opening a bottle when he said, casually, "Charles wanted me to apologize again to you on his behalf."

"For what?" she asked absently, searching for plates. She removed two from the cabinet above the silverware and placed a piece of fish on each one.

"Do you not remember his asinine concerns about us?" he asked. "It's been less than a week."

She shrugged. "Honestly, I haven't really given him much thought.

Clearly, you are comfortable with me. As *you* trust me, I don't much care about Mr. Charles Bingley."

Will grimaced. *Perfect time to talk about an investigation, Darcy*, he thought. The cork came away from the bottle with a soft pop and he set it down while he drew out two wineglasses.

"Well, funny you should say that," he began with some trepidation. "I should have spoken with you sooner, but I wanted to speak with the advisory board first. I did that today."

"Why?" Elizabeth teased, turning to face him with her hands on her hips. "Do they think I'm engaged in some sort of corporate espionage?" She returned to tossing the salad with a bit too much abandon, though Will noted that, while it was a near thing, she did not lose any food to the floor.

"No, of course not," he said, shaking his head. Elizabeth lifted her head and met his gaze. He tried not to look guilty.

She laughed, slapping one hand on the counter. "They do, don't they? At least Charles does. That's hilarious."

Will shook his head again, stymied. "I can never predict your reactions to things, Elizabeth."

She grinned and set the salad out on the table. "I love these salad tongs," she said, turning them over in her hands. "What are they, teak?"

"I think so," replied Will, confused at her sudden change of subject. "Can we talk about Charles?"

Elizabeth sighed. "You caught me in the glow of victory, Will, and now you're ruining it." She cocked her head at him. "What does Charles want, some sort of background check?"

Will thought he might actually blush. "Um, a little more thorough. It doesn't usually happen this early, but Charles is nervous."

She grinned and waggled her eyebrows. "Do I scare him?"

Will chuckled. "No, I think my response to you scares him."

She sidled over to him and put her hands on his hips. "Oh yeah?"

He groaned. "I've already taken one cold shower today, Elizabeth. Please, be kind."

She laughed and released him. "Sooo," she said, drawing out the word and giving him a peculiar look, "how many women have warranted a background investigation in the last, say, three years?"

"Well . . ." Will scratched the back of his head as he considered that. "One. I dated other women, but only one made it past the 'arriving at a restaurant in separate cabs' stage."

Elizabeth rolled her eyes. "So you've not used a background investigation on anyone in the past three years?"

"My lawyers . . ."

Elizabeth held up one hand, palm out. "Stop. I don't care about your lawyers. When was that last report done?"

Will rolled his eyes up to the ceiling to think about it. "Maybe two years ago? Little less?"

She moved to the table and began dishing out the salmon. She pursed her lips. "How many of these investigations have you had to run for Charles?"

Will picked up the wine bottle and set it on the table. "Four."

Elizabeth's eyebrows rose into her hairline. "*Four?*" she responded with some surprise. "Four serious girlfriends in three years? Do they have an expiration date?"

Will winced. It had been about two and a half years, in truth. "They worked at competing businesses." *I suppose that is a lot. But it's Charles.*

Elizabeth spooned rice onto the plates, filled two salad bowls, and gestured for him to sit down. He took out a bread knife and cut several pieces before he took a chair.

"Here's the deal, Will," Elizabeth said, clearly annoyed that her meal was taking second place to their discussion. "I was a Marine for six years. My work by the end was largely to protect American and allied installations from cyber-attacks by finding vulnerabilities before the bad guys did. I also did some tracking of said bad-guys via online channels. I had to have security clearances for those things, including a certification from the NSA. I had to file forms in triplicate if I so much as wanted to change my underwear. A background check instigated by little Charlie Bingley doesn't worry me—I've got nothing to hide." She then leveled an icily intense glare at him. "But at the same time, he is not *entitled* to any information about me. When it comes back, I don't want Charles Bingley anywhere near that report. I don't trust him. It goes to you, and you only—you can inform the advisory board when it comes back clean, which of course it will." She dropped her gaze and her voice modulated. "When you have it, bring it to me and we can discuss anything you like. But this is for your eyes only."

Will let out a huge breath. *That was easier than I thought it would be.* "Agreed."

Her brows pinched together. "I should tell you now that there *are* things about my time in the service that I can never tell anyone. I'm sure Richard has the same problem, and I know Uncle Ed does. Nothing scary, no black ops." She laughed at the very thought of it. "Just sensitive information." She met his gaze steadily and he nodded his agreement. "Okay, then, investigate away."

She plopped herself down across the table from Will and reached for a slice of bread before asking abruptly, "Are you really a billionaire?"

Will was caught off guard. "Uh. . ."

She laughed softly at his shock. "I read it in the *Post* article. Not exactly a bastion of journalistic excellence, but *are* you?"

He tilted his head. "Well, it depends . . . it's more like I manage assets in that amount. It wouldn't be a billion if I actually tried to cash it all out—taxes would eat up at least half of it."

She hooted, her hand, holding a piece of bread, suspended in mid-air. "It depends," she said with a chuckle. "That's a good one." Then she took a bite, chewed thoughtfully, and swallowed before saying, "No wonder you need to check everyone out." She frowned and stared at him before adding, "I plan to be a millionaire in my own right before I hit thirty. Six years," she said firmly, "I have plenty of time."

"So you're twenty-four?" he asked, glad to change topics.

"Almost," she replied distractedly, "I turn twenty-four on November 22nd. Sagittarius, if you want to know. What about you?"

She was young, but he'd known that. "My sign is Aquarius," he said with a grin, "and I feel like I've just been transported back to the 1970s."

Elizabeth ignored him to pick apart her fish with her fork. "Look, it's flaky just like it's supposed to be!" she exclaimed, lifting a forkful to her mouth. She grinned as she chewed, and when she was finished, she held up her hand for a high-five. Will gave her a strange look but complied.

"This is *good*," she gloated. "One major step away from eggs, and it only needs to cook for fifteen minutes. Bennet scores!" She looked at him. "Seriously, it was frozen foods and eggs at my house for nearly a year before Aunt Maddy arrived. That's probably what stunted my sisters' growth."

"They aren't that short," Will said wryly.

"That's because I also bought the cheap milk with the growth hormones," she replied, eyes sparking with mirth.

Will gazed at her. She was truly finished with the conversation he had been dreading since Charles mentioned the report. He shook his head. "You never cease to amaze me, Elizabeth," he said, a small laugh at last breaking through, his mood improving substantially as he tucked into his food. *She's right*, he thought happily. *This is good.*

"I know," she said playfully, lifting one shoulder and smirking. "You're lucky to have me." She took another bite as he grabbed her free hand and held it tight.

"I am," Will said seriously, leaning over to place a kiss on her cheek.

"I cooked, you clean," Elizabeth said airily as she cleared the table and left the dishes next to the sink. "I'd put the leftovers away, but we ate it all," she continued with a self-satisfied smile.

Will shook his head, trying to hide his grin. It was difficult not to smile when Elizabeth was around. "You really are unreasonably smug about this."

"Smug, yes," she admitted, entirely unapologetic. "Unreasonably so? I think not."

He stood at the sink with the dish soap in his hand, and she approached from the back to throw her arms around him. "Have you ever washed dishes before?"

He rolled his eyes. "Yes, and I did my own laundry, cleaned my own room . . ."

She squeezed him tight and then released him. "So you aren't a poor little rich boy, waited on hand and foot?"

He snorted. "My father would never have allowed it. He didn't want me to grow up soft."

Elizabeth thought about that. "You're more like your mom, aren't you?"

Will turned his head so he could peer at her over his shoulder. "What do you mean?"

"Nothing, it's just that your dad seemed to want you to be more like him, and the way you talk about your mom—you know, a quiet captain of the ship—seems more like you." She jumped up on the counter as he washed and set the dishes in the stainless-steel dish rack. She hadn't made much of a mess, so cleaning up was easy.

"I suppose," Will replied. "I'm still like him. I'm competitive like he was, but Mom and I both liked building things up more than taking them apart and reassembling them."

"My father wasn't . . ." Her voice trailed off. Will waited patiently, hoping she'd pick up the thread of her thought. Eventually, she did. "My father was *not* the captain of the ship, and neither was my mother. We were. . ." She paused, seeming to search for the word. Then she tipped her head up to meet his gaze and finished her sentence. "Rudderless."

She wandered into the living room after that, and Will hurried to dry the dishes and put everything away. Elizabeth had discovered his sound system and was examining his collection when he joined her.

"You have a lot of old vinyl here," she said approvingly. "What's your favorite?"

He pulled out a few albums. "We even have some 78s from way back. I can't ever choose a favorite. Depends on my mood. Blues, jazz, rock."

She arched an eyebrow at him. "No opera?"

He grinned and reached over her head to the top shelf of records, plucking out a few and showing her. "I like opera, too, when I'm feeling melodramatic."

She laughed, and her green eyes sparkled up at him. "That happen often, does it?"

"I raised my sister through her teen years," he said, placing the records back in their place. The very reminder made him feel tired. "I'm very familiar with melodrama."

She nodded, still smiling. "I have *three* teenage sisters, so thank goodness for Aunt Maddy." She pulled an album out of the jazz section. "I don't think I've ever heard of this one," she said.

"Oh, that's Artie Shaw," he said approvingly. "Clarinet." He put it on the turntable and held out a hand to her. "Where or When" began to play. "Dance with me."

She took his hand, but her expression was doubtful. "I don't know how."

"It's not difficult," he assured her. "Just let me lead."

Letting Will lead was tougher than she'd thought it would be. She tried to wait a split second to figure out what he was doing and follow, but it took too long to direct her feet. He was laughing at her, but in a comfortable way.

"Here," he said at last, "let's try a waltz." He demonstrated as he counted. "One, two, three, one, two, three."

She stared at his feet and then up at him, dubious. "How did you learn to dance?"

"It was a required course in the Darcy household," he said. "We attended lots of formal events for my father's business and my mother's charity work. Everyone always expected me to dance with their daughters."

"Awww," she replied, trying to picture it in her mind while her feet seemed to move on their own. "Did you dress in a suit?"

He flushed a little and tightened his hold. "A tux."

"I bet a lot of those girls had a crush on you after." She was just moving in step with Will now, not paying attention at all.

He shook his head, "Sadly, no. I think most of them were just trying to protect their toes." He gave her a wink. "I had the same size feet then as I do now."

"Should I be worried?" she asked playfully as she took his hands again. They successfully moved through two more box steps and an underarm turn before she remembered they were dancing and moved in the wrong direction.

"Not if you let me *lead*," he said, his exasperated voice rumbling in his chest.

It was still gray outside when Will heard his bedroom door open and felt a tickling breath in his ear. He swatted at it and heard a chuckle as he turned on his side.

There was a gentle breeze in his ear again, and he swung harder this time. Another laugh finally made him open one eye a bit.

"Will, it's time to get up," he heard Elizabeth croon. "You want to go on our dirty date, right?"

"I thought we already had it," he said, his voice still husky with sleep. Their dancing had improved the night before, leading to what he considered a reasonable make-out session. He had been dreaming of what might come next. He hoped she was ready for more soon. He had fond hopes of being able to take a *hot* shower again.

"Nope. Get dressed, something you can really move in," she sang, then the sheets were tossed back.

"Nooo," he said, turning to reach for her. He reluctantly opened both eyes and pushed himself up, watching her make her way across the room.

"You know," she said, stopping to open a dresser drawer, "we have to resurface sometime. We can't just stay in your apartment for two weeks."

"It was only one day," he complained. "And why *can't* we stay here for the whole two weeks?"

She shook her head and threw a pair of shorts and some sweats at him. They hit him in the face.

"As wonderful as this apartment is, Will, there's a whole big world out there." She gave him a quick kiss on the lips. She was in running clothes. They fit her well, especially around her . . . He groaned, flipped on this stomach, and buried his face in the pillow.

"What's wrong with you?" she asked, perplexed, and then blushed. "Ah. I'll just step outside." He grabbed for her, but she was successful in dancing away. "You are very good for my ego, Will," she said with a smile.

"I may be good for your ego, but you are very hard on mine," he whined.

Elizabeth laughed at the unintentional pun. "I'll drive," she told him. "Put on your clothes."

"Why?" He grabbed his blanket back and burrowed under it, curling into a fetal position.

She sighed as she pulled her hair back into a tight bun. "Because you can't go outside in your boxers and a t-shirt?"

"Why do *you* need to drive?" he growled.

She grinned. "I'm driving your precious car because I know where we're going, and it's a surprise. Get up."

His mind was still foggy, but now certain other parts of him were awake. "I already am," he grumbled into his pillow.

Elizabeth harrumphed and left the room. Without her presence, Will was finally able to get himself under control. By the time she returned, he was plotting his revenge.

As they drove into the Camp Warwick parking lot, Will spied the banner that finally clued him in.

"The Warrior Dash Mud Run?" he asked drily. "*That's* your idea of a dirty date?"

Elizabeth laughed gaily as she whipped the car into a parking space. "This is *everyone's* idea of a dirty date, Will." She put the car in park and leaned over to place a chaste kiss on his lips. "You'll love it, I promise. Besides, it's for charity." Then she all but leapt from the car in eager anticipation.

"Okay," Will said, emerging from the car and folding his arms across his chest, "let's place a wager on the outcome."

Elizabeth arched a single eyebrow. "What kind of wager?" she demanded eagerly as she locked the car and closed her door.

"The winner is the one of us who crosses the finish line with the best time."

She considered that. "You're much faster than I am." She glanced over at the grounds. "But there *are* obstacles . . ."

"Hey, this is your race. I don't even know what to expect, since you didn't prepare me."

She shrugged and nodded. "Okay. What are the stakes?"

Will's expression grew cocky. "Whoever finishes second has to . . ." He leaned over and whispered in her ear. Her eyes grew wide and she pulled away, averting her eyes.

"Win-win, then," she replied, attempting to play it cool but thoroughly discomposed. Such efforts were fruitless in any case, as a deep red flush was rising to color her face and neck. Will grinned and waggled his eyebrows at her.

"Don't mess with the bull, baby," he said glibly, "or you'll get the horns."

CHAPTER TWENTY-THREE

As they walked towards the check-in to receive their numbers for the race, Will took Elizabeth's hand. She squeezed it, still too embarrassed to look him in the eye, and he wondered, not for the first time, how she could be so entirely confident and competent in every area of her life but be so shy about her body. She had told him she wasn't a virgin, but honestly, she might as well have been. He'd never been able to make a woman blush like this merely from a suggestion, and he found he rather liked it.

He smiled as he recalled him teaching her a few ballroom dances. She was athletic and had taken to them quickly, if not with ease. She may not have been the most accomplished dancer he'd ever partnered, but with Elizabeth in his arms, the dances just made sense. His mother had always said that being fond of dancing was a certain step towards falling in love, and he thought he finally understood what she'd meant. His feelings for Elizabeth were deep and powerful. They frightened him a little, to be honest. But he still wasn't sure she felt the same. If running in the mud would help her make up her mind in his favor, so be it.

Elizabeth handed him a bib with his number, and they moved to the holding area near the starting line. Their wave was the first and would begin in about thirty minutes, so Elizabeth started to stretch. He ought to stretch too, he thought, but it was difficult not to watch her raise her bottom in the air as she touched her toes. Instead, he tried to read over the map. It was a 5K course with twelve obstacles, several of which took them directly into the mud. He rubbed the back of his neck. The running was no problem, but some of these obstacles would absolutely slow him down. His height would be an advantage for a few, but he was a good fifty pounds heavier than Elizabeth, maybe a little more. That meant more trouble moving through the muck. He shrugged and jogged in place a bit before beginning his own stretches.

He was a little taken aback when Elizabeth grabbed his hand and led him into the group of runners massing at the start. He'd assumed she'd want to get a better starting position than him. As the horn sounded and the group began, he trotted to the first obstacle, the Fisherman's Catch, and realized he'd entirely mistaken the purpose of the race. While some of the competitors were serious about their time, most were not just rushing through and moving on; they were turning back to help other competitors. Some of them were running in defined teams, and it struck him as he was reaching for the rings at the first stop that Elizabeth had meant them to be running as a team, too.

He saw a blue blur to his right and then, out of the corner of his eye, Elizabeth was away, swinging from one ring to the next like a monkey, legs swinging to help her momentum. As much as he enjoyed watching the lean muscles in her arms tensing as she moved from one ring to the next, he'd laid down a wager, and now he had to make every effort to win. He grabbed the rings and began to swing, slowly gaining on her.

Having easily completed the first obstacle, he caught up and ran alongside Elizabeth for a moment before giving her a pat on the head and moving past, his long legs eating up the ground as he reached the next obstacle, a giant slide named Goliath. He scrambled up the wooden frame behind it, and as he reached the top, he glanced back to judge Elizabeth's position. She had paused about halfway up to call encouragement to a slighter woman just below her who seemed to be having trouble. He would have gone back down to assist, but there were swarms of competitors coming his way. He'd have to go down the slide just to get out of the way. He swung his legs over the top and dropped onto the slick plastic.

He jogged along a bit to the next obstacle, but Elizabeth was soon at his side.

'You caught up quick," he grunted.

"You have no idea, old man," she replied, blowing past him and diving into the Pipeline, a tube constructed of rope. Will groaned and dove in after her, but the enclosed space was tight, and while Elizabeth could bend and scamper through relatively quickly, he had more trouble. She was out the other side and running hard a good thirty seconds before he extricated himself.

By the time they arrived at the halfway point of the run, Will pulled even again on an obstacle called the Warrior Summit, launching himself up the incline with a rope and long strides. He cruised through the next five obstacles, including the trenches and the mud mounds, reaching back to help those behind him, accepting help from those in front. Every so often, he'd see Elizabeth approach an obstacle as he was finishing. As Will ran, he could feel the mud splattering his face and chest, caking on his shoes, hardening in his hair, and found himself happy that Elizabeth had dragged him out of bed. He was having a great time.

The final obstacle, the Warrior Roast, was a thin line of fire about a foot and a half high followed by a mud puddle at least twenty feet wide and thirty feet long. Just beyond it was the finish. Will cleared the flames easily enough but stopped to help when the runner in front of him slipped in the water and went flying. It took a little longer than he thought, as the runner had fallen hard, and by the time he was ready to turn and finish the race, Elizabeth was leaping over the Roast and heading straight past him. She reached out to tag him mockingly, but he was faster, sticking out one arm to catch her.

"Oh no you don't!" he yelled, grabbing for her waist.

Elizabeth hit his arm harder than he intended. She tried to recover as she lost her footing but wound up sprawling into the mud puddle face first, taking Will with her. He heard the whoosh of air being forced out of her as he landed flat on his back. Water splashed up over his face, into his mouth and nose. He sat up spluttering, grabbed the back of her shirt and hauled her out of the water.

"What the . . ." she coughed, her face streaked with mud and dirty water. A large clump of mud was making its way down her neck and she swiped at it. "Unsportsmanlike conduct, Darcy!"

He laughed at the sight of her as he sat up. "No way are you taking advantage of my good Samaritan act to sneak past me and win."

She glared at him. "Fine," she said, scooping up a handful of mud and shoving it in his face. As he spat it out, Elizabeth leapt up and ran for the finish. Will stuck one hand out blindly, coming up only with her shoe as she ran through the puddle without it.

"Damn," Will cursed, and jumped up to chase her.

She had a bit of a lead on him now, and the finish was close. He put on a final burst of energy and caught her right at the line. He grabbed her as they crossed together, Elizabeth laughing so hard she could hardly stand up and Will in only slightly better shape. The volunteers at the end handed them their medals and rolled their eyes.

"Keep this area clear, please," an older woman said, shaking her head and gesturing with her thumb to the bleachers some way behind her. "The showers are over there if you want them."

"First," Elizabeth gasped, knee bent, socked foot lifted behind her, "I need my shoe."

"Bleachers," chuckled Will, watching Elizabeth hop away between a number of other finishers. "You know your sock is already muddy, right?" he called sarcastically.

"Oh," she said, shrugging and putting her foot down. She walked to the bleachers and sat on the lowest bench. "My shoe, sir?" she asked, extending her leg. She wiggled her toes.

Will crouched in front of her and took her foot gently in one hand, caressing it, leaning in, sliding the shoe on her foot as his lips hovered just above hers. Elizabeth moved to meet the kiss but suddenly drew back, screeched, and stood up.

"Mud!" she screamed, laughing, grabbing at her foot and trying to yank the shoe off. "You filled it with mud!"

Will had wrapped the laces around the sole and then double-knotted them in record time. He stood to the side admiring his handiwork as Elizabeth worked on the wet, filthy knot. Finally, she was able to remove the sodden shoe, tapping the toe with the palm of her hand, tipping it over, and watching the mud slowly drip out, landing on the asphalt with a "plop." She dug in with her hand to clear out the rest, rubbing her muddy foot on her leg before shoving the shoe back on her foot.

"Okay," she said, nodding sagely. "Now I know who I'm dealing with." She arched an eyebrow at him. "You'd better watch your back, Mr. Darcy."

Will raised an eyebrow in imitation of her. "I am not afraid of you." He lifted the medal hanging around his neck and scrutinized it. "What is this, exactly?"

Elizabeth looked at hers more closely and guffawed. "It's a medal *and* a wall mountable bottle opener." She met his eyes and smiled, and Will found himself wishing they were alone in his shower at home. "They know their audience." She grabbed his hand and tugged him forward.

"Where are we going now?" he asked, bemused.

"There's a whole festival to explore," Elizabeth said, then turned, reached up, and patted his cheek. "Besides, we have to pick up our free beer and fuzzy Viking hats."

"I will never live this down," Will groaned, looking at the Polaroid photos they'd been handed. Will had thought Elizabeth was joking about the Viking hats, but she'd been in earnest. Red, fuzzy, with horns. And a beer. At ten in the morning because, Elizabeth had said flippantly, it was lunchtime somewhere. And all of this was commemorated in two instant Polaroid photographs.

They wandered for a while, Elizabeth only finishing half her beer before tossing the rest and showering. After they were both clean, they changed into their race t-shirts, bought some food, and listened to some music before stopping by the shoe recycling tent where Elizabeth dumped her trainers.

"They're done for, I'm afraid," she said, tying them together and tossing them on the pile.

Will felt a little guilty about that. "I'll buy you new ones," he said, kissing the top of her head.

She waved him off. "Nah, they were old. Don't worry about it."

Will didn't say anything, but he knew the shoes weren't old. She'd barely broken them in, and they weren't cheap. Though she always looked good, she didn't spend a lot of money on her clothes. But she didn't skimp on her shoes.

"Early birthday present. C'mon," he cajoled, "you know you want to go shoe shopping with me."

"You don't need to get me anything for my birthday, Will. My family's never done presents," she said off-handedly.

He clutched at his heart dramatically. "No presents?" She laughed, and he dropped his hand. "I think the world would literally stop rotating on its axis if Georgiana didn't get at least three gifts from me on her birthday. Expensive ones."

Elizabeth nodded. "Uncle Ed and Aunt Maddy buy for the kids, but once you're eighteen, you're sort of on your own," she said. "I aged out of the system." She shrugged. "I get birthday cards, which is fine. Aunt Maddy always writes something nice. And if they have a gift to give, it doesn't have to wait for the birthday."

Will tilted his head, pretending to be puzzled. "So you *don't* want to go shoe shopping with me? I just don't want there to be any misunderstandings."

"I'd go anything shopping with you, Will," she replied. Her face showed her horror that she had been so honest, and she tried to recover. "I mean, except for, um . . ."

"Don't try to amend that statement," he commanded. "Just agreeing to go shopping at all is a big concession from me. Take the win."

"I may as well take *that* win," Elizabeth scoffed, back in form. "You *stole* my race win."

Will shook his head, incredulous. "I was way ahead of you, Bennet. You had no chance."

"I was passing you, and you practically tackled me!" Elizabeth cried, eyes alight.

"Give it up, Marine. You tried to gloat, and you were properly taken down."

Elizabeth stopped walking to place her hands on her hips and glare at him. "What was that little head pat at the beginning of the race? That wasn't gloating?"

Will shook his head solemnly. "That was a love tap."

"Love tap, my . . . donkey," Elizabeth muttered.

Will blinked. "What did you just say?"

"Donkey," Elizabeth replied hotly. "You know, it's another word for . . ."

"I know what it's another word for," he said with a snort, tossing his still damp hair back from his forehead. "Why did you use donkey instead?"

Elizabeth frowned. "I can't swear."

Will laughed out loud at the petulant look on her face. "Are you telling me you're physically incapable of swearing? You were in the Marines for six years."

She made a disgusted sound in her throat. "I didn't say it was easy." Will continued to stare at her, waiting for an explanation, and she huffed. "I lost a bet."

"Oh *really?*" Will asked gleefully. "And when did this earth-shattering event occur?"

Elizabeth sighed. "A few days before I moved into my apartment."

Will was a bit surprised he hadn't heard about it. "And may I ask who you lost to?"

"Aunt Maddy," Elizabeth said with a scowl.

"What was the bet?" Elizabeth shook her head. "No, I need to know this. It's vitally important."

She stopped, removed her Viking hat, and buried her face in it. She said something that Will couldn't understand, muffled as it was.

"Beg pardon?" he said lightly.

Elizabeth tried to scowl, but she couldn't hold it. "She out-ate me."

Whatever Will had expected to hear, it wasn't this. He blinked. "She what?"

"A hotdog eating contest," Elizabeth sighed. "She challenged me, and I mean, look at her! She's tiny. I thought I would beat her easy." She glanced at Will ruefully. "If I won, I was promised a gym membership. If I lost, I had to go one full year without swearing." She rubbed her forehead, "I guess I'd gotten pretty bad about it. The Marines consider swear words a normal part of the lexicon."

"How many hotdogs did she eat?" Will pressed, entertained beyond belief at the notion of the petite Maddy Gardiner hiding such a talent.

"Nineteen. And a half. In five minutes."

Will coughed in shock. "That is seriously impressive."

Elizabeth sighed theatrically. "Gifted. She's gifted, Will."

Will imagined being in the Gardiners' kitchen as Maddy ate one hotdog after another, and Elizabeth began to realize she'd been had. "This is good stuff, Bennet," he burst out exultantly. "I can dine out on this for years."

"That was a terrible pun." Elizabeth's eyes narrowed as they fixed on him. "*One* year. Well, a little less now."

"And you'll hold up your end?" Will asked skeptically. He leaned in. "Will you be able to avoid calling me an ass?"

"Don't tempt me, Will," she retorted with a smirk. She paused to take her hair down, shaking it out as it unfurled. "I *have* already messed up twice. But I'm trying."

"I might have to inform Maddy to reset the clock," he started to say, but was distracted for a moment as he watched her hair tumble down her back.

Elizabeth punched his arm, forcing him to focus on her. "Donkey," she said.

Will had gone out for food again, and Elizabeth was surfing the Internet searching for more easy recipes. *He's spending a fortune on take-*

out, she clucked. When her phone buzzed, she set down her laptop, stretched out on the sofa near the glass doors to the terrace, and glanced at the screen. *Warrior Dash?* it read.

"Richard!" she cried, and then typed, *How did you know?*

The Post.

He forwarded a link, and she followed it to a picture of Will, face still streaked with mud, kneeling in front of her, about to replace her shoe. She had a large smear of mud running down her neck and arm. He was leaning in, appearing for all the world as though he were about to kiss her. Her heart began to pound, and she felt a cold sweat on the back of her neck. She hadn't even seen the photographer this time. She peered at the picture. It wasn't sharp, like the previous photo had been. *A phone camera*, she thought, feeling exposed. Her phone buzzed in her hand.

Bennet?

She blinked and typed: *Here.*

You okay?

Not really. She felt like there were a million eyes on her. It was unsettling at best.

Are you staying with Will?

She smiled softly. *Yes. Did he tell you?*

Yeah. Me and G. It read as though he approved. She hadn't met Will's sister, so she couldn't say for sure about her.

What could she say? *K.*

The phone buzzed again. *Is he there?*

He'll be back in a few. Hopefully he wouldn't be upset. This one was her fault.

Steer into the skid.

Good advice. But how? *K.*

Richard stopped texting, and Elizabeth guessed he was contacting Will. She drew up her knees and crossed her arms over them, dropping her head and squeezing her eyes closed. *Breathe, Bennet,* she told herself sternly. *People have cameras everywhere. It's not a big deal.*

After a moment, she picked up her head and read the article accompanying the photo.

Our royal couple is at is again, but NOW we know which Prince and Princess we're following. They crossed the finish line together at the Camp Warwick Warrior Dash, but not before Cinderella lost her slipper and Prince Charming was required to chase her down to replace it. Of course, this slipper isn't made of glass, and it's six inches deep in mud, but could they be any sweeter? Keep reading this column to follow their happily-ever-after.

Elizabeth moaned and pushed her phone away. There had been any number of times in the past few weeks she had truly regretted losing a hotdog eating contest to a woman no bigger than a pixie. This was by far the worst.

CHAPTER TWENTY-FOUR

Elizabeth was in the middle of setting up an aggregator to push any future images or articles to her phone when the door opened. Will was talking to someone. She heard him setting something down on the kitchen island while he continued speaking.

"Yeah, not too horrible, I guess," he was saying, sounding irritated but not angry. He paused, listening, and then said tiredly, "Shut up, Richard."

Elizabeth smiled, though she didn't much feel like it. *I'm looking forward to having Richard back*, she thought fondly. *Some help teasing Will would be much appreciated.* She considered how much attention she herself would be garnering from him and frowned. *Then again . . .*

Will set down his phone and called out, "Food's here!"

She joined him in the kitchen. "Hey, Charming," she said apologetically. "Guess I should have used fake names when I registered. With our names linked to our numbers, we were easy to find."

Will sighed and ran a hand through his hair. "It could be worse," he said grimly, then peeked up at her mischievously. "They could be calling *me* Cinderella."

She moaned loudly. "All those years of military training down the drain for a fairy godmother with severely limited magic and a carriage that smells like squash. Not the best exchange." She worried about what her clients would say—nobody wanted Cinderella running their security. She hoped nobody important was reading the *Post*.

"The horses are nice, though," Will said, digging into the bag.

"Oooh, Thai food!" exclaimed Elizabeth excitedly. "Did you get coconut soup?"

"Did I get coconut soup?" he asked, feigning affront. He pulled out a container and set it in front of her. "It's like you don't know me at all." He grinned. "By the way, it's called *Tom Kha Gai*."

She grinned. "Whatever." She laid her head partially on her arm, cheek pressed against the cool stone counter. "Kit and Lydia are super excited about this tabloid business. It's gaining them all sorts of 'popular by proximity' points with their crowd at school."

"That's a lot of alliteration for one sentence," Will replied, removing the other cartons and setting the bag aside.

"Nerd," she said fondly, raising her head. "Kit had already asked me to volunteer for some career day thing next week. I told her I would, so I guess I can expect lots of phone pics there." She glanced, askance, at Will. "Though since you won't be there, maybe it won't be so bad."

"I beg your pardon?" he asked, lifting both eyebrows.

"Well," she snickered, filling a bowl with some of the soup and grabbing a spoon, "who wants pictures of Cinderella without Prince Charming?"

———

"Charming," Will sighed, shaking his head. "Richard gave me grief about that. Of all people to wind up with that moniker, you'd think I'd be dead last."

"Why?" Elizabeth asked as she lifted a spoonful of soup to her mouth.

Will stared at her. Her expression was curious but not teasing. *She's serious.* He deliberated about that. By the time he opened his mouth to respond, Elizabeth had set her spoon back in her bowl and was patiently waiting for him to speak.

Will cleared his throat and reached for the noodles. "You know how I spoke about you at the interview?"

"You mean the non-interview?" Elizabeth asked, confused.

He nodded. "Yes."

She shrugged. "Okay, yes, I remember. Donkey boy came out to play. I still think of you as the surly CEO, you know. But that's not you."

Will winced. "No, I have to say donkey boy is pretty much my real personality." He opened one of the cartons and spooned some vegetables onto his plate.

Elizabeth laughed disbelievingly, filling her plate with chicken, vegetables, and a summer roll before picking up her spoon again. "No, he's not." She carefully swallowed the soup and hummed a happy little tune.

"Sadly, he is. You can ask Richard or my sister."

"You're like that with them?" Elizabeth asked doubtfully.

Will shook his head. "No, no. Just with people I don't know well. Or don't like. Which, when you add them together, is nearly everyone. I mean, I can fake it with clients because there's a defined topic, but I am definitely not the face of the company."

"Why not?" she asked.

"I suppose the long and short of it is that people tend not to be genuine around me," he replied, trying to sound nonchalant. "It's too difficult to try to tease out who's for real and who just wants money or social cachet or something I haven't even considered yet."

"Social cachet," Elizabeth repeated quietly. *What a lonely way to live.* Finally, she shrugged. "So dressing you down in front of your assistant actually recommended me to you?"

You can dress me down anytime, he thought, *dress me up, undress me.* Instead, he gave her a little smile. "Yep." He saw her inquisitive expression and explained, "If you were there to convince me to do something for you, you'd have done whatever you needed to do to keep that interview. Instead, you told me to get over myself, gave me a death glare, and walked out." He got himself some water and sat down. "Of course, not before very politely thanking my assistant for arranging the appointment."

Her lips twisted in consternation. "I can't see it, but if you say so." She reached over the counter with her chopsticks to take some noodles from his plate and drop them in her mouth.

"You know," he complained, "there's an entire container of noodles right in front of you."

"But it's more fun to take yours," she said with an impish smile.

"Okay," he replied, reaching for her soup.

She positioned her upper body to block her bowl. "Not the soup," she said threateningly, brandishing her spoon. "Soup is out of bounds."

He smiled and speared some of the chicken from her plate, which she observed without comment. They ate in companionable silence for a bit.

"When Richard called to ask if I'd seen the paper, I thought he was talking about Bulgaria," Will said, shaking his head. "Only in America does a muddy sneaker take precedence over five million people having their personal information hacked."

"Yeah, I saw that too," Elizabeth replied. "I'm betting on an inside job. The Bulgarian systems aren't a soft touch."

Will popped a piece of chicken into his mouth and chewed thoughtfully. He swallowed and said, "Can you imagine getting your data stolen from the IRS? I mean, you can't just say 'I'm not filing my taxes until you improve security.' Not unless you want to go to jail." He lifted his beer. "What a nightmare."

She lifted her shoulders then let them drop. "It happened to twenty-six million vets who used the VA back in 2006, and still very little's been done to make those systems more secure." She ate more of the soup and then put down her spoon. He looked up at her and she smiled. "You know," she said, changing the subject, "it makes me feel good that you're different with me."

He grinned widely, "So you believe me now?"

Elizabeth reached over to place her hand on top of his. Her green eyes gazed up at him. "I believe you. But you'll always be Prince Charming to me."

"And you'll always be my Cinderella," he replied, with an expression of innocence plastered on his face as he continued to eat.

Her eyes narrowed, and she frowned. "Serves me right for being sweet."

"Yeah," Will said, mouth full of noodles, "you can't really pull it off."

Will was in his study working on one of the proposals he'd come home with, and Elizabeth found herself pulling on a sweatshirt and walking outside to the terrace. The temperature had dropped precipitously, putting a decisive end to the warm weather the area had been enjoying. *Now it feels like fall*, she thought, remembering the glossy beauty of the autumnal leaves and the forested paths around the Bennet home in Meryton. It had been a farm once, but the acreage hadn't been worked in that way for two generations. The house was paid for, and her father had leased land to several business concerns, including a wedding organizer, a photographer, and a local horse breeder to fund upkeep and property taxes. That income, in addition to his salary from the university and a trust fund from his parents, was all they had required. Some of the land had been sold, but most had been maintained, making it a wonderful place to be a child.

Despite the way her childhood had ended, she had many fond memories of living at Longbourn. She'd loved growing up in the country, hiking, riding horses, swimming at the country club pool and the local swimming hole in the summers. She wondered whether the tire swing in the front yard was still operational or whether the rope had at last given out. Her father had hung it up for her and Jane when Mary was born, and they'd made good use of it.

She checked her watch. Will had said he'd work for a few hours, so she figured she had at least another hour left. She pulled out her phone and hit speed dial. A sleepy voice answered.

"Fitzwilliam."

"Whoops. Sorry," Elizabeth said apologetically. "I forgot about time zones."

"Bennet?" she heard him sitting up, imagined him rubbing his eyes. "Everything okay?"

She fought the urge to send him back to bed and end the call. "What do you know about Charles Bingley?" she blurted out.

"Uh," Richard said slowly, "you mean Batboy?"

Is he awake? "What?"

"Sorry." He yawned. "Will always wanted to be Batman as a kid."

No way. "You're joking."

She heard a soft chuckle. "No. The wealth of knowledge I have on that man is truly astonishing."

Elizabeth's eyes lit up. "We'll have to canvas that subject when you get back. But if Will is Batman, wouldn't Bingley be Robin?"

Richard cleared his throat. "Whatever. Is Bingley giving you problems?"

She hesitated. What had Charles done, really, other than be a nuisance and ogle Jane? "Not really, but he ordered a background investigation on me. If it had been Will who ordered it, I don't think it would have bothered me as much."

"It still would have bothered me," Richard replied.

"Well, okay," Elizabeth reluctantly admitted, "it did, a bit, after I thought about it. But it would have been worse if Will hadn't told me about it right away." She sighed. "I want Will to feel comfortable, to know I'm not out to get his money or anything. If this is what it takes . . ."

"Then he's an idiot."

She laughed a little, then, relieved. "There seems to be some of that going around," she confessed, thinking about using Will's real name at the race. "I suppose it might be for the board more than for Will. It's just that I get a strange read on Charles. He's charming and my aunt says he's funny, but what's his story?"

Richard grunted. "You realize I'm not even in the same country. You have a better sense of him than I would."

Elizabeth sighed. "Consider this my background check on him."

Richard sounded clearer now. "Well, my admittedly biased read has always been that he's not dangerous, just young. Even for his years. But he thinks he knows everything. Wants to be treated like an equal."

"He's not *acting* like an equal," she said defensively. "He's giving Will a lot of grief, actually. And he's not young. He's older than I am."

"Bennet," Richard said tiredly, "there's hardly a Marine alive who isn't older than Bingley. But you were born older."

"No," she replied instantly in a low voice, not sure herself why she was so adamant. "I was built that way."

She could almost see Richard rubbing the back of his neck as he tried to figure that out. After a few seconds, he responded, "I've not been impressed, though he's good at the business end of things, and Will likes him. He was Will's first real protégé, and he's got the gift of gab that Will doesn't."

Elizabeth was surprised by this. "Will doesn't have a problem talking to people."

This produced a barking laugh. "'Richard's cast-off' ring any bells?"

"Well, okay," she admitted. "But when he's not p—" She bit her lip. "—Angry at you, he's smart, and funny, and mostly relaxed . . ." *Playful. Romantic.* She recalled what Will had said at dinner, about how the arrogant man she'd met at the aborted interview was the real Will. If he had to run investigations before he could convince himself that a woman cared for him and not what he could give her, it was no wonder he had to put up a front. Still, he couldn't be that conceited, arrogant man and still be the caring, kind, wickedly humorous man he was with her. Maybe he'd used the front so much he'd forgotten. The very idea made her feel a bit forlorn on his behalf.

This silence was longer. Elizabeth was about to ask if Richard was still there when he finally spoke. "I think I need to view this phenomenon in person before I comment, Bennet. Nobody, not even Will's sister, has ever said that about him before, and G idolizes him. Or did, until she decided he was cramping her style. Either he's had a personality transplant, or the man's in love."

"I hope it's the latter," she quipped, trying to get off the topic.

Maybe he just feels safe to be himself with me, she thought. *I love him. I'm sure of it now. Not even the background check made me question him. I'm just not sure he feels the same way. He said he's serious, but what does that mean, exactly?* She'd never had anyone be serious about a relationship with her before. She didn't want to read too much into it in case she was wrong. Her heart, though . . . her heart wasn't listening to her head.

Richard took this as his cue to end the conversation, but Elizabeth was left with the impression that he wasn't fooled.

She wandered back into the house and spied her boxes of computer equipment by the door. She picked up one box and headed for the stairs. She'd agreed to stay for the two weeks Will was off work, so she might as well set up a work space. It made sense, since they intended to be doing things together every day, but she was determined to return to her apartment afterward. She didn't want Charles Bingley or anyone else to get the idea that she was looking for a free ride.

Elizabeth tried to stretch her legs. "I have too much energy," she complained. "I've been inside all day. I need to walk. Or run." She took Will's hand. "Can we go pick up a pair of running shoes tonight?"

"Well," Will said, checking his watch, "we *do* have an appointment to make."

Elizabeth's shoulders sagged. "An appointment for what?" *I need to move.*

His eyes were dancing. "For shoes."

"Will," Elizabeth said slowly, as though he was confused, "you don't need an appointment to buy running shoes."

He smiled enigmatically and would say no more.

Thirty minutes later, he was pulling the Audi into a parking garage and walking her to a storefront with a sign identifying it as *JackRabbit Sports*. Elizabeth bounced up and down on the balls of her feet.

"Now *this* is my kind of place," she gushed.

Will rolled his eyes. "Got it. No Tiffany's. JackRabbit instead."

Elizabeth didn't respond, just walked to the door and then turned to face him, disappointed. "They're closed."

Will smiled and shook his head at her fallen expression. He took her chin in his hand and touched her bottom lip lightly with his thumb. "Don't pout."

Elizabeth frowned. "I don't pout." She pulled away from his hand and started to walk back to the parking garage when Will grabbed her arm. She turned to tell him to leave her alone when she saw an employee open the locked door. *Appointment*, she thought, and would have slapped her forehead if she didn't think Will would laugh at her.

"Rich boys," she muttered, brushing past him, but stopped to smile at the employee, a woman about her age dressed in black workout clothes.

"Good evening, Mr. Darcy," the woman called. "It's nice to see you again."

"Thanks, Megan," Will replied seriously. "I owe my friend here a pair of shoes."

Megan smiled and ushered them in.

Friend? Elizabeth couldn't help feeling a tiny twinge of jealousy when Megan gazed at Will when she thought nobody was looking. The woman was on the short side, but fit and pretty. She flipped her red hair and even tried batting her eyes once, but to Elizabeth's great satisfaction, Will didn't seem to notice.

Megan may have been disappointed, but she was a professional. She spent the next thirty minutes discussing gait analysis, arch support, and overpronation. After they'd selected a pair of running shoes, Elizabeth turned in her chair and blinked at Will, who was leaning against the wall watching her. "I never knew there was so much to consider in a pair of trainers," she teased him, and then smiled softly. "Thank you."

Will couldn't stop staring at Elizabeth as she chatted excitedly with the saleswoman. Her emotions were always clearly expressed on her face. Even when she shut down, as she had earlier, it was clear that something was wrong, even though he couldn't have said what it might be.

He hadn't ever met anyone like her. Even Georgiana, who was a wonderful person, took the privileges of their lifestyle for granted and expected a great deal from her big brother. Elizabeth had come from a very different place, but was intelligent and funny and fiercely loyal, grateful for the smallest thing he did for her, kind and compassionate to those around her. There were no games with her. *Elizabeth has a temper,* he thought fondly, *and she's not afraid to use it, but even that's not so bad. She just has to run it off.* He considered her actions at the hospital. *Maybe we should get two pairs of shoes.*

He had no doubt she'd be just as gracious in the most expensive stores in the city as she was here, purchasing running shoes. And she was so very beautiful. He couldn't wait to take her to the Christmas fundraiser and Uncle Terry's New Year's Eve Ball. He'd talk her into shopping with Georgiana. *Maybe she can model everything for me after.*

Finally, she turned to face him, holding a foot aloft for his inspection. "I think we have a winner." As she turned back to Megan and began to remove the shoes, he caught Megan's eye and held up two fingers. She nodded, and he prepared himself to defend his decision. Elizabeth would roll her eyes at him, but she'd give in eventually. He looked forward to the debate.

CHAPTER TWENTY-FIVE

"Thank you for my shoes," Elizabeth said happily, swinging her bag as they entered the apartment. "I'm going to go run right now. Do you want to join me?"

"I thought you ran to have time alone," Will replied. "Wouldn't running with me defeat the purpose?" He tossed his keys in the bowl where he always kept them.

"You know," she said, abruptly changing the subject and indicating the bowl, "leaving them there makes it easy for a thief to find them."

Will nodded gravely. "Yes, and if he's looking for a car to steal, I'd rather he find the keys two steps inside the apartment and then leave instead of ransacking the place."

Elizabeth considered that. Assuming the intruder was only looking for a car, it made sense. She was pretty sure that anyone who broke into an apartment like this wouldn't just be after a car.

Still, any thief would have to breach a good deal of security to even get into the elevator, let alone into the apartment. Will had an alarm. The building had a doorman and security staff. Unlike many she'd seen in the city, the personnel here appeared well-trained, often former military or law enforcement.

She let it drop. "I don't need to be alone tonight," she informed him.

He motioned to the bag. "Well, go change into the shoes, then. We'll break them in."

Twenty minutes later, they had stretched and were standing in the building's gym. The room took up a quarter of the third floor, and the wall overlooking the park had been replaced with glass. There were several rows of treadmills, elliptical walkers, and bicycles, as well as rowing and weight machines. Free weights had their own space in one corner, and there were two rooms off the main floor used for classes.

Elizabeth turned to Will. "You are so lucky," she said. "So much better to run inside during the winter." She frowned, a crease appearing between her eyes at the top of her nose. "Where's the track?"

Will just smiled, placing one gentle finger under her chin and tilting her head up. The track was on the upper level, the center space fenced with clear plexiglass but otherwise left open so that anyone running could see the rest of the gym below them.

"Clever," she breathed, her eyes sparkling. She gazed around her to find the stairs and spied a door she thought must conceal them. "Here?" she asked, moving towards it.

Before Will could reply, she had darted through the door and up to the track. He followed at a more leisurely pace. As he exited onto the track, Elizabeth was bouncing up and down on the balls of her feet. "It's spongy," she grinned. "I love it. Thanks for showing me."

Then she was off, loping gracefully away. Will just watched her go, feeling content, happy. He hadn't run on the track since Georgiana left for Stanford. She had decided in the ninth grade that she wanted to try out for the track team in high school. She hadn't made the cut, but they'd kept up running a few times a week. Still, the gym was something they'd always had, and he'd long taken it for granted. Not that he wasn't grateful for what he had, he told himself, but seeing his home through Elizabeth's eyes made him happy. He didn't think he'd ever smiled as easily or as often as he did when he was with her. When Elizabeth finished her first lap, she called to him to run with her, and he did, matching her shorter strides easily.

"I love these shoes," she told him as they ran. "Thanks again. You didn't need to buy me new ones."

"I did, actually," he replied, rolling his shoulders as he tried to loosen up, "I'm the one who filled your old ones with mud." He glanced over at her and admired the rosy hue her face was taking on as she ran.

"I deserved it," she said with a grin, "but I love the shoes anyway, so thanks."

"Really, it's fine."

She huffed a bit and glanced up at the ceiling. "Let me remind you how this simple social interaction is meant to go, Will." She sounded amused, but also annoyed, and Will wondered what he'd done this time. He couldn't think of anything between buying the shoes and beginning the run that could account for her shift in mood.

"Excuse me?" he asked, confused.

She started to laugh a little. "I say 'thanks,' and then you say, 'You're welcome.'" She shrugged, "It's really not hard."

He felt his face grow warm, and it wasn't from the running. "I tend to have trouble with small talk," he explained.

"I know," she replied bluntly, "which is why you need to practice."

They'd completed two laps by now. Will noticed that Elizabeth's stride was growing stronger, and he lengthened his own a bit. She grunted appreciatively and made an adjustment to keep up.

"So . . . Thank you for the shoes," she repeated teasingly.

Will pretended to think about it for a moment before relenting. "You're very welcome."

"See?" she laughed, "Simple."

Only with you, Elizabeth, he thought, but instead began to run backwards in front of her. "Race?"

"Against those basketball-player legs? Are you crazy?"

He snorted. "Afraid?"

"No," she shot back instantly with a toss of her head, "just absolutely certain the deck is stacked on this one, and not in my favor." She kept running at her steady pace as he began to pull away. No matter the taunting, she could not be influenced to take him on. She just smiled and let him go.

After eight laps, Elizabeth slowed considerably, running a final circuit in a slow jog as she cooled down. Will ran another lap before finishing with his own cool-down. When he made the final turn, he saw Elizabeth, her back to him, flexing her left knee as though it was bothering her, and he frowned.

"You okay?" he asked as he jogged to a stop in front of her.

She nodded. "New shoes, new track. Just a bit sore. It happens." She shook her head, and her lips twisted briefly into a grimace. She said something softly. He thought he heard "three-thirty-seven," but that didn't make sense.

"What was that?" Will asked, as she began to stretch.

Elizabeth shut her eyes briefly. She gazed out the window at the dark sky and the illuminated park, and replied, with a single shake of her head, "Nothing."

No matter how Will tried, he could get no more information from her. When they reached the apartment, she wrapped up some ice in a towel and elevated her leg, refusing to let him help her. Instead, she opened a notebook and grabbed a pen. With a flourish, she paused, pen at the ready, and asked, "So what's on our highlights of New York City list, Mr. Darcy?"

Will slumped into a chair next to her at the table and swiped at his face with a towel. He held two bottles of water in his hand, passing one to her and opening his own, guzzling down half of its contents before taking a breath. She shook her head at him.

"Worn out from all that showboating?" she grinned.

"Hey, I'm old compared to you," he told her. "You shouldn't be so afraid of racing an old man."

"Right." She snorted. "You're absolutely decrepit."

"Still," he pressed, "you were a maniac at the mud run. It's not like you to back down from a challenge." He grinned. "Disappointing, I have to say."

She tapped the notebook and ignored him, writing as she said, "I'd like to see the Statue of Liberty, for sure, and Ellis Island." He glanced over at the paper to see that her handwriting was tight and even. "Oh, and I have to take you for dim sum, but according to Jane, the best place isn't actually in Chinatown."

Will gazed at her. "Elizabeth," he said in a low voice, "what's wrong?"

She ignored him, continuing to write. "I do have to attend that school thing for Kit."

He almost growled this time. "Elizabeth."

She tossed the pen down and sighed. "Do I really have to spell it out?" He looked at her blankly and lifted his shoulders in an apologetic shrug.

Elizabeth's expression grew guarded. "There was a time when I wasn't so slow, you know," she explained defensively. "Six months ago, even, I would have taken you up on that race." She raised her chin as she stated baldly, "and I would have stood a chance of winning, too." Will held her gaze, and she laughed, relaxing. "I said a *chance*. You know, if I kicked you in the ankle or something."

She broke the connection, casting her eyes to the ice on her knee before speaking again. "I feel pretty fortunate to even have a leg." Unconsciously, she rubbed a very thin scar just above her eyebrow, trying not to notice Will's guilty expression. She failed. "See, that's why I don't bring it up," she said, irritated. "I was lucky, Will. Most of the time I don't even have to think about it. Complaining would be an insult to all the Marines who've suffered so much worse."

There was a short silence, and then Will said sternly, "You sound like Richard." It wasn't a compliment. "It's not an insult to be honest if you're in pain. You don't need to compare your suffering with anyone else."

"Fine." *He doesn't get it.* "I will let you know if I'm in pain as long as you trust me to manage it."

"Deal," he replied. "Just don't leave me hanging out there acting like a prick."

"But it looks so good on you." He tossed his empty plastic bottle at her. She grabbed it in mid-air and set it on the table in front of her.

"Nothing wrong with your reflexes," he grumbled.

"I'm not the old coot here," she replied coolly. "Now, where do you want to go?"

Elizabeth's phone buzzed. She sighed, fairly certain who was contacting her.

"You okay?" Will asked from across the table.

She nodded and read her text message.

Strike three, Dutch. I got a call from my guy at The Markham. They wanted to replace you. I convinced them to hang in there for now, but I couldn't get York to sign you on.

Elizabeth grimaced. The Markham was a really good job. She didn't want to lose them as clients. And she'd been counting on York. *I'll speak to The Markham.*

You do that.

Abby didn't write anything else. Elizabeth was concerned. Abby wasn't generally so abrupt. *Maybe she's out on a job.* She glanced at Will, who was jotting down notes so he could purchase tickets or have Wanda arrange things. *Or maybe she thinks I'm not listening.* Maybe taking this time to spend with Will wasn't such a great idea.

"Do you want to catch a show?" he asked. He smiled at her, and she could tell he was excited at the prospect of having time, just the two of them.

She smiled back. She wasn't any less excited, and she'd promised—she couldn't disappoint him. She'd work around their schedule as she planned, and with any luck, there would be no more princess references. Elizabeth just nodded.

Elizabeth finished her workout but could still feel the stress knotting the muscles in her shoulders. She had to speak to Will about the text Abby had sent last night. She wasn't sure what could be done about it, but she was worried about her business. She knew Uncle Ed and Aunt Maddy would take her in if everything collapsed, but she couldn't bear the notion of moving back into the house because her business had failed. It simply couldn't happen. She wouldn't let it.

Will had done this a long time, he'd said. He had to have some clue about how to get it to stop.

Will Darcy had very nearly groaned when he saw Charles's number on his screen, but he answered dutifully. "What do you want, Charles?" he asked with a sense of foreboding.

"Is that any way to talk to your Vice-President of Operations?" replied Charles, who did not sound upset at the brusque greeting.

"It is if he's about to give me bad news." Will put the phone on speaker and leaned back.

"I know you're on vacation," Charles began, and Will pinched the bridge of his nose between his thumb and forefinger.

"What do you *want*, Charles?" Will repeated.

"I want to use this press you're getting. It's millions in free advertising, Will, an amazing opportunity for us. You *are* FORGE, but you're normally so camera-shy nobody really knows it."

As Charles spoke, all Will could think about was how he'd just told Elizabeth he wasn't the face of the company. Now that was exactly what Bingley wanted to make him. Everything they did over the next two weeks would be selectively leaked to the press. Charles was bargaining on the belief that a huge increase in visibility for the two weeks before the holiday season would mean that interest would lessen somewhat afterwards. *Controlled overexposure*, he called it. In addition, the more available they made themselves, he explained to Will, the less money those photos of them would be worth, and the less attractive a target they would become. But their image, Charles argued, would already be firmly entrenched in the minds of the public. "So long as you mean to make a go of this thing," was Charles's caveat.

Will growled at the flippant reference to his relationship with Elizabeth, but he couldn't deny that the idea had merit. If the photographers were going to follow them anyway, it would be better to hire professionals to manage them. But what Charles was talking about went beyond that. He meant to create a media brand from which FORGE would benefit, an image of a company that helped innovators create Cinderella stories just like the one its CEO was supposedly living.

Richard had laughed out loud when he'd read about Prince Charming because he knew as well as anyone in Will's inner circle that it wasn't a role he was born to play. Richard, or even Charles, would be far better candidates, and Will was certain at some point he'd revert to form and undo any work Charles had done. Not to mention, Elizabeth had to agree to be a part of this, and she was unlikely to appreciate being dragged down this particular rabbit hole with him.

He covered his eyes with one weary hand. It struck him suddenly that Prince Charming wasn't the only role being cast against type. *Elizabeth. She'd have to play Cinderella.*

He ended the call with Charles, promising him they'd speak again in the morning, and sat for a time just staring at the walls of his study. He had promised Elizabeth he'd be no more than a few hours, and it was already thirty minutes past.

"She's going to kill me," he told the ceiling, then pushed himself up and headed for the door.

CHAPTER TWENTY-SIX

E lizabeth stared at Will. *He wants to make it worse?*
"No," she said succinctly.

Will sighed. "I thought this might be a hard sell," he admitted, rubbing the back of his neck.

He can't possibly think this is a good idea. "I can't believe you would even *ask*." She stood, hands on hips, shaking her head, her ire and her volume rising in tandem. "Are you *kidding* me?" She pressed the heels of her hands into her eyes, searching for an appropriate word to replace the string of curses she was desperate to let loose. "Have you *any* idea . . . Gaaah!" she exclaimed in a strangled voice, throwing her hands in the air and heading for the stairs. *Aunt Maddy has ruined me.*

"Where are you going?" Will asked, sounding irritated. As if he had the right to be upset with *her. He* wasn't losing jobs because his credibility was shot. *Everybody loves a Prince Charming. Cinderella, though . . .*

"To get my shoes," she said curtly. She'd worked out earlier as she tried to decide how to broach this topic with Will, but now she needed to run and the track in the gym wouldn't do it. She nearly flew down the stairs. When she stomped back up, trainers on her feet, shoving an arm into a navy-blue hooded jacket, Will was waiting, his own coat in hand.

"I'll come with you," he said firmly.

She shook her head. "No." *That would defeat the purpose.*

"Elizabeth," he said reprovingly, "it's dark out. You can't go out by yourself in the city after dark."

"Ah, but I can," she shot back, eyes afire. "Because I am *not* some frail damsel in distress created to increase male self-esteem or improve your profit margin while mine disintegrates." She moved past Will to grab her shoulder bag, removing her license and some money and shoving them in a pocket. "I highly doubt Central Park West at night is as dangerous as . . ." her voice trailed off and she clamped her lips together.

"Dangerous as . . .?" asked Will.

I don't know, almost everywhere I've been in the last six years? She knew he was only trying to keep her talking but it just made her angrier. What planet was he living on that he thought he could talk her into this completely asinine idea?

"Never mind." She pushed past him to the door, and Will put his hand on her arm.

"Elizabeth, please, let's just talk about this." There was a note of pleading in his voice, but she refused to feel sorry for him. He tightened his grip a little.

She grew very still as she looked at his hand on her wrist and then at him. Her voice, when she spoke, came out in a slow, icy growl. "Remove your hand or lose it, Will Darcy."

Reluctantly, he dropped her arm, but as she stormed out, he followed.

"Don't follow me!" she yelled as she stomped to the elevator.

Will's voice was aggravatingly calm. "I won't say a thing if you don't want to discuss this, Elizabeth, but you are not going out alone."

"*Unbelievable,*" she muttered, stalking into the elevator and standing in the corner, face to the wall as she continued to talk. "Insufferable. It's not enough that Batboy wants a background. Now he wants a performance?"

Will sighed from behind her. "I see you've spoken with Richard." She faced the back wall, trying to calm down. "Are you even going to turn around?" he asked, his tone becoming less repentant and more aggravated.

She heard him talking, but the words didn't really make sense. She needed quiet to think. *I'm already losing work, and he wants me to do more? Just hand me a shovel, Will, and I can bury my entire career.*

They rode in silence after that, and when the doors shushed open, she turned without a word to stride out of the elevator and into the lobby.

"Good evening, Ms. Bennet, Mr. Darcy," came the very low voice of Jeremy, who was running the security desk. He stood, unfolding his broad, 6'5 frame, and nodded at the doorman who placed one hand on the door's brass handle.

Elizabeth stopped. "Hello, Jeremy," she said kindly. She'd spoken to him a few times while she waited for Will to finish a phone call upstairs. "It's good to see you. How's your grandmother?"

Jeremy smiled a brilliantly white smile. "They released her this morning, thank you for asking."

Will seemed puzzled. Didn't he know Jeremy? "That's excellent news," Elizabeth said quietly.

Jeremy turned to Will and nodded. "Mr. Darcy."

Elizabeth turned to look at Will, and the smile dropped from her face. She walked through the open door, Will trailing behind her. She broke into a run, dove into a waiting taxi, and was gone, leaving him standing alone on the sidewalk.

"Damn it," Will said, watching the cab turn the corner.

Jeremy glanced up with a sympathetic expression as he reentered the building and made for the elevator. He wondered when Elizabeth had gotten to know the nighttime desk staff, but then, she was always interested in people and their stories. As he passed by the desk, Jeremy said, to no one in particular, "Ef greedy wait hot wud cool."

Will stopped and looked at the security officer, waiting. Jeremy smiled, a smaller smile than he had given Elizabeth, and translated. "Patience," he said, rocking up on his heels and down to his toes, "will be rewarded."

Fifteen minutes later, his phone buzzed and he grabbed it, hoping Elizabeth was returning to the apartment to talk.

The voice on the other end was slurred. "William?"

He frowned. "Who is this?"

"Caroline, darling."

The only Caroline Will knew was Charles's sister. She was coy and ridiculous, and he'd never spent time with her unless she accompanied her brother. How had she gotten his number? Charles swore he always had his phone locked up tight.

"I'm at The Dakota Bar," she said slowly, "and I thought you would like to come and join me."

He cleared his throat. "It sounds like you've gotten a pretty good start on me, Caroline. Let me call your brother to come pick you up."

"Nooo," she protested, drawing out the word. "Charles haaates me. If you don't want to come, I'll just wait a bit and drive myself home."

He pinched the bridge of his nose. He couldn't let *anyone* get into a car if they were drunk and he could stop it. "Can I speak to the bartender, Caroline?"

"Heee's busy," she giggled. The ambient noise increased, and then he heard her muffled voice saying, "Oh, hello!"

"Caroline," he called into the phone. "Are you by yourself?"

"Of *course*, darling," she sang. "Jealous?"

The bartender should stop serving her, but he might not notice— the Dakota was always busy, and people generally didn't go there to drink alone. Will didn't want to leave the apartment, but she *was* Charles's sister, even if his friend did dislike her. *I'm not exactly thrilled with her right now, either.* "Caroline, don't drive. Just stay put."

He ended the call before she'd finished her boozy innuendo and tried to reach Charles. It went straight to voicemail, meaning he was probably at the end of a successful date. Will didn't have the other sister's number. In a fit of desperation, he even tried her father's work number, but unsurprisingly, there was no answer. He grabbed a coat and prepared to hoof the several blocks.

"Not like I don't have other things to be doing," he groused.

Will arrived at the bar a short time later. It was packed and hot and loud, all the things he disliked about going out on the weekend, but it wasn't difficult to find Caroline Bingley. She was dancing by herself in the corner of the front room, a martini glass held high. He rolled his eyes and began to make his way over to her.

"William!" she called loudly. "You came!" As he approached, she threw her arms around his neck, splashing some of her martini on his back, and placing a sound kiss on his lips.

Shocked, he pushed her away. "What the hell do you think you're doing?" he asked, wiping his mouth with the sleeve of his coat. "Give me your keys, Caroline."

"Oooh," she cooed, "I knew you'd want to take me home, lover."

"I'm taking you to your apartment so you don't kill anyone with your car," he replied angrily. *But leaving you to the mercy of a taxi driver is looking better and better.* "Give me your keys."

She opened her clutch and poured out the contents on the table. He refused to look at them other than to grab both her phone and her keys. He took the purse from her and swept the other items back into it, snapping it shut and handing it back.

He scrolled through her contacts, found his number, and deleted it. Then he scrolled back up. "Is Louisa your sister?"

"Yes, but you don't want her," Caroline purred, sliding her hand down his arm. "She's married to her job."

Will shrugged her off and placed the call. It went to voicemail. "Louisa Bingley, this is Will Darcy. Your sister drunk-dialed me, and I can't get in touch with Charles. I am driving her to her apartment, but I will not stay there. You'd better have someone meet me to help her in the next thirty minutes, or I'll just drop her at an ER to make sure she hasn't poisoned herself."

Caroline laughed loudly and grabbed his arm. He removed it, instead holding her by her upper arm and guiding her out of the crowd onto the sidewalk.

"Which car is yours, Caroline?" he asked, realizing she might be parked some distance away. He was beginning to suspect there was a reason she'd chosen to drink at a bar so close to his apartment when there were far more options near her own in the Lincoln Center area. She waved ineffectually, and he feared the worst. Fortunately, when he pressed the unlock button on her key fob, the lights of a black Jaguar lit up just across the street. He took her to the corner and waited for the light, then led her to the car, got her inside, helped her with her belt, and asked, with no little trepidation, "What's your address?"

Caroline fumbled in her purse for what seemed like forever, but finally handed over her license so Will could plug the address into his phone's GPS. Before he started the car and pulled out into traffic, he checked his voicemail.

Nothing.

Under other circumstances, he might have enjoyed driving the Jag, but all he could think about was first, killing Charles, and second, tracking down Elizabeth. Had she returned to the apartment only to find him gone?

When they arrived at Caroline Bingley's very modern apartment building, he maneuvered her car into the spot she blearily pointed out. He jumped out and caught hold of her arm, marching her to the lobby, where he was relieved to find a woman waiting for them. She was shorter than Caroline and perhaps a few years older. She appeared to have dragged herself out of bed and didn't appear any happier about it than he felt.

"Caroline Augusta Bingley," she said furiously, "what are you doing, overindulging in this manner? You know better than this."

"Shhh," Caroline said, staggering to one side and lifting a finger to her lips. "Will is going to come upstairs with me. Go home, Louisa."

Will scowled. "She's all yours, Ms. Bingley."

Louisa sighed. "Thank you for seeing her home, Mr. Darcy. I'll be sure to let Charles know."

"Nooo," Caroline cried. "Don't send him away! Daddy won't like it!"

Will eyed Louisa carefully. "What was that?"

She shook her head. "No idea."

He held up his hands, palms out. "I don't want to know. Please tell your sister I am blocking her number."

Louisa was herding her sister towards the elevator. "I get the point, Mr. Darcy," she told him wearily. "Thank you and good night."

Elizabeth stood in the doorway, unsure she should enter. The train had taken forever, and she'd considered walking the two miles from the station. The heat of her anger had cooled somewhat on the ride, though, and she was beginning to feel foolish for ditching Will in front of the apartment. *I told him I didn't want company*, she thought, trying to defend her position, but a moment later, she sighed. *It's Will. I could have had a grenade launcher, and he still couldn't let me to go out on my own.* She huffed a little. *Maybe if I had a tank.* In the end, she'd gazed around the nearly empty train car, spied a few men in hoodies, and recalled the feeling of being followed on her run. She'd taken a taxi.

"Lizzy?" Jane called softly.

"Yes," she responded. Elizabeth removed her shoes and jacket, then padded over to the bed. The mattress sank a little as she sat on the end of it. She didn't say anything. Jane moved over towards the wall and held the blankets up so Elizabeth could join her, and the invitation was immediately accepted.

"What happened?" Jane asked.

There was a pause before the words came. "He made me angry."

Jane put her arms around her sister. "I suppose you'll explain how."

Elizabeth was silent for a moment and then asked, "When do you have to go back to work?"

"Around ten," Jane replied sleepily, putting her hair back.

"Can I tell you in the morning?" Lizzy asked.

Jane shrugged. "Sure." She touched her forehead to Elizabeth's.

Elizabeth sighed. "Can I ask a favor?"

"Of course," replied Jane.

Elizabeth moved her forehead to Jane's shoulder. "Would you text Will and let him know I'm here? I don't want to talk to him, but I don't want him to worry, either."

She could feel Jane smile in the darkness. "Give me your phone," she said, holding out her hand.

Will stood in front of the apartment door, frowning. He was sure he had closed and locked it when he left for the bar, but it was slightly ajar. He called downstairs. "Jeremy?" he asked. "Has anyone come upstairs since I left?" His first thought had been that Elizabeth was back, but he didn't think she was careless enough to leave the door open in the middle of the night.

"Not a soul, Mr. Darcy," the man said. "Is there a problem?"

"No," Will replied. "Thanks." *I must have left it open. I could have sworn . . .* He thought he heard something, but it didn't sound like voices, exactly. He cracked the door open a bit more and seeing nothing, stepped inside. He tapped a small square on the wall just beneath the hall table and reached in for his gun. He checked it to be sure it was loaded and stepped into the next room. On the other side of the kitchen, music was playing. He'd left The Flamingos on the turntable but had turned it off when he and Elizabeth went out earlier. That he knew for certain. He'd never thought "I Only Have Eyes for You" was an eerie song, but the words stuck with him as he checked every corner of the upstairs while the music played. When he was satisfied there was nobody around, he turned it off.

He realized then how stupid it had been to come into the apartment alone. He needed to sweep the lower floor but didn't want to involve the police, knowing they would probably just hang up if he told them he'd come home to an unlocked door and doo-wop music. He couldn't ask Jeremy to help—that wasn't his job. He wished Richard was home.

Oscar. Will moved back towards the front door and made a call.

Within fifteen minutes, there were three armed men pushing their way inside and telling him to wait in the hall until the house was secured.

His phone buzzed.

Are they there?

Yes, Will typed. *Where are you?*

In DC. I sent them from Dad's place. The senator's New York apartment was not far from Will's. *You can trust them. Let me know if you need anything else.*

Thanks, O. He could have swept the downstairs himself, but it wasn't smart to do so alone. He knew Oscar would tease him about it, but he decided it was the right decision anyway.

No problem. Remember to lock your door next time.

By the time the men from his uncle's private security team had given him the all-clear, Will felt a little foolish. Maybe he *had* forgotten to lock the door. But what about the music? Maybe it was just a power surge? He said good night and thanked them before closing the door and locking it.

He jumped a little when his phone buzzed. "Elizabeth?" he asked aloud, digging it out of his pocket. But it wasn't a call. "A *text?*" he protested to the empty room, staring at the screen. "You're going to *text* me now?"

He read Jane's message and sat again, leaning his head against the back of the couch. "She took the train back to New Jersey. Good God, woman." He hoped, but did not expect, that she had called her uncle for a ride home from the station.

What a night. Will mentally ran through the conversation he'd tried to have with Elizabeth. He had laid out Bingley's plan but had only said he thought it worth discussing. He hadn't insisted they do it or told her she needed to change her behavior in any way. She'd just gone off the deep end and run away. He reviewed it again and came to a slightly different conclusion. *If you'd let her go, she'd have come back on her own,* he chastised himself. *You might as well have pushed her into the cab yourself.* He released a sigh. *But no matter who she is, it's not safe to be out at night alone in the city.* He covered his eyes with one arm. "Maddening woman."

Elizabeth was sitting on one of the chaise lounge chairs with the hood of her sweatshirt pulled over her head, chin resting on her bent knees as she stared out at the sickly gray sky. She didn't turn her head when Jane sat down but gave a little grunt by way of a greeting.

"You're up early," she told her older sister without looking at her. "It's only five. I thought you didn't have to go in until later?"

Jane laughed softly. "I'm up early because someone who should be in my bed isn't there." She reached over to gently move Elizabeth's hair away from her face and tuck it further back in the hood. "Did you have a nightmare?"

She sighed. "Yes."

"Well," Jane said soothingly, "you're having them less often, yes? Same one?"

Elizabeth sniffed. "A little weirder this time. Same stuff from overseas, but do you remember Bill Collins?"

Jane's eyes widened. "The maladroit pastoral student from Meryton?" she asked. "The one you *warned* to leave Mary alone?"

Elizabeth rolled her eyes. "Maladroit? He wasn't just awkward, Jane, he was a pervert. And you know what he said to Mary. Even if she didn't understand it, I couldn't let it stand."

"Yes," Jane replied drily. "I remember. I don't think his nose ever healed right, and he couldn't walk properly for a month. We got a visit from the Sheriff, and you had to do community service."

Lizzy chuckled then. "Oh right, Sheriff Anderson. Totally worth it —he introduced me to Mrs. de Bourgh, the bigwig at Rosings Manor, remember?"

"Mom was really mad at you." Jane didn't continue.

Elizabeth closed her eyes. "Mad" hadn't begun to cover what had happened in the Bennet household once the Sheriff's car was safely down the drive. Her mother's response had been much worse than what she had done to Collins. "Anyway," she continued, "he was in the nightmare too, with a camera, taking pervy photos and calling me names. After that, it was all the same stuff."

"How's your head?" Jane asked. "You seem to get migraines along with the nightmares now. It's likely tied to your stress level."

Elizabeth massaged her temples. "Likely."

"So are you ready to talk about what compelled you to flee a Central Park mansion to share a twin bed with me in New Jersey in the middle of the night?"

"You know," Elizabeth said ruefully, cracking open one eye to give her sister a contrite glance, "when you say it that way, it just sounds stupid."

Jane smiled. "One thing you never are, Lizzy, is stupid. Opinionated, judgmental, quick to anger, maybe a little impulsive . . ."

"Stop," laughed Elizabeth contritely. "I get it, I get it."

Jane stuck her nose in the air. Elizabeth mirrored the movement.

"Obstinate, headstrong girl!" they cried together, their voices pitched and nasally.

"Oh," said Elizabeth, pressing one hand to each side of her head. "Ow."

Mrs. de Bourgh, or "Lady Catherine" as she liked to be called, had warmed to Elizabeth immediately. She had worn huge floppy hats and ancient business suits with white gloves, black heels, and the same single strand of perfect white pearls. She was a character. But she was also an heiress, and her husband had left her even more money. It was a generous grant from the de Bourgh Foundation that provided opportunities for "troubled youth" in Meryton and surrounding towns. Their mother had pitched another nervous fit when Elizabeth was given that label and assigned to the program.

She'd gone cheerfully about her business, helping out in the convalescent wing of Rosings. The residents told her wonderful stories about their lives, even if they did tell them to her more than once. She often brought those stories home to her sisters, who enjoyed them, too. In the summer, Elizabeth had risen early to meet Mrs. de Bourgh where she sat on the same bench in the city park and brought her a glazed donut. Always glazed. For some reason, Lydia adored the old widow too, and Elizabeth often took her youngest sister along. Jane and her other sisters had been a little afraid of the old lady.

"Catherine de Bourgh," Jane said quietly. "Whatever became of her?"

"I think her family moved her to the city," Elizabeth said. "To keep her close by after her last de Bourgh relation passed away. At least, that's what I was told." Elizabeth closed her eyes. "She wasn't doing so well on her own anymore."

"She really liked you, you know," Jane said as she reclined on the chair and pulled her robe tight around her.

"Yes, another of my legions of adoring fans," Elizabeth said. "She was a pushy old broad." She hid her face in her arms. "I liked her, too."

Jane cleared her throat. "So, you haven't answered my questions."

Elizabeth shrugged. "I forgot what they were."

Jane laughed in disbelief. "You, Elizabeth Bennet, are a dreadful liar."

Elizabeth placed the back of one hand against her forehead and carefully leaned back. "No future for me on the stage, then?"

Jane placed a gentle hand on her sister's other arm. "Stop deflecting. Do you have a migraine?"

"Yes," Lizzy mumbled.

Jane stood and disappeared into the house, reappearing with a bottle of acetaminophen and a glass of water. She shook out two pills and handed them to Lizzy with the water.

"Another, please."

Jane frowned. "You shouldn't need three. Maybe you need your prescription refilled."

"No," Elizabeth protested. "I hate taking that stuff. This is fine. I just need three to get started."

Jane pursed her lips and held out another pill. When Elizabeth set the glass down, Jane sat and folded her hands in her lap, waiting.

"Your silence is deafening," Elizabeth complained. Jane did not reply, just waited expectantly until she huffed. "Fine."

"You know," Jane said, when Elizabeth was finished, "it's not a *horrible* idea to have a PR company come in to work with the press."

"It wasn't that part I was objecting to, Jane," she protested.

"Mmm," Jane replied serenely. "Does Will know that? Or did you just do that thing where you get too angry to speak and then fly off the handle?"

Elizabeth fell back into the chaise and stretched her arms out over her head. "That thing."

"Poor Will."

"Poor Will?" Elizabeth whispered indignantly. Speaking out loud hurt. "He shouldn't even be considering making me play nice for the paparazzi."

Jane shook her head. "More like he wants you to help play them, I think."

"I can't do it," Elizabeth declared. "I'm trying to get a serious business up and running, Jane. What company is going to hire Cinderella over Staff Sgt. Bennet?"

"*Tell* Will, Lizzy," Jane said firmly. "If he doesn't respect that, then you know he's not the guy for you. But I think he will. Respect that, I mean." She took her sister's hand. "You are so good about keeping everything that bothers you to yourself. *Too* good, I'm sorry to say. You can't expect Will to read your mind." She moved to the chaise and looked her straight in the eye. "Sweetheart, I have a constant parade of man-children trying to get me to go out with them. I am not ashamed to tell you I am insanely jealous of you."

"You're jealous of *me*? That's rich," Elizabeth muttered.

Jane snorted. "I'm not blind, Lizzy. I saw how worried Will was when he showed up here the other day, how he couldn't sit still without touching your hand to reassure himself you were okay." She kissed Elizabeth's cheek. "And my lord, that man is handsome." Jane shook her head. "Don't mess this up," she warned, "or the next time you run home and get into my bed in the middle of the night I may put my cold feet all over your back." She smiled. "I know how you love that."

Elizabeth tossed her arms around Jane's neck and gave her a quick squeeze. "Warning received. Thanks for talking me down, Janie," she whispered with a brief laugh.

"Of course," was the reply. "Now, since you're here, go get me breakfast, please. And no glazed donuts."

Lizzy rolled her eyes. "I'll get right on that. You want eggs or eggs?"

Jane went back inside, and Elizabeth got up and stretched before starting to make her way inside through the family room. Jane returned at that moment and gave her a wink.

"I believe you have a visitor," she said, her blue eyes twinkling. Elizabeth bit her lip and walked to the door. She took a deep breath and let it out slowly, then opened the door.

Standing before her was Will Darcy, one hand suspended in the air ready to knock, the other awkwardly balancing two coffees in a carrier and a very large bag of Murray's bagels.

CHAPTER TWENTY-SEVEN

Will stood unmoving as his eyes searched Elizabeth's face, trying to gauge her reaction to his presence. "I, uh," he began disjointedly, "I got some very good advice last night, but I'm afraid I've ignored it."

Elizabeth closed her eyes and rubbed one ear against her shoulder, making Will frown. "Whatever it was, I'm glad," she said quietly. "Come in."

She led him to the still empty kitchen, where he set down the coffee and bagels. He started to say something, but Elizabeth interrupted him.

"I'm sorry," she said hurriedly. "I was angry and impulsive, and I didn't let you talk. So just let me say—I'm really sorry."

Will's entire posture relaxed the moment he heard the words. "I think if I'd given you more room to process, it wouldn't have gotten so bad. I'm sorry too," he replied. Elizabeth stepped close and tossed her arms around his waist and he wrapped his arms around her in an embrace. They stood there for a few minutes until there was the sound of a throat clearing.

"Good morning," came Uncle Ed's voice. "I thought I heard you come in last night, Lizzy."

"Yes, sir," she said, pulling back. "I had to talk to Jane."

There was humor in his tone, but not in his expression as Ed Gardiner flicked his gaze from Elizabeth to Will. "I am assuming she helped you see reason?"

Elizabeth smiled and nodded. "She always does."

"Must have been some argument," Ed said briskly, "I see Will has brought bagels. Murray's, even."

"Help yourself, sir," Will said. "I brought enough for everyone."

"Just two coffees, though," Ed teased, "so I guess I'll go start a pot."

"I couldn't carry that many cups," Will admitted bashfully, proving he'd considered it, and Ed laughed.

"You brought the important ones," he said, and then addressed Elizabeth. "You might want to take your food downstairs before we're overrun."

"Yes, sir," she replied gratefully.

Will grabbed two bagels and dropped them in the toaster while Elizabeth sipped her coffee. "This is still hot. You didn't get this coffee at Murray's," she said, trying to make conversation while they waited for the bagels to toast.

Will turned. "No," he replied, staring at her unabashedly. "I remember you mentioning The Corner, so I stopped there once I was in town." He shrugged. "I was here kind of early."

"When did I mention The Corner?" she asked, trying to remember. It made her head pound, but the medication was beginning to dull the pain.

"The *first* time I came over here to apologize," he said, tapping the toe of one foot against the floor absently. "You said it was too late to go to The Corner."

"You remember that?" She looked surprised.

"Astonishing, I know," Will replied, "I wanted you to have coffee with me, so I was listening very carefully."

"Even then?" she asked, surprise in her expression.

He shrugged. *Might as well own it.* "Yeah, even then. I wanted to get to know you better, but I'd already dug a pretty deep hole for myself."

He grabbed the bagels as they popped up and carried them to the island. They both spread cream cheese on thinly and wrapped them in paper towels. The silence was growing tense until Elizabeth tugged the bag over to look inside.

"No lox?" she asked playfully.

"Uh, no," he replied tentatively, with a tight smile. "I didn't know you liked it."

She gave him a small but comfortable smile. "Next time."

He let out a deep breath. "Right."

"Should we go downstairs?" she asked. "Aunt Maddy will make sure Sarah doesn't attempt a hostile takeover."

"Okay," he said, picking up his bagel and coffee and followed her to the basement.

Elizabeth flipped the light on, and they settled on the couch, placing their food on the coffee table. She blinked a few times, then got up to turn the light off again.

"Migraine?" Will asked softly. She nodded. He held out his hand, and she took it uncertainly. He pulled her down to sit with the back of her head against his chest and sank his hands into her hair to gently massage her scalp.

"Ohhh," she sighed, melting against him. "That feels *so* good."

He kissed the top of her head. "And that's with my clothes *on*."

"You have a one-track mind, Donkey," she said affectionately. He could feel her body sag into his.

"Jarhead," he replied gently. *I'm a man, Elizabeth, and you don't seem to have any idea how beautiful you are.*

"Will," she whispered, "we have to talk about this."

"Mmm hmm," he responded wryly. "I think that was *my* line."

Her voice was almost a whisper, but it was firm. "I can't do it."

"Okay," he said, moving his hands to the back of her head and neck and continuing the massage.

"Okay?" she asked, lifting one eyelid to peer at him. "That's it?"

"No," he shook his head, "but it can wait. 'Ef gravy wait hot wud cool.'"

She snorted. "What was that supposed to mean?"

He grinned, though he knew she couldn't see it. "I'm sure I've messed it up, but it's supposed to mean patience is a virtue. Or has a reward. Or something. I'll have to ask Jeremy to repeat it for me. Where is he from, anyway?"

"I see you have my ear for languages," she said teasingly, but then blanched and winced. "Barbados, I think."

"Shh," Will said. He gazed down at her face and lightly traced the dark circle under one of her eyes with the pad of his thumb. "I didn't sleep much either. Maybe we should just take a nap before we talk? You apparently get cranky when you don't have enough sleep."

Elizabeth tossed her hand back to slap him lightly, but then closed her eyes and replied, "Okay." Will could see she was beyond tired—she was exhausted. She folded her legs up on the sofa and fell asleep almost immediately. Will sighed, content, feeling the warmth of her cheek against his chest, her body curled up into his. Soon his eyes were drifting shut, head resting atop the back of the couch, one arm around Elizabeth. Neither heard Sarah's wails about being denied access to the basement, nor were they awakened by the family getting ready for their day. The telltale sounds of doors shutting, car motors turning over, and the opening and closing of the garage door went entirely unremarked.

It was only the crash of something being dropped in the kitchen above that eventually caused Elizabeth to stir, and her movements woke Will. She glanced at her phone where it lay on the table next to a cup of cold coffee and realized it must be Jane getting ready for work. She sat up.

Will disentangled himself and stood to stretch his back, then returned to the couch.

"Feel better?" he asked her. She nodded.

"The massage helped," she replied. "Thanks."

"Of course," he said. "Now . . ." He gazed her very seriously.

"I know," she nodded. "We need to talk about it." *I hope I can say this clearly.*

Will sat up and took her face between his hands, carefully turning her face up to his without getting too close. "We do. I need you to understand that I am not going to push this one way or the other, but I *do* think we should look at the entire plan and make a decision."

"Will," she insisted in a low, firm voice, "I've heard the plan. I'm not a doll to dress up, and I'm nobody's princess. Never have been."

This statement seemed to strike Will hard, which confused her. His expression softened as he gazed at her.

Elizabeth sighed and rubbed her forehead with one hand. "More importantly, though, I have my business to protect. How many clients are going to entrust their cyber-security to Cinderella or ask Miss Glass Slippers to track down hidden accounts in the Caymans? I'm in a serious business, Will." She paused before saying evenly, "I was about to talk to you about how we could *stop* this story, not enhance it. I've already lost a potential job over this, and one of my best clients is getting nervous, even though I've done good work for them." She pursed her lips. *I have to make him understand.* "FORGE is already well established. The extra press might help you expand, but your business doesn't need it to survive." She put her hand on his arm. "Following this scheme will almost certainly kill *mine*."

Will looked dismayed. His face had paled, and his forehead was furrowed. "I am sorry to say that I didn't even think about that," he told her. "I was completely focused on FORGE and on us and not on your business. I apologize again."

"Will," she said slowly, solemnly, "I don't want you to apologize. I want you to understand."

He nodded and waited. She bit her lower lip for a second before she began.

"Apart from my professional concerns," she said, "it would make me a terrible fraud. How could I ever hold up my head among all those female Marines who've worked so hard for credibility? How could I even face my younger sisters?" She shook her head. "It's one thing to be unfairly labeled by the press. I can't help what they do. But you're asking me to participate willingly, to accept that label, to celebrate it." She let out a deep breath. "No. It goes against everything I stand for, and I won't do it."

Will took her hands. "Okay."

She snorted at the repeated answer from earlier. "That's it?"

"No," he chuckled, "but I get it. I do. I'll tell Charles we won't be implementing that part of the plan."

"And which part are you going to try to talk me into now?" She crossed her arms over her chest.

He shook his head. "Easy, Staff Sergeant. We need to talk about the part where we call in a professional public relations staff to manage the media for us."

She let her arms drop. *That doesn't sound so bad.* "What does that mean, exactly?"

"Elizabeth," he told her calmly, "I've been doing this a long time. We would just include you in what I've already got set up." He saw her frown and added, "With your permission, of course."

She stared at him dubiously and he smiled a little. "We send them our itineraries, and if PR thinks the press would like photos, they schedule something formally." He saw that she was considering it. "It's cheaper for the papers if they know where we'll be, and they can send a staff photographer. If we are offering them something they value, we have something to negotiate with."

Elizabeth supposed that made a twisted sort of sense.

"Part of that negotiation can include a contractual obligation not to purchase pictures from freelancers," he explained. "Buying photos on spec has gotten pretty expensive, and Charles is right—if there are pictures of us readily available, there's less incentive to spend money to have stringers track us down."

"Supply and demand," Elizabeth said simply. It still bothered her, though it wasn't the most outlandish idea she'd ever heard.

Will nodded. "But at least somewhat controlled."

"No more sneak attacks?" she asked expectantly.

"No guarantees," he replied with a small lift of his shoulders. "Sometimes there may still be the odd freelancer. But that's the idea. They only want photos now because I'm a wealthy recluse who has emerged from his cave, and after Brussels, you're a media darling. That doesn't stack up against movie stars or the royal family, or—"

"Aliens and UFOs?" she interjected.

He smiled. "Right. So I'm guessing that this level of attention is temporary."

Elizabeth thought that through, laying her head back on Will's chest. She remembered Richard's advice to steer into the skid.

"Okay," she said.

He smiled and stroked her hair. "That's it?" he asked.

"No," she replied sarcastically, "but we'll talk about it."

"Good," he said, "because that whole talking to the corner thing was a little freaky."

Elizabeth laughed quietly at that. "When I get overwhelmed like last night," she clarified, "I have to let off steam somehow. Usually I go out for a run and it helps me figure out what to say. I couldn't do that last night, and I was ready to explode."

"I thought you incredibly composed," he said sarcastically. "But why didn't you just use the gym in the building?"

Elizabeth rolled her eyes. "I needed to be away—running in circles isn't the same."

He kissed her forehead. "Why didn't you just do that last night?" she asked, gazing up at him innocently.

He shrugged. "I was told I might lose a hand."

"You have to be more assertive, then," she said, deadpan, and shrieked with laughter when he pushed her over on her back, pinned her to the couch, and began tickling her mercilessly. When he stopped so she could catch her breath, he grinned down at her.

"We just effected our first compromise," he told her proudly.

She rolled her eyes. "I can't believe this is how we're spending your vacation." Her stomach gurgled, and she glanced over at the half-eaten bagels. She turned back to Will.

"Dim sum?" she asked hopefully. "My treat."

"Are you always thinking about your next meal?" he asked teasingly.

Elizabeth's eyes raked over him from head to toe. "Nooo," she said, reaching up to touch his cheek, "sometimes I'm thinking about . . . dessert."

She began to say something else, but was cut off as his lips crashed down on her mouth.

———

Major Richard Fitzwilliam glanced up as another stack of files was dropped on his desk. He was busy analyzing the potential for more kidnappings in Syria, and the data was coming through in printed communiques and reports. *God, I hate paper reports*, he thought, trying not to think about his separation date less than two weeks away and failing miserably. *Thanksgiving with Will and G*, he told himself. *Maybe even Dad and Oscar.* At least at FORGE, the reports and spreadsheets would be digital. *Mostly.* His cousin did, after all, wear a wristwatch and have an actual newspaper delivered to his apartment every morning.

He wondered idly if Bennet would be at Thanksgiving. The last he'd heard, she'd laid down the law with Will about Bingley, and he'd just seen the *Post* article about running shoes the other day. He'd laughed so hard he'd nearly thrown up when he saw they were calling Bennet "Cinderella," and "The Jersey Princess." *Oh man, gotta send her a tiara*, he thought affectionately, and then, *she's lucky she's not from Queens*. He missed her unique brand of cheerful snark more than he'd thought he would.

Richard genuinely liked Bennet and thought she would be good for Will. She'd also been a mystery to him for months, and mysteries didn't sit well with him. Bennet had worked under a Captain Carter for about six months and requested consideration for the Enlisted Commission Program before being abruptly transferred to Brussels, but there wasn't much else. After speaking with her and learning about her education, he'd been unclear why she'd never been offered a chance to attend

ECP. She seemed a perfect candidate. He frowned. He usually had more access than this to personnel files.

When he'd first met her in the office working on her inspections, he'd thought she was too exuberant to be a serious Marine. But the more he spoke to her, the more he had realized that she hid a sharp intelligence beneath the wit. Furthermore, beneath all the banter was someone who had some steel, something he'd never been more grateful for than on that evening in De Roos.

Richard tapped his pen on the desk. They never spoke of it, but he wondered how she was doing, whether she was having nightmares or trouble sitting in a bar if she wasn't facing the door. He'd been through combat situations before, but somehow this had been different. He'd not been protecting civilians before, perhaps. Or maybe it was that he had gotten soft, spending more time working with men in suits than in uniforms.

His phone buzzed. A text.

"Bennet," he said with a grin. "Speak of the devil."

I know you heard about the Jersey Princess thing. Whatever you're planning, stop.

He locked up the office and stepped out into the street. When he was home, beer sitting on the coffee table and his feet up on the sofa, he took up his phone to answer.

Bennet, he typed, *you know that's not possible.*

He waited a second before her answer popped up.

You should be prepared for reprisals.

He nodded. *Always.*

He could almost hear her sighing from across the Atlantic, and it made him smile. When the phone buzzed next, he read: *Beware. I have Will on my side. He knows things.*

"Please," he scoffed. *I'm not afraid of Batman, Bennet. What kind of amateur do you take me for?* He chuckled. This was more fun than planning something. She was winding *herself* up.

As my friend Catherine used to say, I shall know how to act!

Richard chewed that over. Weird. *My Aunt Catherine says that, too.*

Must be the name. I'm just warning you, Dicky. No sudden moves.

Dicky, is it? Lizzy? Lizard? Dizzy Lizzy? Frizzy Lizzy? Stones, glass houses.

You're a riot, major. I bet the general gets a real kick out of you. Has she asked you out yet? You know, as her very personal assistant?

Low blow, Bennet. He hit send before he sat up abruptly and cried out, "No, no! Shit! That's not what I meant!"

There was a pause, and now he could almost hear her laughter. Then her last message came through.

Gotcha. Bennet 1, Fitzwilliam 0.

Richard nearly threw his phone across the room. How could he have let her win that exchange? He'd had her right where he wanted her and she'd wriggled free. He guzzled almost the entire bottle of beer and set it back on the table with a thud.

"All right, Bennet," he said to the empty room, a mischievous gleam in his eye. "You want to keep score? This is war."

Will poured popcorn into a large bowl and punched a button on the remote. The opening credits began to roll for *Roman Holiday.* Elizabeth dropped her phone on the coffee table and leaned back against the leather couch.

"Fair warning," she said. "I may kill your cousin."

Will handed her the bowl and sat down next to her. "What's he done now?"

She shook her head. "Nothing yet, but I know how he thinks. I tried to warn him off, but . . ."

He grinned. "That's not really the best way to handle Richard."

"That's not the best way for *you* to handle Richard," she replied. "He's always known you as his younger cousin. He's *afraid* of me."

"Oh really?" Will asked, a skeptical expression on his face.

"Mmm hmm," she responded, chewing. She swallowed and said, "He's seen me shoot."

Will laughed. "He's seen *me* shoot. Many times."

Elizabeth gazed at Will. "Oh Will," she said with a shake of her head, "I love you, but it isn't the same thing. At all."

He felt his breath accelerate and removed the bowl from her hands to set it on the table.

"What did you just say?" he asked.

She stared blankly at him, and then her eyes widened, and her cheeks flushed pink. She bit her lip. "It isn't the same thing?"

Will raised his eyebrows.

Elizabeth reached for his hand, and Will took it, feeling the slight dampness in her palm. "I hope it doesn't change things for you," she said, and took a shaky breath. She let it out. "I love you."

Will could feel the smile splitting his face. He brushed some hair from Elizabeth's forehead and leaned in to kiss her before pulling slightly away from her face and replying, "That's excellent news, Elizabeth." He moved to kiss her neck and reveled in the shudder it produced. He moved back to her lips before saying, "I love you, too. I just wasn't sure you were ready to hear it."

Her face lit up like a firefly. "I wasn't sure *you* were ready," she said, laughing quietly. She reached up to touch his cheek. "You make me happy, Will. Really happy." She glanced up at him through her eyelashes, and this time, he knew she wasn't being playful or teasing. "Will you say it again?"

He helped her up from the couch and put his arms around her, pulling her close. "I love you, Elizabeth Bennet," he whispered in her ear between kisses. "I am hopelessly in love with you."

Will woke later than usual the next morning. Through the window in his bedroom, the autumn sky appeared gray and dismal. For a moment, he panicked, thinking he was late for work, but as he bolted upright, he remembered. *Vacation.* When he threw himself back down on the bed and pulled the down comforter over himself to return to sleep, he heard a muffled protest and recalled that not only was he on vacation, he was not alone.

"Hey, cover hog," came Elizabeth's sleepy voice, and he grinned.

"Sorry, not used to having to share."

"Clearly," she said, sitting up. Her hair stuck out at all angles, creating a jagged cloud around her head until she tamed it with her hands.

"Aw," he teased, "it looked good up there, like a spiky halo."

She snorted. "More like horns."

Will was quiet then, just watching her. Her cheeks were flushed pink from the warmth of the bed, and her lips were red and full. *She has perfect lips*, he thought, running his eyes along their curves. As Elizabeth snuggled into his side to counteract the unceremonious loss of her blanket, she crinkled her nose and brought her hands up to his chest. He flinched a bit—her hands were cold. He tucked the comforter around them both and tossed an arm around her. She hummed happily.

"You know," she said, once she was warm again, "you can disagree any time."

"There's no good answer," he replied, sanguine. "If I say you're the devil, you'll hit me, but if I say you're an angel, God may strike me down for the lie."

She huffed and buried her head under a pillow, emitting enough sound that he knew she was saying something, but not what. He lifted the pillow and his eyebrows at the same time.

"Care to repeat that?" he asked, trying not to laugh.

"I said," she reiterated, speaking with emphasis on each word, "that a lot of angels were soldiers for God. Scary ones. Like Marines."

This time he did laugh. "I'll call my cousin an angel when he comes home. We'll see how well that goes over."

"You show him pictures of Michael the Archangel, and he won't mind." She clutched the comforter to her chest and sat up. Then she thought better of it and fell back on the pillow. "I don't want to get up this morning."

"Then don't," Will said, stroking her hair and pushing it back from her face. He let his thumb carefully trace the thin white line just over her eyebrow before planting a little kiss on the end of her nose. "I like waking up this way," he said, leaning his forehead to touch hers.

"You mean stealing the covers so I'm out here shivering?" she replied with a dazed smile. She tossed an arm over his side and hugged herself to his bare torso. "You're so warm." She yawned widely. "I guess it's not so bad."

"No, love, that's not exactly what I meant." Will kissed her on the top of her head and then burrowed under the covers until they were eye-to-eye, inches apart. "Your eyes are so deeply green," he said quietly. "I don't think I've ever seen anyone with eyes quite that color before. They're beautiful."

Elizabeth smiled. "Thank you."

He laughed softly. "Is that another lesson? How to take a compliment graciously?"

"Of course," she replied with a giggle.

"It freaks me out a little when you giggle," he said, bemused. "You're usually so formidable. It throws me off my game."

"Will Darcy," she said with a sigh, returning his penetrating gaze, "please. You have no game."

"True," he agreed solemnly, though his lips quirked up. "Only too true."

Elizabeth brought her hand up to touch his face. "Thank God. Despite what I said about you being a prince, I wouldn't know what to do with a charming man." She flushed as the meaning of her words hit her. They stared at each other blankly for a few seconds before they both began to laugh.

Elizabeth finally pushed herself up and perched on the edge of the bed, her back to Will. She flexed her knee, seemed satisfied, and made as if to stand, but he grabbed the elastic waist on her pajama bottoms and pulled her back to bed.

"Will!" she squealed. "What are you doing?"

"You said you didn't want to get up," Will reminded her.

"I changed my mind," she told him with a shrug.

"But who said you could leave the bed?" he asked.

"I did," Elizabeth said indignantly, trying to wrest her pants out of his hand. "Let me up."

Will thought about it for a long minute, but did not release his hold. At last, he spoke. "No."

"What do you mean, no?" she asked, beginning to get annoyed.

Will saw the line appear between her eyes and smiled mischievously. He put his arm around her waist and pulled her fully back onto the bed, where she sat up with her arms crossed over her chest.

"Sweetheart," he said just above a whisper. "I want to get to know you."

He watched her eyebrows pinch together. "You do know me," she replied, sounding confused.

With one hand, he pushed up the left leg of her pajama pants and ran one finger lightly over the scar just to the side of her kneecap.

"Was this from De Roos?"

"Mmm hmm. Three-inch metal splinter." Her voice was steady.

Will tried to imagine it and couldn't. "Does it still hurt?" he asked softly.

"No," she said, shaking her head. "It just gets sore. They had to remove some cartilage. I don't get too much pain from it anymore." He wrapped both hands around her calf and kissed the scar. He glanced up to see Elizabeth blink and her lips part slightly. He placed another kiss on the fine line just above her eyebrow.

She was wearing a tank top, and Will next skimmed some fading white lines on her forearms with his fingertips and then a crescent-shaped scar that curved just at the point where her collarbone met her shoulder. "What's this one from?" he asked softly, moving his lips to her neck, just under her jaw, then behind her ear.

"Mmm. Shrapnel," she mumbled, squirming under him. "Not really pillow talk, Will."

He gently pressed his lips to the scar on her shoulder. Elizabeth's eyes closed, and her head tipped back. Her breath came a little faster.

"So, your eye, your knee, and your shoulder," he continued, kissing a spot behind her ear that made her shiver. "Anywhere else?"

She placed her hands lightly on the small of his back, her heart pounding. "Uh, scars?" she asked, distracted as he nibbled her earlobe.

"Mmm." He dropped his head to her chest.

"Oh . . ." She sighed, wrapping her arms around his neck.

"What else?" he insisted, turning his attention to her breasts. Her hands wound themselves into his hair.

"Ah . . . concussion." She moaned and began to arch her back as Will moved farther down her torso and began to kiss her sides, her stomach. Her next sentence came out in short gasps. "Your. Cousin. Threw. A. Bomb. At. Me."

"I'll have to speak to him about that," Will replied in a low voice as he moved in to capture her lips with his own.

Afterward, just before they both fell back into a deep slumber, Elizabeth's phone buzzed. She flailed around for it without any urgency. When she finally grabbed it, she thumbed through a few notifications before letting out a groan. She showed the headline to Will, who just laughed at the photo of the two of them outside the shoe store. "*Sole* mates? They didn't have anything better than that? I'm keenly disappointed."

Elizabeth scrolled through the other stories and began to laugh. When she started hiccupping, Will sat up.

"What is it?" he asked, holding out his hand. She passed the phone over and pointed out the last headline.

Will tossed the phone on the bed and flopped back on the pillows. "That's just perfect," he said sarcastically. "Richard will *never* let me live this down."

Elizabeth rolled her eyes. "He's already seen 'Jersey Princess,' and I have two teenaged sisters trolling the internet for this stuff. It's your turn."

"Great," he said wryly. "I hadn't even thought about Georgiana seeing this. I feel much better now."

Elizabeth leaned over and planted a kiss on the back of his neck. He shuddered.

"I love you," she said softly. "Think about that instead."

They kissed for a good long time before she lifted the covers, glanced down, and told him mischievously, "I need to check out the merchandise." She was silent for a moment, contemplating. "Nope, the originals still look pretty good to me."

Will put his hands on either side of Elizabeth's face and drew her down to his lips. Her arms snaked around his neck, and he rolled over on top of her. As their lovemaking grew heated, her phone bounced off the bed and hit the floor. The contact made the screen light up, revealing the last headline for a few seconds before the display went dark.

DASHING DARCY BUYS A PAIR

EXCERPT FROM HEADSTRONG BOOK 2: ADAPT

Elizabeth was sitting in the kitchen with two empty beer bottles in front of her on the counter, her head pillowed on her arms, when she heard Will opening the front door. There was the sharp clink of the keys being tossed in the blue bowl, but she didn't lift her head, not even when she heard his footsteps and a soft laugh a few feet away.

"It went that well, huh?" he asked playfully.

She looked up, her chin resting on her forearm. Will was wearing a thin blue sweater over a white oxford shirt and light tan slacks. He had already removed his sportscoat. *He always looks good. Jerk.* "Where've you been?" she asked. "I thought you were working from home today."

"I was," he replied, "but I had some things to take care of." He returned the conversation to its original topic. "How'd it go?"

"This day has been surreal," she said and sighed. "Like, Salvador Dalí surreal."

He pursed his lips, unsure how to respond. "Jerry told me you called him to pick you up."

She grunted. "I had to speak with my aunt, so I went home with the girls and missed the express." She closed her eyes, then opened one to peer up at him. "I didn't have it in me to take the long train, and I needed to talk to you. Plus," she tapped one of the bottles, "I can drink here without anyone commenting."

Will sat across from her. "Want to talk about it?"

Elizabeth shook her head from side to side. "Not particularly, but I think it's important that we do."

"That's a dramatic announcement," he said cautiously. "Was it your speech? I thought it was pretty good, myself."

"Didn't give it."

He waited but she didn't say anything else.

"I could just call Kit and ask, I suppose," he said thoughtfully, peering down at her.

Fine. "She's just as confused about it as I am. Lydia, on the other hand, may very well be planning a hit on you . . ."

Will stopped teasing. "What are you talking about?"

Elizabeth stood and turned to the refrigerator. She reached in for another beer, which she set on the counter and Will immediately grabbed.

"Hey," she protested as the bottle flew out of her reach.

"No 'hey,' Elizabeth Bennet," he said seriously. "You never get beyond a half a bottle of beer and you've already finished two. Explain."

She resumed her original position and grunted. "I've been waiting for almost three hours, Will—a few beers isn't a big deal." She sighed. "I know we need to talk, but I don't want to have another huge argument where I get mad and I don't want to go run tonight."

Will's eyebrows pinched together suspiciously. "You have to be careful with your alcohol intake because of the concussion."

She frowned. "Who told you that?"

"I looked it up," he said flatly.

She rolled her eyes. "It's been months, Will."

"The alcohol limits never go away," he insisted. "Once you've had a TBI, you really shouldn't drink at all."

"Will," she huffed. "I'm allowed to drink a beer or two if I spread it out and drink water. Which I have."

He narrowed his eyes at her. "I don't like the sound of that. Have you had more than those two?"

"Mmmph," was all she said. Elizabeth heard him step on the lever for the recycling bin. She'd put the first bottle in there hours ago.

"Okay, that's it," Will said sternly. He took two bottles of water out of the refrigerator, hooked one hand under Elizabeth's arm and hauled her up despite her protests, half supporting her down the stairs to the bedroom. He sat her on the bed and handed her the first water. "Drink it," he commanded. "And then start talking." She frowned but lifted the bottle to her lips. He changed while she drank. He watched until she finished it, then came back to the bed in his t-shirt and some sweatpants, opened the second bottle, and handed it to her. "Sip this," he directed.

"Bossy," she complained.

"Apparently, I have to be the grown-up," he shot back unapologetically.

"Really?" she asked. "*You're* the one acting like an adult?"

"*Elizabeth*," he said sharply, arms crossed over his chest, "what is going *on*?"

Elizabeth pulled out her phone, touched the screen, and handed it over.

He stood there, staring at it. His lips parted slightly, but he didn't say anything.

"Who is Caroline Bingley, Will? Is she related to Batboy?" Elizabeth asked insistently. "And why were you leaving a bar with her the same night we had our fight?"

ACKNOWLEDGMENTS

Many people were instrumental in the writing of this novel, which began as a story on A Happy Assembly in 2016. I thank all my reviewers, readers, and supporters, those who pointed out errors or inconsistencies, and the experts in many areas who contributed their knowledge. A special thanks goes out to the women veterans and those in active service who commented on Elizabeth's experiences. Thanks to you, the story is better and stronger than it would have been without your assistance.

As always, a heartfelt thanks to my intrepid beta Sarah Maksim, whose incredible brainstorming skills, keen eye for humor, and quick turn-around had a great influence on the development of this story. Thanks to my editor, Sarah Pesce, at Lopt&Cropt for keeping the writing lean and clean.

Finally, I must thank my family, who put up with my many hours spent typing away on my computer when I might have been cooking, cleaning, or doing the million other things it takes to run a house. Thank you for your love, support, and the invaluable gift of time.

ABOUT THE AUTHOR

MELANIE RACHEL is a university professor who first read Jane Austen at summer camp as a girl. She was born and raised in Southern California, but has lived in Pennsylvania, New Jersey, Washington, and Arizona, where she now resides with her family and their freakishly athletic Jack Russell terrier.

Facebook: facebook.com/melanie.rachel.583
Website: melanierachel.weebly.com

Made in the USA
Coppell, TX
07 May 2020

24468128R00169